ROOKIE COP

America, June 1940: Nick Train has given up his dreams of a boxing championship after a brief and unsuccessful career in the ring. When one of his pals takes the examination for the police academy, Nick decides to join him. But what started out as a whim turns into a dangerous challenge, as Nick plays a precarious double game of collector for the mob and mole for a shadowy enforcement body . . . Will the rookie cop's luck hold?

RICHARD A. LUPOFF

ROOKIE COP

Complete and Unabridged

LINFORD
Leicester

First published in Great Britain in 2012

First Linford Edition
published 2015

A catalogue record for this book is available
from the British Library.

ISBN 978–1–4448–2339–4

Published by
F. A. Thorpe (Publishing)
Anstey, Leicestershire

Set by Words & Graphics Ltd.
Anstey, Leicestershire
Printed and bound in Great Britain by
T. J. International Ltd., Padstow, Cornwall

This book is printed on acid-free paper

1

First Day on the Beat

It's one thing to have guts and another to be plain dumb. During Nicholas Train's two-year career as a professional pugilist he won accolades like 'plucky,' 'tough,' 'gutsy,' and 'courageous.' What he didn't win was a single match.

He'd been the best boxer at William Seward High School, the third or fourth best high school in Brooklyn, New York. He didn't know what he wanted to do after he'd got his diploma, but a canny manager had seen him in the amateur bouts and urged him to turn pro. His father had been in favour of the idea. He'd been a boxing fan since the days of Jim Braddock. He was personal friends with Battling Levinsky. He knew Barney Ross. He figured it was a way out of poverty if you played your cards right.

Of course, Nick's father was already in

failing health by then; the chemicals he breathed all day at the dry cleaning plant were taking their toll. But he still got up every morning and dragged himself to work.

Nick's mother was dead-set against Nick fighting for a living, and his sister, Marie, lobbied against it for all she was worth; but a combination of male solidarity, the chance to make some quick jack, and a certain glamour that seemed to attach to the enterprise, carried the day.

Between the summer of 1936 and the autumn of 1938 Nick fought as a welterweight, performing in clubs in New York and New Jersey, compiling a record of no wins, thirteen losses, and one draw. His total take-home earnings, after buying equipment and paying his manager, trainer, gym fees, and travel expenses, was $134.58. The draw had been in his first bout, a bottom-of-the-card three-rounder against a washed-up bum, in a gym in Paterson, New Jersey. That had encouraged him to go on with the fight game. The thirteen losses convinced him to give it up. Especially the last of them, from which he emerged with a broken nose, cuts over both eyes, a bruised left orb courtesy of his opponent's resin-coated thumb that took weeks to return to normal, recurring headaches, and a sore kidney that leaked blood into his piss for a month.

Some wealth.

Some glamour.

He still followed the division, went to see Babe Risko fight Freddie Steele, Steele fight Fred Apostoli, Apostoli fight Al Hostak, and Hostak fight Solly Krieger. They handed the crown around like a reefer cigarette at a party. Nick wasn't too impressed by any of them. Then he heard about a kid named Tony Zale from the Indiana steel mills and started following his career. A ruffian named Jimmy Clarke knocked Zale out in the first round. Zale turned around and decisioned King Wyatt, then kayoed Bobby LaMotte in five, then got a rematch with Clarke and punished him for eight rounds before putting him away.

No more dreams of a fight crown for Nick Train.

His father could have got him a job at the dry cleaning plant, but he saw where that was leading the old man. His brother-in-law, Jocko Sullivan, was a stevedore and that looked like steady work and only moderately dangerous, but Nick didn't get along too good with his brother-in-law and he didn't want to have to rely on him for his livelihood.

One night he was sitting in his pal Benny Jensen's basement playing poker with Benny and a few other Seward High buddies and Benny said, 'I'm gonna take the police exam. I'm goin' down Monday morning and take the exam. Who wants to come with me?'

Marty Macon and Pudgy Watterson started hooting and making faces. Jackie Goldstein took off his Coke-bottle glasses and squinted at the others and said, 'I ain't inclined to waste my time and there's no way they'd take me for a cop.'

But Nick Train said, 'Where do they give the exam?'

Benny told him the time and place, and

what he'd need to bring with him — namely his birth certificate and high school diploma — and said he'd meet him at the BMT station. 'And bring a nickel for your fare; I can't treat you to the ride.'

Pudgy said, 'If you two sweethearts have made your date now, how about playing poker? Goldstein is dealer. Come on, Jackie, don't call one of them crazy games of yours. Play it straight; I need to make some scratch.'

Jackie Goldstein grunted something that might have been, 'Okay.' The ante was in the middle of the table, beers scattered around. Goldstein reached for the deck, clipped his can of Trommer's with his elbow and sloshed the table with beer. Everybody jumped up. Jackie grabbed his beer to keep more of it from spilling. Pudgy Watterson raced to the bathroom and returned with a couple of towels. Once he'd wiped the table the only visible damage was a bunch of water — or rather, beer-logged cards. They were deposited in a wastebasket.

Benny went to an old desk and

returned with a cellophane-covered deck. He slit the cellophane, broke the seal, and handed the cards to Goldstein.

Jackie started to cackle. 'Look at these — Benny has one of them girlie decks.'

Everybody got a good laugh. Benny put the cardboard package back in his desk and the game resumed. Later, when they broke up, Jackie eyeballed the stack of chips in front of each player and announced who was in the hole, and how deep, and who had gelt coming to him.

Marty Macon was the big loser. 'You sure that's right, Jackie?'

Goldstein said, 'Absolutely. You want to count all the chips and figure it out, that's okay by me.'

Macon shook his head and reached for his wallet. 'Nah. I remember from Seward, you were the math wizard, Jackie. How the hell do you do it?'

Goldstein shrugged. 'Search me. It's just a talent. You know, some guys can put a basketball through a hoop every time. I sure can't. But I know numbers.'

'Okay. You going to use numbers to make a living?'

Another shrug. 'I don't know. I'm certainly gonna try. I'm studying accounting and I've already got a part-time job with the phone company. They need mathematicians there, that's for certain.'

★   ★   ★

It was late autumn by now. Nick Train felt a tug when he walked past William Seward High School, even though he'd been out of there for two years. He missed school, missed spending every day with boys and girls his own age, but now he was a man. By the age of twenty he had a failed career behind him, scars on his eyebrows and a slightly crooked nose to show for it. At least he'd regained the use of his injured eye and his urine was no longer red.

He took the police exam along with Benny Jensen and they both passed and enrolled at the Police Academy; by the end of autumn they were both probational patrolmen. Benny barely made it through the academy and was assigned to a beat in Cop Siberia, aka Staten Island.

Train finished on top of his class and got a beat in Brownsville, the most densely populated section of Brooklyn. That was a break. He could walk to work.

Department policy dictated a vacation at the end of academy studies. Train played poker with his buddies, went to the movies, read some pulp magazines, and took in a couple of football games.

His first day on the job, Officer Train was welcomed to the precinct by Lieutenant Kessler, who turned him over to his shift commander, Sergeant Charlie Garlington. Sergeant Garlington said, 'You're a local boy, Train. You know the ropes around here. I'm glad to have you working for me. I'm sending you out with Officer Winger. You know Winger? Dermott Winger?'

Train said, 'No, sir.'

'No, Sergeant. Sergeant, not sir. Just like the army. Lieutenants are sir and sergeants are sergeant. Winger's a good man. His old man was a cop. Young Winger joined the force same time I did, 1923. It was a different world then, Train. Everybody's gone soft now. First they got

Depression-shocked, then they got New-Dealed and they think life is supposed to be a free ride. It ain't, Train, it ain't. You stick with Winger. A good man, he is. A good man. He'll teach you everything you need to know. Everything they didn't teach you at the academy.'

Train stood at attention in the line-up. Sergeant Garlington inspected the shift, then they hit the street. Train had been issued a Police Special. He'd done well at weapons training and marksmanship at the academy. He hadn't been raised around guns but by this time he was comfortable with the revolver strapped to his hip.

Winter had set in by now. There had been three or four good snowfalls. Every storm left the city looking like a Currier and Ives print for the first couple of hours and after that like Pompeii after Vesuvius blew up, except the gray sludge in the street was cold slush instead of hot ash. The police were wearing heavy overcoats and it wouldn't be easy to reach their revolvers. Nick had done all right in nightstick drills and figured if he had to deal with some rowdy he'd rather not draw his firearm anyhow.

'First thing you have to do is forget everything they taught you at the academy,' Winger told him. 'You got that?'

'Sergeant Garlington said you'd teach me plenty, Officer Winger.'

'Yeah. Dermott. Can the officer guff. That's for citizens. You know this neighborhood, Train?'

'A little.'

'Mostly Hebes, some Syrians, some wops, some Moors — whatever the hell they are — and blacks over by Rockaway Avenue. We got all kinds here. You got a problem with that, Train?'

'No problem.'

'Chinese.'

'No problem.'

'Just a few of 'em. They got a chop suey joint on Junius Street near Linden Boulevard, and a laundry. They don't make trouble; they're okay with me. Okay with you, Train?'

'Okay with me, Officer Winger. Dermott.'

'All right, Train. Look, we might as well

10

start at one end of the beat and just walk it. You got good heavy brogans on? Good thick socks? Okay. Look, I'll give you a hint, kid. Say, wait a minute, let me look at your kisser.'

Train stood straight and let Winger study his face.

'Got your nose on crooked, don't you, kid?'

'Got it broken, Dermott.'

'No kidding.' Dermott stared at Train for a while, then nodded as if he'd solved a puzzle. 'I saw you fight. Wait a minute. Saint Nicholas Arena. You was a prelim boy.'

'That's all I ever was.'

'Wait a minute. I saw you fight Cyclone Carson.'

'That's right.'

'He beat the crap out of you.'

'That's right.'

'You give up the racket?'

'Yeah. That's why I enrolled at the academy.'

'Smart move. Okay, what was I saying?'

'About wearing the right shoes and socks.'

'Yeah. Carry a spare pair of socks with you, Train. In fact it wouldn't hurt to carry a couple of spare pairs. It's a long day, kid, and your dogs are gonna start shivering after a few hours. You'll want to change your socks. Find a nice warm place, maybe take a little something to warm your insides, get your dogs warm and dry, put on fresh socks.'

'Makes sense, Dermott.'

'Okay, let's go.'

The sun was trying to break through the clouds, but the best it could manage was a small bright spot where the gray looked a little less dead than the rest of the sky. Stand in the right spot and face the right way and if you were tall enough you could see the top of the Woolworth Building in Manhattan, and the Chrysler Building and the new Empire State Building farther uptown. Train was tall enough.

There was foot traffic on the sidewalk and cars and trucks passing in the street. They were on Junius Street and there were tenements and businesses lined up shoulder-to-shoulder all along the street. The only open space Train could see surrounded St. Columba's Catholic Church. There must have been a grassy plot in front of the church, but it was completely covered with snow. The snow was gray. A few flakes were drifting down now, and if enough of them fell they would cover the gray snow and turn it white again.

Tombstones, most of them shaped like crosses, stuck up out of the snow. Some of them must have been old; they weren't shaped like crosses but were simple round-topped markers. Three or four of them had statues of angels. There were even a couple of mausoleums, stone crypts shaped like little churches themselves. The individuals inside, Train thought, were lucky. They didn't have any idea how cold they were.

'You'll get to know the people around here,' Dermott Winger told him. 'You get to know who's crazy, who's dangerous, who's a lush, who's a whore. I'll introduce you to the local merchants, the priest over there at St. Columba's, the rabbi at the shul. You know what a shul is, Train?'

'Yes.'

'Good. Look out for the Jews. They have the toughest gangs in the city. Smart, too.'

They were strolling down the sidewalk. You could tell the recent immigrants from the ones who had been in New York longer and the ones who had been born in America. The greenhorns backed away from Winger and Train, tipping their caps and ducking their heads. They were used to the Old World, to the Czar's police or the Emperor's bullies. The ones who had been here longer smiled and offered polite greetings. The kids who had grown up on these streets either scampered out of the way or snarled.

Winger swung his billy club like a schoolteacher's pointer. 'See that, Train? That's progress.' A minute later he said, 'You need to know where all the call boxes are. Keep an eye out. Remember them. You need to call in routine reports every two hours but you mainly need 'em if something nasty is going on. You can signal with your billy club but it don't always carry far enough.'

The call box was attached to a

14

telephone pole in front of the Kings County Citizens' and Workers' Bank. Train already had a savings account there. The account was worth something like six dollars. He'd heard enough lectures on the importance of thrift at home and in school, so this nest egg would surely see him through the tribulations of old age if he ever made it that far.

The two police officers entered the bank and Winger led the way through a swinging gate to the higher-ups' area. They found the manager of the branch in his private office. Winger already knew him. He introduced Train and the manager handed him an elegantly printed business card. It read: *Morris Finch, Manager, Brownsville Branch, Kings County Citizens' and Workers' Bank*. Finch had brown hair, wore a brown suit and a brown tie, and sat in a brown-paneled office. He was next to invisible.

On their way out of the bank, Train introduced himself to the uniformed guard, a retired cop named Mike Calvert. Train had seen Calvert in the bank since he was a kid. He'd always been afraid of him. Now things were different.

Winger and Train stopped in front of the marquee of the local movie house. The theater was called the Junius Street Variety, a survival of the days of vaudeville. Movable letters on the marquee spelled out the name of the current feature, *The Life of Emile Zola*.

'See that, kid? You wouldn't expect a picture like that to go over in a Hebe neighbourhood; you'd expect 'em to show something like *Captains Courageous* or that Jeannette MacDonald thing, what's-it, with all the singing. But Paul Muni is one of them. So they all gotta see him chew up the scenery. Come on, you ought to meet the guy who runs this place.'

The theater hadn't opened yet, but when Winger rapped on the door with his billy club the manager opened it and let them in. Winger introduced Train to the manager. He was clearly trying to look like Adolph Menjou and doing a pretty good job of it, except that Menjou managed to make his little moustache look elegant. The theater manager, a wiry forty-year-old named Victor Tremont, wound up looking more like a nervous rodent.

There was a coloured man sweeping up the lobby, stopping every so often to go to his knees. Each time he would pull a putty knife out of a loop in his overalls and scrape some chewing gum off the carpet. The candy girl was running a popcorn machine. The smell was tempting and comfortingly warm on this frigid day.

Before they left the theater the manager asked, 'You got a girl, officer?'

Train said, 'Nobody special.' He noticed the candy girl perk up when she heard that. She was pretty, with long brown hair and an ample figure. She smiled at him and he smiled back.

'Any time you want to see the picture, just come around,' the manager said. 'Bring your girlfriend, bring your parents. Any time.'

Train thanked him. He winked at the candy girl and she blushed and smiled. She wasn't coy.

Before they left the theater the manager and Winger disappeared into the manager's office for a few minutes. Train ambled over to the candy counter and exchanged names with the candy girl. They shook hands. The popcorn popper was bouncing away. The girl asked Train if he'd like a free sample and he said he thought he'd better not, not right now, but maybe some other time.

Winger came out of the manager's office and they left. Outside the theater the snow was coming down a little more heavily. At least it was falling in dry flakes. Train didn't mind snow; it was sleet that bothered him.

Next stop was the old Brocklyn van der Zee Hotel. Winger asked, 'You know this place, Train?'

Train did. The hotel was a landmark, the first building in Brownsville with an Otis elevator. It was far past its prime, but still busy.

'Lots of action here,' Winger said. 'Bootleg liquor during Prohibition. Some dope now, and the manager runs a string of whores for customers. Name's Alf

Corona. Call him Fatty. Cocktail lounge in the building, Alf's brother Bobby runs it. Skinny. They'll send a bottle up to any room in the hotel, any time. We collect twice, Train — once from the hotel and once from the bar. Service from the girls, too. A very nice deal.'

The lobby of the Brocklyn van der Zee was musty. It looked like a movie set from the silent era. Winger introduced Train to the brothers. They could have passed for Laurel and Hardy. Skinny invited Winger and Train into the lounge for a drink. Winger had a boilermaker. Train abstained.

Winger pulled a watch out of his pocket and consulted it.

'Got an appetite, kid? What do you feel like? All kinds of food around here.'

'Anything. I've got a pretty good appetite.'

'Yeah. You must have got in the habit when you were fighting, eh?'

'It burns up a lot of nourishment, yeah.'

'Okay. Might as well introduce you to a couple more friends.' Train thought

Winger put a funny emphasis on the last word, but he didn't ask any questions.

They stopped at St. Columba's Catholic Church. The building was a typical piece of gray granite with a small steeple. A smaller building was visible behind it, probably a rectory. The priest was a Father Dempsey. Why the Church put an Irish priest in charge in a neighborhood with hardly any Irish people was a mystery.

Winger introduced Train to the priest. Father Dempsey said, 'I've seen you box, Nicholas. I follow the sport. Hardly have a choice, have I, with my name? No relation, though.' He clapped Train on the shoulder. 'Well, I think you made the right choice, Nicholas. Some of us are cut out for one profession and some for another. I'm sure you'll be more successful as a police officer than you were in the ring.'

They stood in the churchyard until Winger said, 'Oh, food, that's what you're thinking about, Train. Don't be afraid to speak up. Come on, we'll head for the Chinese.'

The snow was accumulating on the roofs of parked cars, but the sidewalk was pretty clear. The Chinese restaurant was called the Imperial Palace. It had something like a dozen tables. Half of them were occupied. The owner greeted Winger and Train and they sat away from the door. It was warm inside. The two cops hung their uniform caps and overcoats on metal hooks. They kept their revolvers and billy clubs.

The owner handed them menus, then he went away and a black-haired, green-eyed knockout in a Chinese dress took his place.

Winger said, 'Hello, Susan, how are you?'

The knockout said, 'I'm just fine, Officer Winger, thank you. What will you have today?'

'Say, first, let me introduce my new partner, Officer Train.'

Train stood up. The knockout extended her hand. Train shook hands with her. 'I'm Nicholas Train, Miss — is it Susan?'

'Chen Shu,' she said. 'English, Susan Chen. Please to meet you.' Her accent was half Chinese, half Brownsville. Train had never heard anything like it. When she took her hand back he felt himself blushing. He sat down again.

'The usual for me,' Winger said.

Susan Chen waited for Train to order. He tried to read the menu, then gave up. 'Same for me.'

She walked away.

'Sit tight, kid.' Winger stood up, crossed the restaurant, bent over the owner, and whispered something. The two men disappeared through a beaded curtain. Train studied the restaurant, the other customers, the passing foot traffic out-side. He tried not to be too obvious when he looked at Susan Chen.

Winger came back through the beaded curtain. There was a small bulge in his uniform tunic. He pulled out his chair and sat opposite Train. A minute later their food arrived. The waiter was a male equivalent of Susan Chen.

'Larry, this is Nick Train.' They shook hands. 'He's her brother,' Winger told Train after the waiter left. 'Old man Chen, Chen Ching-kuo, owns this place with his wife. Susan and Larry are their kids.'

The next stop was the Four Star Kosher Butcher Shop. Train had been in the shop before he walked in with Winger. He'd even been there as a customer, buying a freshly killed chicken or a brisket of beef at his mother's direction. The sawdust-strewn floor, the chill in the air, and sight of fresh cuts of meat were all familiar. He recognized the owner, a German immigrant who'd lived in Brooklyn longer than Train had been alive. His name was Henry Little, formerly Heinz Kleinmann. He was an odd mixture of the assimilated and the traditional. He still wore a Jewish *yarmulke* and his English was accented, but he talked about Mayor LaGuardia and President Roosevelt and the sensational stories in the *Eagle* and the popular movies and radio shows of the day.

As usual, Winger disappeared briefly with one of the men behind the counter, Henry Little himself in his black *yarmulke* and a bloodstained apron.

Next was Walker's Bar. When Winger

and Train walked in, there were half a dozen drinkers leaning against the mahogany and as many more scattered at tables. The lighting in the room was dim and the place smelled of stale tobacco smoke and liquor. A huge portrait of the former mayor held a place of honour above a stone fireplace. There was no evidence of the present mayor or of the two short-timers who had come between Gentleman Jimmy and the Little Flower. The bullet-headed bartender wore the regulation white shirt and bow tie.

Winger said, 'Dinny, this is Nick Train, used to be a middleweight fighter.'

'I remember you, kid. Dinny Moran. Pleased ta meetcha.' The bartender extended his hand and Train took it. Obviously he was pretty well known from his fighting days. Maybe that was a good thing, maybe not.

Conversation had stopped in the room when Winger and Train strode in. Winger said, 'Train, Dinny and me got a couple of topics to discuss. We'll be right back.' The two men disappeared through a doorway. Train tried to be inconspicuous.

One of the drinkers at the bar said, 'Hey, I remember you, too, kid. Saw you fight that coloured boy last summer. When was it, Bert?'

The drinker next to him said, 'I remember that fight. It was the day after we split that doubleheader with the Bees.' He turned toward Train. 'I'll say this for you, kid, you never let your manager throw in the towel. I don't know how far that coloured boy is gonna go, but he sure looked good against you.'

Train nodded. 'Yeah. He was tough.'

The two drinkers turned away. Train observed them in the back bar mirror. The one on the left was heavyset. He wore a ribbed sweater and a knitted cap. He might once have been an athlete but he was obviously out of shape. He had a definite weight problem. His companion was half his size, but when he spoke he was twice as loud. He wore a red plaid lumber jacket and a stained porkpie hat.

There was no bartender present now, but Train figured that nobody would try to reach across the mahogany and rob the till with a cop in the room.

Apparently the big man in the sweater and the little man in the plaid jacket had been arguing about the Dodgers before Winger and Train arrived. The little guy was saying, 'Grimes may have been a great pitcher but he don't know a thing about managing. Even Stengel was better. They need a new skipper or they'll never go anyplace.'

The big guy shook his head. 'Not Grimes' fault. The team got no talent. Looka their rotation. Fitzsimmons is washed up, Hamlin's an old man, Posedel's a late bloomer, and Presnell's another Methuselah. Tamulis is their only decent arm. Camilli's their best hitter, Ernie Koy's got some power, and Lavagetto is okay, and that's all they got.'

'They ain't that bad. They got some talent. Look at Phelps, he's a .300 hitter. They just gotta settle down. They need some leadership. Grimes ain't it.'

'No they don't. For cripes sake, even Uncle Robby couldn't win with this team. They — '

Dermott Winger and Dinny Moran the bartender re-emerged from the back room. Winger was buttoning his overcoat. He had his uniform cap on. The bartender slid behind the mahogany and looked sadly at the guy in the sweater and the guy in the jacket. 'You two geniuses settled the problems of the world yet? What about Hitler and Mussolini, you got them solved?'

Winger took Train by the elbow and steered him out of Walker's Bar. They made more stops; called in a couple of times; stopped at a Hungarian restaurant for a hot pastrami sandwich, a beer for Winger and a cup of coffee for Train; and headed back to the precinct house.

Train went home. His father was sitting in front of the radio. Edgar Bergen and Charlie McCarthy were trading wisecracks. The old man had a copy of the Brooklyn *Eagle* in his hands, but his eyes were closed and his chin was on his chest. The *Eagle* was opened to an article by the old man's favourite writer, a reporter named Barney Hopkins, who specialized in crime and Borough Hall corruption stories. Train couldn't tell if the old man was awake or asleep, so he left him alone.

His mother was cooking. Train went in the kitchen and gave her a kiss. She looked up at him and said he looked tired.

'Did a lot of walking, Mom. And it's cold outside. I think I'll take a bath and put on dry clothes. Pop okay? He's snoozing in front of the radio.'

'He's okay.' She didn't sound confident.

'Marie and Jocko gonna be here?'

'Not tonight.'

'Better give Pop a glass of Scotch. That always perks him up. He's too skinny. What's for dinner?'

'Never mind. Go take your bath.'

Train took his bath. Twenty years old, living in the apartment with his parents, taking a bath when his mother told him to. He put his service revolver in a drawer and pulled on some woolen pants and a sweatshirt so he'd be comfortable for dinner.

Pop had his Scotch in the parlour. He dropped the newspaper on the floor and turned off the radio when Mom called him to come eat. He wanted to know all about his son's first day on the beat and Train told him. Pop was most interested in the argument about the Dodgers.

'Thank God for the Phillies. Seventh place ain't so good but at least it ain't eighth.'

2

Screaming in Chinese

The next morning Train reported to work at the precinct. The snow had stopped falling and the sky was bright blue. The sun was as bright as a brand new penny. If you kept your eyes turned up it was a beautiful day.

The day went quickly. Winger asked him about life as a boxer. He didn't really enjoy talking about it much. It was a closed chapter in his life, a failed ambition, and it wasn't much fun to dwell on it. But he figured he had to keep his partner happy.

There were no more disappearances into back rooms. Winger and Train made it from one end of their beat to the other and started back. They stopped at the Imperial Palace again. Train ordered sizzling rice soup, wontons in hot oil, and something called dragon and phoenix.

He'd never had anything like it before. It was the best meal he'd ever eaten.

Susan Chen took their order and brought the dishes from the kitchen. Train wanted to talk to her but all he could think of was the food. He told her he was crazy about it. She seemed pleased. He spotted her brother giving them the evil eye. He'd heard that the Chinese were clannish. They didn't like their young people getting involved with white Americans. But Susan seemed to like him.

On Saturday he got Pop to go to the doctor. The doc looked him over, pounded on his chest, listened to his heart, made him stick out his tongue, poked a tiny light in his ears and up his nose. Pop didn't like his son being there during the examination, but Train insisted. The doc said the old man was doing as well as could be expected and should be okay if he took care of himself. He didn't say what that meant and he didn't say how long the old man would be okay.

Pop insisted on stopping at Walker's

Bar on the way home. With Train wearing civvies the atmosphere was more relaxed. Dinny waited on them. They had a couple of rounds to the background mutter of a basketball game on the radio. Then Train took Pop home.

Winger and Train didn't have too much action on their beat. There were domestic squabbles. Usually a husband with a load on beat up his wife. The neighbours heard the racket and called the precinct. Next time Winger and Train phoned in they'd get sent to the apartment and they would soothe the wife, warn the husband, and leave. They never arrested anybody.

A couple of times a week some kid would get caught shoplifting and the storekeeper would complain. Train figured they followed up about one call in ten. They'd threaten the kid with Riker's Island or worse if he wound up in juvenile court, then march him home, and his father would whale the daylights out of him and the kid would go on to bigger and better crimes.

Major excitement was a stabbing in front of Walker's Bar. Winger and Train didn't have to wait for word from the precinct on this one; there was so much excitement in the street you'd think Dinny was handing out free samples. It turned out that the victim was Train's pal, the big guy who liked Burleigh Grimes. The knife was wielded by his girlfriend, a dirty blonde with a dirty face. No, Train thought, that was unfair. Her face was streaked with tears. The dark stuff was mascara, not dirt. She was laying all over her boyfriend's body trying to stop the bleeding with her hands and crying up a storm. Dinny Moran and the little Dodgers fan and some other Walker's regulars were standing around.

Winger said, 'Train, you handle this one. I'll watch.'

Train got out his notebook and started asking questions. It seemed that the big guy had a new girlfriend, and his old one found out about it and warned him to cut it out or he'd be sorry. He hadn't cut it out and now it was his old girlfriend who was sorry. The big guy wasn't feeling anything.

Dinny and his flock drifted back

toward Walker's. Train managed to drag the woman off her victim's chest. There was blood on her coat and in her hair. Train put her in handcuffs. He spotted a call box nearby and kept her under control while he called for the meat wagon for the victim and the paddy wagon for the stabber.

He got home late that night; the paperwork had been awful. But Marie and Jocko were over for dinner and Mom made her special, pot roast and potatoes with red cabbage. Pop was doing okay. It was a good evening.

Once a week Winger would slow down their routine. He did his visiting the back room with the boss at most of the establishments on their beat. Never with Father Dempsey at St. Columba's, never with the rabbi at the shul — only with the businessmen in the neighborhood.

Train's old William Seward High School gang still assembled for card games. Usually the games were at Benny Jensen's house. They drank beer and ate sandwiches and played penny ante poker. Pudgy Watterson was working for the

Brooklyn Union Gas Company. He said it was boring and he was thinking of going to college. Jackie Goldstein was working for the phone company days and studying accounting nights. He was engaged to be married as soon as he got his accounting degree. Marty Macon wasn't doing anything special, picking up a few bucks here and a few bucks there. Benny Jensen was still pounding a beat in Staten Island.

After the game Pudgy Watterson and Jackie Goldstein went home. Marty Macon hung around for a while, acting as if he wanted to be invited to stay. Finally he gave up and headed into the night. That left Nick Train and Benny Jensen.

Benny Jensen said, 'There's something the matter, isn't there, Nick?'

'Yeah.'

'Must be cop stuff, right? You didn't want to talk about it with the other guys here. Pudgy and Jackie and Marty.'

'Right.'

'I thought Marty was never going to leave. Sometimes I wonder if that guy is all right. I saw your old man the other day. He don't look so good. Is that it?'

Train scrabbled for a church key and jerked the top off a bottle of Trommer's. He inhaled a sizable portion, then shook his head. 'I don't know about this job, Benny.' He searched for what to say next, but Benny Jensen saved him for the moment.

'I wonder about it myself, Nick. I mean, Staten Island ain't exactly Times Square. It's a hell of a long trip out there every day and I don't get paid for riding the train or the ferry. It's colder than a witch's kiss out there, too, with the wind blowing from every direction. Sometimes I think it's coming from Jersey and sometimes I think it's coming from Russia.'

Train managed a feeble grin.

'Trouble is, I don't know what else to do,' Jensen said. 'I mean, if I quit the force, what do I have? I wasn't exactly an 'A' student at Seward.'

'What about your old man, Benny — could he get you a job where he works?'

'At the DeSoto dealership? He's a partner now. Soon he'll have his name on the place. But they're not making any money, Nicky. I talked to him and he and Mom really need me bringing in an outside paycheck. Ever since they tried selling those Airflow cars back when we were still in school, the dealership's been in the dumps.' He shook his head. 'You know what? My old man bought one of those Buck Rogers things for himself. He got a great price.' He laughed. 'And it's a great car. He still has it, won't part with it for love or money. But nobody wanted the things, and DeSoto never got over it.'

He held out his hand and Train gave him the church key. He popped a Trommer's for himself and drew on it. 'So I guess I'll stick with this thing for a while. I don't know.' He yawned and stretched, his feet sticking out in front of him. There were holes in the bottoms of his shoes. 'I'll stick with it for now. The way things are going, there's gonna be another war, you can see it coming. That dust-up in Spain was just the preliminary. Wait till Stalin and Hitler start going at it, Nicky, it's going to be something crazy.

The Japs are kicking the Chinese around already. It's gonna be all over, just wait and see. Roosevelt says he's gonna keep us out of it, but just you wait and see, Nicky.'

Train stood up and walked a trifle unsteadily to the window. The streetlights' glare kept him from seeing much of the sky, so he couldn't tell whether it was cloudy or not; but a few snowflakes were drifting down — he could see that much — so he figured it wasn't exactly a clear and starry night. 'I got this partner,' he told Jensen. 'I don't know what to make of him, Benny.'

'What's the matter? He on your case?'

'No.' Train shuffled back to his easy chair. He had his Trommer's in his hand, had had it there all along. He held the bottle up and shook his head, then put it down and found another for himself. He had to get the church key back from Jensen to open the bottle.

'No,' he said again. 'He seems to be a decent mug. Kind of a geezer, past thirty, but not so bad for an old guy. But I think he's up to something.'

Jensen made a face. 'You gotta tell me more than that.'

So Train told him about Winger and Dinny Moran's back room disappearances and the other little side trips on their beat. Jensen asked how often that happened. Train told him once a week.

'How many places on your beat?'

'I don't know. Let me think about it.'

Jensen waited while Train counted on his fingers.

'You mean everything?'

'Just the commercial establishments. Don't count churches or schools.'

Train closed his eyes. When he opened them he said, 'Must be close to a hundred. Restaurants, bars, candy stores, groceries, couple gas stations, got a Chinese laundry even. Yeah, close to a hundred.'

'And he does this once a week, no more and no less.'

'Yeah.'

'Jeez, Nicky, how old are you? Don't tell me, I know. You are the most innocent baby I've ever met.'

'What? What?' Train pushed himself

out of his chair, or tried to — but fell back into it, the Trommer's bottle still in his hand, but nothing in the bottle.

'Holy smoke, Nick, do I have to spell it out for you? The guy's on the take.'

'On the take?'

'Jesus Christ on a crutch, pal, wake up, will ya? You got a hundred joints on your beat. He's shaking 'em down. Probably been at it for years. He's smart; he's not too greedy. He probably gets five bucks a week from the groceries and the laundry. Probably ten or even fifteen from the liquor stores and bars. He's pulling down five hundred smackers a week, Nick.'

Train blinked. 'He's dirty.'

'Oh, my gosh. Don't act so surprised. Nick, if you're shocked by that, listen, I've got a really nice bridge I'd like to sell you.'

'I better talk to Sergeant Garlington.'

'He your watch commander?'

Train grunted something that might have been a yes.

'Don't do it.'

'Don't do it?'

'Don't do it. Not if you like your job,

Nick. Not to mention your skin.'

'But — '

'But me no buts, pal. Didn't they teach you nothing at Seward?'

Train made another noise that might have been a no.

'Look, Nicky, I don't know how you lived this long without wising up even a little bit. Maybe you took one too many hard rights to the kisser. If your partner, what's his name, Wagner — '

'Winger.'

'Yeah. If Winger's on the take, you can bet your watch commander — '

'Garlington.'

'Right, he knows about it. He'll be getting a cut of everything Winger takes in and everything the senior cop on every beat on his watch takes in.'

'Then I'll go to Lieutenant Kessler.'

'No you won't. Nicky, Nicky, Nicky, do you know enough to wipe your own nose when you sneeze? If Winger's on the take then he's paying a cut to Garlington and Garlington's paying a cut to Kessler. Who knows how far it goes, maybe to the commissioner, maybe all the way to

Hizzonor.' He paused. There was a row of narrow, ground-level windows in Jensen's basement. Train turned his head and watched the snow falling.

'No,' Jensen said, 'not Hizzonor. Fiorello is such an honest guy, he wouldn't keep a dime if they gave him too much change at the A&P. But anybody else, you can bet they're all on the take.'

'Then what can I do, Ben?'

Benny gave him one of those looks. One of those *If you're that dumb there's no hope for you* looks.

'You think I should call in Internal Affairs?'

'Nick, Nick, you know what happens in the big house if you rat on another con? Death, my friend. Death. You can get away with almost anything in prison except squealing. That gets you the death penalty every time.'

'Yeah, but — '

'Don't gimme no yeah-buts, Nicky. The force is like one big happy prison yard. You call IA, you squeal on Winger, Garlington, Kitzler — '

'Kessler.'

'Katzenbaum, I don't care what his name is. You squeal, you're going to have an unfortunate accident. I tell ya what, you want to call IA, just make out an insurance policy with me as your beneficiary. I'll pay the premiums for you, won't cost you a dime. I'll be able to retire from the force and move to Florida.'

Train finished his bottle of Trommer's, swapped it for a fresh one and popped the cap. 'Okay, Benny. You tell me, then. What can I do?'

'What you can do is relax and enjoy it, Nicky. Sniff around. See if Wanger — '

'Winger.'

' — is due for a promotion. Some of these old-timers, they just homestead a beat and stay there forever. But Wanger might be ready for a bump and then you start taking home the extra mazuma. I wish there was something like that on my beat, but all I got out there is a bunch of poor slobs what can barely stay alive, no less support a business district. But I'm keeping my eyes and my ears open. I'm gathering information, Nick. You know the old saying: knowledge is power. I'm saving up, and one day I'll be as big as Con Edison.'

Train let his eyelids slide shut as he contemplated that. Next thing he knew, Benny was shaking him by the shoulders. 'You want to stay over, Nick? Or you want to head for home?'

'I'm okay. I'm okay, Benny. Feed me some coffee and I'll go home.'

The next week he asked Susan Chen if she'd like to go to a movie with him, and he was astounded when she said she'd like it a lot. They agreed that he'd pick her up at the Imperial Palace. The restaurant occupied the ground floor of a two-story building. The Chen family lived upstairs.

Train worked through the week with images of Susan in his mind. He had to go to court for a proceeding in the stabbing death of the baseball scholar. That was a nice break from his routine. When he and Dermott Winger visited Walker's Bar, Winger and Dinny Moran disappeared into the back room. The skinny Dodgers fan in the plaid jacket had found a new companion, a red-faced Irishman in a battered fedora, and continued his complaints about the baseball team as if nothing had happened.

Train's old man was still going to work almost every day, reading the Brooklyn *Eagle* every night, dozing over Barney Hopkins' exposés, listening to his favourite radio shows or maybe sleeping through them, and leaving his dinner untouched. Train found his mother in the kitchen, her face hidden in her apron, too many times. Marie was coming around more often, usually with her reluctant husband in tow. Train hugged his sister, shook hands with Jocko, and found that he had little to say to Marie and less to say to Jocko.

Saturday night he showed up at the Imperial Palace looking for Susan Chen. Old Man Chen didn't speak a word of English, or pretended not to. Susan's brother, Lawrence, gave Train a look that would have frozen a bucket of molten iron. Mama Chen gave Train a funny look and pointed to a doorway. That led to a staircase and he found Susan sitting in the Chens' parlour, reading a magazine. She jumped up and got her coat from the closet. Train held it for her and she slipped into it. He could smell her hair. It made him light-headed.

Susan asked if they could see *A Star Is Born* and Train agreed. When they got to the theater Morris Finch, the Adolph Menjou look-alike manager, spotted Train standing in line at the ticket booth. He pulled Train and Susan out of the line and ushered them into the theater. The candy girl recognized Train even in civvies and started to give him a big smile, then realized that he was with Susan Chen and went stone-faced.

Halfway through the movie Train put his arm around Susan's shoulders and she didn't object. Near the end of the movie she jumped when Fredric March hit Janet Gaynor. When Gaynor made her big *Missus Norman Mayne* speech, Susan burst into tears and Train even got choked up.

After the picture show Train and Susan walked to the corner, his arm around her shoulders. The night air was frigid. There was a lot of traffic. Train spotted a cop ahead of them, heading their way, recognizing him from the precinct. Train nodded as they passed. The cop started to smile, then looked at Susan and instead frowned.

'He doesn't like seeing us together,' Susan told Train.

'Tough. It's none of his business what we do.' The traffic light was red and they watched the cross traffic. 'You know what would warm us up?' Train asked.

Susan shook her head.

'How about a drink at Walker's?'

'You mean whiskey?'

'Whatever you want.'

'I don't drink whiskey.'

'Whatever you want,' Train repeated. 'You can even get a cup of coffee if you want it, but I wouldn't recommend it. Dinny makes a pot every day when he opens the bar and just leaves it on simmer all day. But it's a nice place. They have a fireplace.'

After a little more coaxing Susan agreed. 'But I can't stay out too late, Nicholas.'

'I'll get you home.'

Walker's was filled with an assortment of barflies bellied up to the mahogany, couples seated at tables with their heads together, and the usual collection of sports fans arguing about their favourite teams. For once the topic was football instead of baseball. Some guy was yammering about Tarzan Druze and the Seven Blocks of Granite. Train could only see him from the back. He bore an uncanny resemblance to the big guy who'd been stabbed outside Walker's, but when he turned around the resemblance disappeared.

Dinny Moran recognized Train. When Train and Susan Chen found a table Train had to go back to the bar for their drinks. There was no table service in Walker's. Dinny told Train their drinks were on the house. Walker's whiskey was okay, probably the same stuff that came in the bottle to start with. Susan Chen sniffed the coffee and put her cup back on the saucer. As usual the reception Train received in civvies was a lot friendlier than when he entered the bar in uniform.

A trio of whores were looking for trade without much success. Train had arrested a couple of them and one of them, a tall blonde who must have looked great thirty pounds and twenty years ago, winked at Train; he had to work to suppress a smile. He was off duty and he was damned if he was going to get involved collaring working ladies for trying to earn a living. Their racket was tough enough.

Susan Chen asked Train if he knew the blonde and what their exchange was all about, and he stammered an explanation. They had a couple of rounds, or he did anyway, feeling guilty that Susan just watched, and then Train walked Susan Chen back to the Imperial Palace. The establishment was dark but there was a light in the window upstairs. Susan got a set of keys out of her purse. She didn't invite Train in, but before she went upstairs she let him put his arms around her and kiss her on the mouth and she kissed him back.

He went home with his head spinning.

Jocko Sullivan was pacing in the living room smoking a cigarette. The radio was turned on and dance music was playing. Train was surprised. 'Where's Marie? Where's everybody?'

Jocko said, 'Your old man collapsed. Marie and me come over for dinner and everything was okay until your old man passed out. Fell off his chair. Hit his head on the table going down.'

'Where is he?'

'Marie called an ambulance for him. She rode along with him. So did your old lady. They're probably at the hospital now.'

'Which hospital?'

'I don't know.'

'What was wrong with Pop?' Train crossed the room and turned off the radio.

Sullivan said, 'I don't know. He seemed okay. He was reading the paper and listening to the radio, and your old lady called him to eat and he sat down at the table and just fell over.'

The phone rang. Train grabbed it. His sister was calling from the hospital. 'I'm glad you're home, Nick. It's Pop.'

'I know. Jocko told me. How is he?'

'Not so good. The doc says he's got a big problem inside. There's something wrong with his guts. The doc says he doesn't want to operate. He says Pop's too weak. He says they want to keep him for a couple of days and then they're gonna send him home.'

Train was holding the candlestick phone in one hand, the earpiece in the other. Jocko Sullivan had plopped himself in Pop's favourite chair and Train was pacing as far the telephone cord permitted. 'There's nothing they can do?'

'The doc says he'll be a little better for a while, that's all.'

'I'm coming down there. What hospital is he in?'

She told him and he left Jocko sitting in Pop's favourite chair. When he got to the hospital he saw the old man. He looked awful. He reached for Train with a hand like a chicken's foot. Train held his hand. The old man's eyes were open when Train arrived but he closed them and Train put his hand down and the old man didn't stir.

Train took his mother and sister home.

His sister Marie and Jocko left after a couple of hours. It was pitch black outside except for a few streetlamps and the traffic lights at the corner.

A few hours later Train grabbed a bite of breakfast and made his way back to the station house. He climbed into his uniform and went to work. It was quiet on the beat. Train didn't know whether he was glad of that or not. He would have liked a little distraction, maybe a fistfight at Walker's or one of the other bars on the street, or an unruly customer at the Four Star Kosher Butcher Shop, or a runaway kid. Even a dogfight would have been a break from worrying about Pop.

He hadn't even remembered that this was Winger's collection day. The older cop was taking his time at each stop. The customers didn't seem very happy. Not that they ever did when they had to pay off. But today they seemed edgy. Train wondered if he should ask Winger about it. Winger had never talked about the payoffs. Train figured he wasn't supposed to know anything about them. If that was so, Winger was certainly doing a lousy job keeping the payoffs secret. They were illegal as hell; they'd talked about them at the academy and a civilian guest speaker from the DA's office had come in to warn the baby cops that going on the take could not only cost them their jobs, it could land them in Dannemora.

All of that had Train wondering just what Benny Jensen knew, and how he had found it out. What was he planning to do with the information once he had enough to act?

Winger spent a long time in the meat room at the Four Star Kosher Butchers before he came out and snarled at Train. Their next stop was the Imperial Palace. Winger didn't take a table as he usually did, but grabbed Chen Ching-kuo, the old man, the owner of the place, and headed for the back. The bead curtain clacked and swayed from their passage. Train wondered what they had to talk about in the back room. Old Chen supposedly didn't know any English. Train figured he might actually know a few words but probably no more than that and Winger, Train was certain, didn't know Chinese.

Mrs. Chen was running the place along with her son and daughter. Susan Chen smiled at Train and asked if he wanted to sit down, but he said he was just waiting for Winger to come back and he'd know what to do then. Eventually Mrs. Chen disappeared through the bead curtain. She came back screaming in Chinese. Her son and daughter ran after her. Then she sat down at a table and started to cry.

She was crying and waving her hands and gasping out something in Chinese, and Susan and Lawrence were trying to calm her down. Finally she got out what sounded like a few sentences in Chinese, and Lawrence left Susan with her and ran to the back room.

Train got up and went over to Susan and Mrs. Chen, Chen Chu Hu. He asked, 'What happened?'

Susan stood up and said, 'I think it's Mr. Winger. You better come.'

She grabbed Train by the hand and pulled him through the bead curtain and into the back room. They left Mrs. Chen sitting at the table, crying. Although there were other customers in the restaurant and the chef was in the kitchen, Susan Chen and Nick Train headed for the back room.

Train had never been in the room before, and he didn't have time to take it in now because Dermott Winger lay sprawled face-down on the floor. His uniform cap had tumbled off and his hair seemed to be disarrayed until Train realized that he was actually bald. He'd worn a toupee all this time, and Train had never known it. He was wearing his full uniform, including his winter overcoat. There was a single small hole in the back of the overcoat. It wasn't obvious, not against the midnight blue of the woolen garment, but it was there and the dark stain around it was slowly spreading.

Old Man Chen, Chen Ching-kuo, was standing over Winger, wringing his hands and yammering away in Chinese.

Train dropped to his knees and put his face close to Winger's. He could see that Winger was alive, his back rising and falling with rapid, shallow breaths. Winger was trying to say something but all Train could make out was a string of violent oaths.

Winger didn't look good. Train asked what had happened, and Winger managed to turn his head so he was looking Train straight in the face. He mumbled something that made no sense at all, and closed his eyes.

Train put his fingers on Winger's neck and felt for a pulse, but there was none. He stood up and covered his face with his hands, shutting out the world for a few seconds while he frantically sorted out his thoughts. He dropped his gaze and surveyed the room. Susan Chen was holding her father's hands, trying to calm him down and having a fair degree of success.

Train said, 'Susan, is there a telephone in the restaurant?'

'Yes.'

'I need you to go call the precinct. Just tell the operator to get you the Brownsville precinct. Whoever answers, tell him that we have an officer down, send personnel. They'll know what to do.'

Susan released her father's hands and

ran to do as Train had told her. His mind was racing, speeding back to his classes at the academy, remembering the ordained procedure for dealing with a violent felony scene. He followed Susan back through the bead curtain and surveyed the restaurant. The lunchtime rush had passed and it was too early for the dinner crowd to arrive, so there were just a few customers. He took out his notebook and told them that there had been an incident and he would need their names and addresses and their telephone numbers, those of them who had telephones, in case it was necessary to contact them.

Most of the customers were cooperative. One henna-haired woman in a heavy coat and a knitted hat called him a Cossack and said she wouldn't provide any information — where did he think he was, Russia? — but he told her he would have to hold her as a material witness if she didn't cooperate, and she gave him her name and address. 'Under protest,' she spat, 'under protest. I'm going to take this up with my union, you hear me? And if I have to sue the city I'll do it!'

Train thanked the customers for their cooperation and let them leave, then had Susan Chen lock the front door. He had her accompany him to the back room to keep her father calm and to translate for him.

Now Train had a chance to look around the room. It was pretty nondescript. The walls were covered with a thick matting that looked like dried straw. The floor was covered with a dark-coloured carpet. It must have had an interesting pattern woven into it at one time, but by now it was threadbare and the pattern was long since obliterated. There were a few portraits on the walls. He thought he recognized the one-time Chinese boss, Sun Yat-sen. He didn't recognize the others in their military get-ups.

The room was furnished with a desk and a safe. The safe was locked. Train knelt beside Dermott Winger. He felt again for a pulse, knowing that he wouldn't find one, and he didn't. The breathing had ceased and Winger's skin was turning cold and clammy. Train was uncertain about touching the body once he'd determined that Winger was dead. He told Susan Chen to take her father out of the room, back to the restaurant. He considered telling her to take both her parents upstairs to the apartment but he decided it would be better to keep them close to the crime scene until precinct personnel showed up. He wondered where Susan's brother, Lawrence, had disappeared to.

The bead curtain clacked as Susan and her father left the back room.

3

Monsters in the Closet

Train studied the hole in Winger's overcoat. It wasn't very big, probably a .25, maybe even a .22, but the bullet had done its work. Whoever had fired was either a damned good shot or a damned lucky one, because the single round had entered Winger's back just to the left of the spine. It must have penetrated his heart and kept on going. That was all it took for a fatal wound.

He rolled Winger over on his back and studied what he saw, seeking evidence of an exit wound. Winger's blue uniform overcoat was buttoned up. There was a small hole just to the left of the center of his chest. There was a little blood around it, making a black disk on the blue wool overcoat. He unbuttoned Winger's overcoat and felt his inside pockets. He'd seen Winger with bulges in his uniform jacket, clearly payoff money. He found a bulge in Winger's top inside jacket pocket and pulled an envelope from the pocket. There was blood on the outside, and a small hole neatly punched in one side and out the other. He looked inside the envelope. It was filled with five- and ten-dollar bills, each of them showing a little round hole. There were even a couple of twenties. Benny had been right, then. Winger was on the take, running his own personal version of a Chicago-type protection racket, except that it was the beat cop and not the bootleggers or mobsters who were running the racket.

He heard someone hammering on the restaurant door. That meant that the precinct people were here. He had to decide, fast, what to do with the envelope. He rushed to the bead curtain and called Susan's name. She responded without delay. For once Train had got lucky: Lawrence Chen must have gone to let the police into the restaurant. Now he had to hope that Susan Chen knew the combination to the office safe.

He pushed the envelope toward her

and pointed to the safe with his other hand. 'Quick, put this in there!'

If she didn't know the combination there was no time to dispose of the envelope, but she did know the combination. She dropped to her knees and had the safe open in seconds, shoved the envelope inside, and slammed the door closed again. She spun the dial and rose to her feet.

Now Train heard voices from the restaurant. He pushed Susan Chen ahead of him and found Lawrence Chen talking with a group of newcomers. He recognized Sergeant Garlington by his rasping voice even before he saw his beefy form. Garlington had gray hair, a florid complexion, and a swaggering manner. Some old cops got beaten down and dispirited — Train had seen that — but not Charlie Garlington, not by a pretty penny. Garlington was strictly old school, a veteran of the day when the beat cop was the king of his own little piece of the city. It might be only a few blocks in length, but it was his domain, and woe to the miscreant who challenged him.

Things were different now, however: there was a New Deal in the land and a clean breeze blew from City Hall; and part of the new arrangement was the notion of the police officer as a public servant rather than a petty tyrant.

Yes, try telling that to Charlie Garlington.

There were a couple of other harness bulls with Garlington. Train recognized them and they all exchanged nods and muttered words. There was a detective with Garlington, too. He wore a camel's hair overcoat over a brown suit, a hand-painted tie and a good-looking fedora and wingtip shoes. Train had seen his face around the precinct but had never met him.

Garlington spotted Train. 'Report, Officer!' This guy didn't waste any words.

Train gave the briefest possible account of the crime. A cop had been killed in the line of duty. This was bad. He didn't say anything about the envelope he'd lifted from Winger's uniform jacket.

The plainclothesman said, 'Thank you, Sergeant. I'll handle this now.' To Train he said, 'You secured the crime scene, Officer?'

Train said, 'No one's been in there except Miss Chen and myself.'

'You brought a civilian into the crime scene?' The detective appeared incredulous.

'Her father was there already. He was acting — ah, he apparently witnessed the crime, but he doesn't speak English. Miss Chen acted as translator.'

The detective grunted. He took off his overcoat and handed it to a uniformed patrolman. He pulled a handkerchief from his trousers pocket, lifted his fedora, and wiped his face. Even though it was a winter day he was sweating. He shoved the handkerchief back in his pocket and replaced the hat carefully on his neatly arranged hair.

'All right,' he said, 'it's your squeal, Officer. What's your name?'

Train told him.

'All right. I'm Inspector Clarke. You're going to see more of me than you want to, starting right now. This is your beat, right? Yours and Winger's. You haven't been here long, have you? When did they turn you loose from the academy?'

'September, sir.'

'Okay. You didn't actually see Officer Winger shot, right? Hey, Lefcourt — ' He gestured to a uniformed cop. 'Take notes on this.' He turned back toward Train. 'Who saw Winger get shot?'

'Mr. Chen.'

'No one else?'

'No, sir.'

'Wait a minute.' He spun away and cleared the space to the bead curtain in long, heavy strides, setting the beads clattering as he barged through. 'Garlington! Who told you to violate the crime scene? Get the hell out of there. Go on!'

Sergeant Garlington emerged from the back room looking furious. He shot a look at Train but he didn't say anything.

'Is there another exit from this place? Is there anybody else in the building?'

Train said, 'I think Miss Chen knows best.'

Inspector Clarke looked around, spotted Susan Chen, and repeated his question. Susan stood up. She'd been sitting with her parents and her brother. She said, 'There's a back door from the kitchen. It's kept locked except to bring in deliveries or put out garbage. The chef is in the kitchen. He's been there all along. I think he heard the excitement and got afraid.'

'Speaks English?'

'No.'

'Okay.' He turned. 'Officer Horowitz, come here.' The uniformed cop hopped to it. 'Accompany Miss Chen. She's going to summon the cook. He doesn't speak English.'

Susan Chen and Officer Horowitz headed for the kitchen. They returned quickly. The chef — Train had never seen him before — turned out to look amazingly like Fatstuff, the comic relief guy in the *Smilin' Jack* comic strip. He looked hopelessly confused. Susan Chen said his name was Lee Hop.

Speaking through Susan Chen, Inspector Clarke asked the chef what he knew about the killing. Lee Hop looked more confused than ever. He spoke rapidly to Susan Chen in Chinese, while waving his

66

hands. She said, 'Inspector, he doesn't know anything about any killing. He's frightened. He says, 'Please don't send me back to China, the Japanese will kill me.''

Clarke told Susan to tell Lee Hop to relax, that nobody was going to send him back to China, and to just sit down until things were sorted out. Susan translated for Lee and he relaxed visibly, bowed to Inspector Clarke, and went to sit with Mrs. Chen. Clarke went through his hat-off, wipe-brow, hat-on thing again. He pulled a cigar from an inside pocket, located a gold-coloured guillotine in a trousers pocket, clipped the end from the cigar, and put away the guillotine. Then he found a matching gold-coloured lighter in his vest pocket, started the cigar going, and put away the lighter. Clearly, Nick Train thought, Inspector Clarke liked rituals.

'Okay,' Clarke rasped, 'here's who I want. Train, you were the reporting officer. I'm going to keep you close. Mr. Chen — ah, he can't understand me, you translate for your father, will you, Miss

Chen? He was with Officer Winger when Winger was shot, is that correct? I want him there and I want Miss Chen there as translator.' He started toward the bead curtain.

Sergeant Garlington moved toward the others. 'I think I should be there, Inspector.'

'No.' Clarke stopped him in his tracks. 'You're in charge here, Sergeant. You and Horowitz and Lefcourt. Nobody in or out. You play baby-nurse to Mrs. Chen and Junior there and what's-his-name, Lop Top.'

'Lee Hop, Inspector.' Train couldn't tell whether Susan Chen was annoyed or just being helpful as she added, 'In China, family name comes first, then person's name. Lee Hop is from family Lee; he's Mr. Lee.'

'Thanks, that's fine. Tell him to stay here with the others, all right? Good. Now, the rest of us — Mr. Chen, Miss Chen, Officer Train, come on.' The beads clattered behind him.

Train watched Clarke in action. The guy really knew what he was doing. He must have had the academy manual memorized. Maybe he'd written it. Using Susan Chen as interpreter, he questioned Chen Ching-kuo. Chen said that he and Winger had been chatting as they did from time to time. Winger was a good policeman, Chen said. He took nice care of everybody. He was honest. No trouble. He saw to it that no trouble happened to good people on his beat. Train wondered how Chen and Winger could chat if Chen couldn't speak English and Winger couldn't speak Chinese, but he kept his suspicions to himself.

Chen seemed pretty nervous as he answered Clarke's questions. Train didn't blame him. He wondered how much of the conversation was edited by Susan Chen. Obviously Chen and Winger hadn't spoken to each other if Chen knew almost no English and Winger didn't speak Chinese. Maybe it was all done with gestures. It certainly seemed odd. Chen Ching-kuo didn't say anything about payoffs to Winger, or at least Susan Chen's translations didn't include any mention of payoffs. Chen wasn't sure whether he had heard a shot or not. There was too much noise from the restaurant and from the kitchen. Maybe he'd heard a sound, something like a pop, maybe not. Winger fell down face first. Chen had quickly looked at him, found the hole in his back, saw that Winger was bleeding, and began to holler. That was when Train and Susan Chen came into the picture.

Clarke examined the body, nodded and grunted, the cigar clenched between his teeth. He told Officer Lefcourt to go fetch Horowitz and start looking for a weapon or other evidence of how the crime had been committed. Then he rounded on Train. 'You stand by, Officer. I don't want you interfering with the other officers, but I want you here. You understand?' Train said he understood.

The room was windowless. Some light penetrated from the restaurant via the hallway, but in fact not much got past the bead curtain. Most of the light in the room came from a single bulb hanging from a cord in the center of the ceiling. There was also a green-shaded lamp on the desk. Train scanned the ceiling. There was no indication of any opening. Besides, if the shot had come from above, Winger would have had to fall before the shot was fired in order for it to penetrate his body as it did; and old Chen indicated that Winger fell after the shot was fired, or at least after Chen thought he heard the popping sound.

Clarke told Susan Chen to have her father stand where he had been standing when he heard the pop, and to indicate where Winger had been standing. When Chen complied, Clarke barked an instruction to Lefcourt. The cop measured the distance from Winger to the wall behind him. He examined the wall carefully. The rough-textured straw-weave covering the wall would conceal a small opening, but Lefcourt managed to find a hole the size of a small-caliber bullet.

Next, Officer Horowitz followed the same imaginary line in the other direction, beyond Winger's body. Crawling on all fours, Horowitz found a bullet lying against the baseboard. 'What do you think, Train?'

Why has Clarke singled me out for the

question? Train wondered.

'Come on, you're a smart boy. I read your academy transcript. You've got a bright future in this here man's police force, Officer. What do you make of this?'

'Officer Winger was shot through the wall, Inspector.'

'Good. How did the shooter take aim?'

'May I take a look over there?' Clarke nodded. Lefcourt stepped aside, looking unhappy. Train studied the wall, fingering aside the woven straw carefully to minimize changing it in any way. Either he could hear a clock ticking or there was one going in his head. Then he smiled. He turned around, indicating his find. 'There's a peep-hole here.'

Clarke grinned. He pulled on his cigar, then exhaled smoke toward the overhead light fixture. 'Anything else, Train?'

'It wasn't made very long ago. Look at this. The wood inside the peephole is still fresh. Wait a minute.' He knelt. 'And look at this. A fresh wood shaving on the carpet.'

Clarke pointed at Susan Chen with his cigar. 'What's next door, Miss Chen?'

Susan tilted her head as if calling up information from a well of memory. 'Let's see. One side, candy store; other side, butcher shop.'

'Which one is on this side?'

'Oh, that's the butcher store. Mr. Little's butcher store.'

Clarke left Sergeant Garlington in charge of the Chen family and Lee Hop in the Imperial Palace. He led the others — Train, Lefcourt, Horowitz — back onto the sidewalk and into the Four Star Kosher Butcher Shop. During the few seconds they were outside, Train caught sight of a police car pulled to the curb, another officer he knew waiting patiently behind the wheel. The sky had turned to a dark gray and once more a few flakes were drifting down. The patrol car's green and white and black patterned paint job showed streaks where flakes had landed and melted and run.

The interior of the Four Star Kosher Butcher Shop was chilly. The floor was covered with sawdust. There were glass display cases filled with whole small dead creatures and pieces of large dead creatures. There was a back counter of heavy wood, stained with blood. There were heavy cleavers and knives that Train imagined could split a man down the middle if wielded with enough force.

Three butchers stood behind the counter, uniformed in white shirts and bloodied aprons and straw skimmers, facing a row of customers waiting to take home fresh meat for their dinner tables. On the wall there was a large framed photograph of a bearded man in ecclesiastical clothing. Beside it hung a fancy certificate in Hebrew.

'Who's in charge?' Inspector Clarke demanded.

One of the butchers pointed to the rear of the shop. In heavily accented tones he said, 'The owner is in the back.'

Clarke didn't bother to respond to the statement. He gestured over his shoulder to the three uniformed officers, a clear *follow me* gesture, and headed in the direction the butcher had indicated. As Train moved to obey Clarke, he noticed that the other two butchers had ignored the exchange. The one who had answered turned back to a customer and began to converse in Yiddish.

There was a heavy wooden door at the back of the butcher shop. Clarke opened it. Beyond was a cooler compartment the size of a small living room. Whole carcasses hung from meat hooks. A short, heavyset man stood at the far end of the cooler compartment. He wore a white butcher's outfit and a paper cap. His apron was stained with blood. He held a heavy butcher's knife in one hand and a small pistol in the other.

He stood blinking at the new arrivals.

Train saw Inspector Clarke make a move toward his shoulder, but before Clarke could draw a gun Train said, 'Wait, Inspector, I know him.'

Clarke shot a glance over his shoulder at Train. 'Your move, Officer.'

Train held his hands up in a placating posture. 'Mr. Little.'

The butcher's expression had been glazed. Now he blinked and shook his head like a dog shaking water from its coat.

'Herr Kleinmann.'

The butcher lowered his hands. He

didn't drop the blade or the gun, but the tip of the knife and the muzzle of the revolver were now pointed at the floor midway between himself and the police.

'Herr Kleinmann,' Train repeated. He tried to remember the few words of Yiddish he'd picked up on his beat. '*Vos forkomen?*'

The butcher blinked again. He shook his head a second time. His face was round and he was wearing wire-rimmed spectacles with thick lenses that made his eyes look the size of BBs.

'*Ich bin eine ro 'tsai'ach.*'

That was the limit of Train's Yiddish, both to speak and to understand. He said, 'Okay, Mr. Little. It's okay. Please put your weapons on the floor.'

Little complied. Clarke gestured. Horowitz and Lefcourt rushed forward. Within seconds Horowitz had collected the butcher's knife and revolver, and Lefcourt had handcuffed Little.

Clarke gritted, 'What did he say?'

Before Train could reply, Horowitz translated. 'He says he's a killer, Inspector.' He grinned. 'Jeez, Nick, I didn't know you were Jewish.'

'I'm not.'

'I could tell.' Horowitz laughed.

Inspector Clarke turned slowly in a circle. Train inferred that he was orienting himself, locating the wall that abutted the back room of the Imperial Palace. He pushed aside a couple of carcasses hanging from a horizontal rod.

'C'mere.' He gestured to Train. 'Look at this.'

There were two holes in the wall. A brace and bit lay on the floor beneath them. One hole was at the height of Train's shoulders. He bent and put his eye to it. He could see into the back room of the Imperial Palace. The hole was just about at the eye level of the short, stout Henry Little. Train dropped to one knee to get a close look at the lower hole. It, too, looked like the result of work with the brace and bit. It was surrounded by a ring of black matte material. Train sniffed. It was gunpowder. There was little question now as to how Henry Little had killed Dermott Winger. The real question was why he had done it.

Clarke had Officer Lefcourt summon the paddy wagon for Henry Little. Then he asked Train what he thought of the incident.

'Beats me, Inspector.'

'Sure it does, Train.' He drew on his cigar, then exhaled. 'You're no dummy, Train.' He studied the glowing tip of the cigar. 'Come on, Officer, we're going to seal this room until the evidence techs can file their report. Then we'll let the providers of victuals to the community resume their honest labours.'

At the precinct, Little refused to answer questions in English. Train's feeble attempts at Yiddish got nowhere. Clarke called Horowitz in to serve as interpreter. Not that this did much good. Little made no attempt to deny committing the crime, but he refused to say why he had killed Winger. He admitted that the butcher's knife was his. He used it in his work. The brace and bit had come from his home. He had purchased them at the hardware store around the corner and brought them to Four Star to use in some amateur carpentry, or so he claimed.

'And the gun?' Clarke asked, via Horowitz.

'I found it in the gutter,' Little replied, via Horowitz.

The questioning went on for a couple of hours, but Little refused to budge. He was perfectly forthcoming about drilling the peephole and the firing hole between the meat cooler and the back room of the restaurant. He even pantomimed his actions in shooting Winger.

How had he become adept at the use of firearms?

Oh, he had been drafted into the Emperor's service as a young man, long ago, long before he left Europe for the Land of Opportunity.

And why had he killed Winger?

Because he had to.

And why had he had to kill Winger?

Because it was necessary.

Clarke had Little booked. He wrote up a report for the DA's office. He tugged back his sleeve to check his Bulova wristwatch, then raised his eyes to the Manishewitz Wine wall clock to get a second opinion. He heaved a weary sigh.

'All right, boys. You're all going to be late for dinner. I'm sorry. Sign out and go home. We'll see you in the morning.'

On his way out of the precinct Train passed Sergeant Garlington. The sergeant looked annoyed but he didn't say anything to Train.

The apartment was quiet when he got home. Train's mother met him at the door. He put his arm around her shoulders and kissed her on the forehead. He hadn't realized how thin she was getting; he could feel her bones through the back of her dress. Even her bones seemed light and fragile. His father was in bed. They had scraped up the cash to buy a second radio, a table model, and it stood beside the bed. It was turned on, its dial glowing orange. A detective play was in progress. A copy of the Brooklyn *Eagle* lay across the quilt. The old man was sleeping, his chest rising and falling gently with each breath.

Train folded the newspaper and tucked it under his arm. He turned off the radio and walked quietly from the room. He sat at the kitchen table, still in uniform; he'd been too tired even to change to civvies at the precinct. His mother brought him a bowl of tomato soup. A dish of little oyster crackers stood on the table. Train picked up half a dozen crackers and dropped them in his soup. He watched them slowly absorb the red liquid and soften. When he realized that he had nearly fallen asleep he rubbed his face and blinked.

The old lady had sat down opposite him and leaned her elbows on the oilcloth. Train had never seen her looking so weary. He reached across the table and laid his hand on hers, and she dropped her face and laid her cheek against the back of his hand. After a minute she pushed herself upright, leaving her son's hand wet with her tears.

Train had already laid the newspaper on the table. A story in the newspaper caught his eye. It was an exposé of corruption in Borough Hall. The byline was that of Pop's favorite *Eagle* reporter, Barney Hopkins. It was obvious that Hopkins's star was rising at the paper. His stories appeared on page one and he always got a byline. He even had a weekend column, not hard news but more of an opinion or analysis piece, with his picture next to it. He wore glasses and he looked as if he needed a haircut. Well, he didn't owe his success to good looks, anyway. He looked more like Donald Meek than Clark Gable.

Train's mother said, 'You look tired, Nicholas.'

He admitted that he was. He picked at his soup. Tired as he was, he didn't have much of an appetite.

'So what happened today, Nick? What's the matter?'

How much should he tell her about Winger's death and the arrest of the butcher Henry Little? Department policy discouraged cops from talking about active cases off duty, even with family members. But Train knew that everybody did it. When he'd told his mother about the stabbing at Walker's Bar, she'd clucked her tongue and sighed and made a comment about people who drank too much.

'Not that I want to bring back

Prohibition,' she added. 'All it did was make people make their own liquor and make themselves sick. And the bootleggers, the gangsters — oh, if people want to drink whiskey, let them drink whiskey. But I don't like it. I don't like it.'

Train didn't say anything about Winger and Little. Instead he said, 'No coffee for me tonight, Ma. I'm beat. You keep Pa company, all right? Listen to the radio, put your feet up, try and rest. I have to turn in.'

He took today's copy of the *Eagle* into his bedroom. He washed up and climbed into his pajamas and sat in bed reading Barney Hopkins's story on corruption for the second time. When he was this tired he could read something and think he understood it and ten seconds later it was gone from his head. He turned to the sports section, but he couldn't get interested in basketball. It was January and the Dodgers would start spring training soon in Florida. That would be fun, he thought, to go to Florida and watch spring training games, see if the Dodgers had any young talent worth bringing up, or if they'd be as bad in 1939 as they'd been in '38.

The next morning there was plenty of scuttlebutt at the precinct house about Winger and Henry Little. Nobody would say anything officially, but Train got in early enough to share coffee with some others on his shift. Apparently Clarke had brought Horowitz back to question Little some more and got no results, so he bucked the case up to Lieutenant Kessler. Kessler called the DA's office and they sent down a Yiddish-speaking assistant DA to talk to Little.

The fat butcher proved to be a tough nut to crack. He didn't deny committing the crime. He didn't deny drilling the two holes from the meat cooler to the back room at the Imperial Palace. He didn't deny shooting Winger. He didn't demand a lawyer, either. Maybe he didn't know he was entitled to one, and maybe he'd never heard of the right not to incriminate himself. He was from the old country, where you didn't have rights. Maybe he thought America worked that way, too.

At the shape-up Sergeant Garlington

announced that Officer Winger had been tragically taken from the ranks of the finest, and an orphans' and widows' fund collection would be taken up. Train didn't even know that Winger had been married. Winger had not been very garrulous, and he never mentioned anything about his home life.

Train was assigned a new partner, a cop named Tim Charters. Charters spoke with a southern accent. He liked to talk. Train thought that was a good thing up to a point. It kept him from dwelling too much on Winger's death, his own complicity in Winger's collection racket, his dying father, his fragile mother, the fact that there was an envelope full of money in the safe at the Imperial Palace with Winger's blood on the outside and a bullet hole through it.

Susan Chen was a smart girl. She would figure things out. She must know that Winger had been on the take from her father, and if she knew that she would realize that he was on the take from every business he could squeeze, which was every business on his beat. Would Susan leave the envelope in the safe? Train doubted that. But what would she do with it? Officially she didn't know that Henry Little had been arrested for the murder, but news spread like wildfire in Brownsville. Surely everyone up and down the street was aware of what had happened by now.

Charters was going on about the terrible northern winters and how much nicer the southern climate was, and how cold and hostile northern people were compared to the gentle manners of friendly southern folks, and especially what was wrong with these uppity northern Negroes who just didn't know their place. He blamed the whites as much as the Negroes because half the time the whites encouraged them to be uppity, especially those Jews who seemed to think that they were as good as anybody else and even that Negroes were, too. 'They ought to try that down in Mississippi where I come from; we'd teach 'em a lesson quick. You want to see happy people, you just visit Hattiesburg some time, you'll see.'

They were walking the beat that Train had shared with the veteran Winger, had learned from Winger. He hadn't cared a lot for Winger, but he had to admit that he'd been a good cop in his own way. He didn't shove people around, he showed up for work and didn't malinger, and as far as Train knew he didn't stab any other cop in the back. He wasn't honest, okay, but he didn't squeeze anybody too hard. No, he didn't deserve to get picked off in an ambush the way he had.

Charters was still going on about the wonders of the South. Train had heard it before and ignored it.

When he got home that night, there was a story on the Winger killing in the *Eagle*. It was bylined Barney Hopkins.

Train picked up the telephone and started to call his friend Benny Jensen. He needed to talk to somebody, and he didn't trust anybody else at the precinct to keep his mouth shut. Pop was too sick to carry on a serious conversation, Train didn't want to add to Mom's burden, and Marie and Jocko were hopeless. But before he got through to Benny he changed his mind. Instead, he called the Brooklyn *Eagle* and asked for Barney Hopkins. He had no idea what kind of office hours Hopkins kept, or whether he would be at the *Eagle* or out covering a story even if these were his office hours, but it didn't hurt to try.

'Hopkins.' The reporter answered in a thin voice, pitched almost as high as a woman's. Between the photo in the weekend paper and the man's voice, Train felt anything but reassured, but he didn't want to give up.

'Is this Barney Hopkins?'

'That's me. Who's calling?'

'Do I have to say?'

'Not yet. Not if you don't want to. Eventually, though, I'll want to know who I'm talking to. What do you want?'

Train squeezed his eyes shut and concentrated. Pop was asleep, he knew, and Mom was sitting by his bedside, her own eyes shut, half-listening to *The Goldbergs* on the radio and half-dozing herself. Certainly no one would overhear his half of the conversation with Hopkins.

'Are you there?' Hopkins asked.

'I'm here, Mr. Hopkins. I read your story in the *Eagle*. Your story about Officer Winger.'

'Okay, thank you, a lot of people read the *Eagle*. What can I do for you?'

'I'm not sure, Mr. Hopkins. I think there are some things you should know about.'

'All right, that's my business. Let's have it.'

'Maybe — maybe we should meet.'

'Listen, I have a job, fella. If you have some information for me, I'm ready to hear it. You don't need to play Mata Hari. Why all the cloak and dagger?'

'I think it might be dangerous. You know about Dermott Winger and Henry Little?'

'Of course. Anybody kills a cop in this town, it's important news. I wish we'd had more details for the late edition. What do you know about it? Give me something good and we'll have it on page one tomorrow.'

'I was Winger's partner, Mr. Hopkins.'

'Holy smoke! Wait a minute, kid. Let me get my pencil.'

'I don't know if I ought to talk on the phone, Mr. Hopkins.'

'Nobody's gonna hear you.'

'Even so, I don't know, I think it might be better if we could meet.'

'All right, kid, if that's the way you want it. What's your name?'

Train told him.

Hopkins said, 'Wait a minute, never mind.'

Train heard a dull sound followed by a scrabbling noise; he guessed Hopkins had put down his telephone and was looking for something.

'Okay, you're Officer Nicholas Train, right?'

'Yes, sir.'

'I recognize your name. You haven't been in the news lately, have you? Wait a second, don't tell me. You used to turn up on the sports page; you were — wait a second — a baseball player? No. Football, basketball? No wait, I got it — you're the boxer, ain't you? Hey, I think I saw you fight a couple of times. You weren't too great, were you?'

'No. That's why I'm a cop now.'

'Good for you, kid. Get out of the racket before you get your brains scrambled. I've seen too many ex-pugs that can't focus, can't carry a thought. So you're a cop now. What can you tell me about Winger and Little? Why'd the little guy shoot Winger?'

'I'm not really sure. But I think I have an idea.'

'Okay, what's your idea?'

'I don't think I can say on the phone, Mr. Hopkins.'

'All right, kid, let's do it your way, then. When can you come down to the *Eagle*?'

'I'm not so sure I can do that, either.'

'Why not, kid?'

'I just — I don't know, Mr. Hopkins. I just, well, I don't want to do that.'

'Okay, you want me to come to your place?'

'I'm not so sure about that, either.'

'Jeez, kid, you call me up and tease the hell out of me, and then you won't talk to me on the phone and you won't meet me here and you don't want me to come to your house. You remind me of my old girlfriend. What the hell do you want?'

'Maybe we could meet somewhere else.'

'Okay. You name it.'

Train rubbed his forehead. 'How about Schrafft's?'

'Sure. Any particular one, or do you want to play hide-and-go-seek?'

Train mentioned a Schrafft's in mid-town Manhattan. It was the most anonymous place he could think of. Hopkins asked when Train could meet him. Train was off in two days. Hopkins grumbled that he wanted to meet sooner, but he agreed. 'How will I know you, kid? You gonna wear your uniform?'

'I don't think that would be a good idea, sir.'

'Okay, how about a white carnation in your lapel? If you can't pass for Robert Montgomery I'll know it's you.'

'No, Mr. Hopkins. Just show up. I'll recognize you from your picture in the *Eagle*.'

Hopkins snorted. 'I knew that had to be good for something.'

They set a time and Train put the earpiece back on the hook. He checked on Mom and Pop. They were both snoozing. What happened, Train wondered, what happened? Yesterday I was a kid fighting with Marie, and Mom and Pop were giants who ruled the world and handed out rewards when we were good and spankings when we were bad and put us to bed and called the doctor when we were sick. And now . . . now, Marie was married and only showed up when she could get her fascist husband to stir his behind out of their house, and Pop was surely dying and Mom was not much better off and Nicholas Train was — he got up and looked in the mirror.

What was Nicholas Train?

He picked up the candlestick phone again and plugged the speaker in his ear. He called Benny Jensen's house and Benny answered. Train said, 'I gotta talk to you, Benny. I wanna come over to your house right now, okay?'

He left a note for the old lady so she wouldn't worry if she woke up before he got back from Benny's place. He bundled up in a sweater and his heaviest coat, pulled on galoshes, and braved the night.

As he left the apartment house a car started its motor and turned on its lights. The car didn't move until he started along the sidewalk. It followed him to the bus stop. The driver pulled to the curb and turned off his lights. The car was still there when the bus arrived and Train climbed aboard and dropped his nickel in the fare box.

He sat down next to a window and tried to decide whether the car had been waiting for him and had deliberately followed him. He couldn't solve that one. Maybe he was going nuts, jumping at shadows, seeing spies under the bed and monsters in the closet like a six-year-old. Or maybe this was real.

4

The Mayonnaise is Starting to Turn

Neon signs in store windows, the new orange glowing sodium streetlamps overhead, headlights and tail-lights of cars in the street, a pattern of weaving colours and images. Train could see faces and figures and animals and buildings in the pattern. He squeezed his eyes shut, held them for a moment, then opened them and discovered that the bus had stopped and an old woman carrying a bag of groceries was climbing painfully aboard. She dropped her fare in the box and hobbled down the aisle to sit next to Train. He pushed himself against the window to give her room. The driver closed the door with a hiss and the bus pulled away from the curb.

Benny Jensen was playing records when Train arrived at his house. Train heard a sweet-voiced siren sobbing through

'Where or When.' Benny turned off the Victrola. He took one look at Train and disappeared from the room. When Benny got back, Train was slumped on the couch. Benny clutched a bottle of whiskey in one hand and a couple of glasses in the other. He poured a couple of fingers' worth and handed the glass to Train. He poured a smaller drink for himself.

'I've seen you worse, Nick, but only after you'd taken a whipping at the Arena.'

Train took a swallow of whiskey, coughed, set down his glass, and grunted something like, 'Yeah.'

'What's the matter?'

'Bad stuff going on, Benny.'

'I coulda guessed. What bad stuff?'

'You know, there have been a couple of killings on my beat.'

'I know.'

'The first one was routine. Stupid. Guy was running around with a broad, got tired of her, started running around with another broad. He didn't bother to tell the first one she was out. She was putting him up and paying his bills; I guess that was why he didn't want her to know about his new squeeze. She found out anyhow, got annoyed, and came down to Walker's Bar and sliced him up.'

'I know.'

Train drank his whiskey, lowered his glass, and put his face in his hands.

'That isn't what's bothering you, Nick.'

'I know.'

'So do I. It's Winger.'

Train nodded.

'Not your fault, chum. Why the hell did that butcher guy kill your partner, what's the Yid's name?'

'Henry Little. Heinz Kleinmann.'

'Yeah.'

This time Jensen paused to swig at his glass. He peered at Train's glass. Train held it up. It was empty. Jensen refilled it.

'Why'd he do it, Nick?'

Train stood up and made a circuit of the room, whiskey glass in hand. He was still pretty steady on his feet. He watched Benny Jensen watch him do it. When he got back to the couch he sat down. He hadn't spilled a drop. He took a healthy swig to celebrate.

'You didn't drive over here, did you, Nick?'

'Don't have a car.'

'Then you won't drive home drunk. Just don't fall in a snowdrift and freeze to death.'

Train managed a hint of a smile. 'Yeah, I promise.'

'Okay, what about Winger?'

'Benny, I trust you.'

'Swell. I trust you too, Nick.'

'I mean, I trust you.'

'Right.'

'What I tell you — ' Train set his glass down. The whiskey sloshed around but didn't overtop the rim. He managed to get his eyes into focus and maybe his brain. 'What I tell you, you don't tell nobody, right? Not IA, not Pudgy or Jackie or Marty, nobody.'

'Right.'

'Benny, is everybody on the take? I mean, everybody?'

He didn't wait for Jensen to reply. He just rambled on.

'I thought Dewey cleaned that all up. I mean, we were just school kids, weren't we, when he started rounding 'em up? When did Lehman bring him in? When did he kick Dodge out and bring in Dewey? Didn't he go after Tammany? Didn't he go after Schultz?'

'Dewey didn't get Schultz,' Jensen said. 'Charlie Workman done it. Workman was a hired gun, you know that. Luciano and Lansky sent the Bug, and the Bug got the Dutchman, and that crazy Dutchman babbled away for two days and then he kicked it. Dewey didn't have nothing to do with it.'

'All right, all right, I don't care who shot the Dutchman. I mean, I mean — ' He stopped and gathered his thoughts. 'I mean, it didn't work. It didn't work. Lucky's in the pen, but it's still going on. Everybody's on the take, Benny. Everybody.' He couldn't go any farther. He put his chin on his chest and closed his eyes.

Somehow Benny must have got him back in his heavy coat and onto the bus. Train somehow stumbled up the stairs and into bed. There was an elevator in the lobby but it didn't work half the time and he wasn't up to dealing with it. He woke up with a hangover but at least he was in his bed. Mom gave him a big breakfast and avoided his eyes. Pop actually managed to crawl out of bed and into a bathrobe and drag himself to the table. He sat there looking like a ghost while Mom shoveled scrambled eggs into his mouth. Like a ghost or like a very sick, very skinny child.

★ ★ ★

Train walked his beat that day with Officer Charters. He got a non-stop lecture on how the Red Communists and the Jewish bankers and the coloureds were all working together to take over the world, and the good white Christian Americans had better wake up and do something about it before it was too late. Look at what happened in Spain. If Hitler and Mussolini hadn't helped out, there would be a Red government in Madrid right now, and France would go next, and then there would be a real mess.

Train closed his ears and let Charters's words roll over him and fall into the slush in the street. He didn't collect any of the five- and ten-dollar pay-offs that Winger had habitually squeezed out of the merchants on their beat. He didn't go into the Imperial Palace because he didn't know what to say to Susan Chen and he didn't want to stand there feeling stupid and looking like a cigar store Indian. He stepped into the Four Star Kosher Butcher Shop long enough to introduce Charters. Nobody said anything about Little and Winger. Train decided that was the way it was, so he dragged Charters out of there as fast as he could.

He hadn't heard anything from Inspector Clarke, but he expected to any day. He avoided Sergeant Garlington at the precinct. He knew he'd have to face him before very long, but he didn't want to deal with that any sooner than he had to.

When he got home his old lady greeted him at the door, ashen-faced. He figured the old man had died but even standing in the doorway he could see Pop sitting next to the radio wearing a bathrobe, the *Eagle* in his lap, some war rumours from England on the radio.

'Benny's gone,' the old lady whispered.

Train didn't know what she meant, or maybe he didn't want to know. 'What, Ma, what?'

'He disappeared. His mother called here. She thought maybe he was here. He's your best friend, Nicholas.'

'Yeah, Ma. I gotta come in the house, come on. How's Pop doing? It's cold as ice outside. I'm shivering. Look at me, I'm shivering. What's this about Benny?'

'I told Mrs. Jensen she should call Pudgy Watterson's house or Jackie Goldstein's house or Marty Macon's house. I know the five of you were friends. You were friends since William Seward High, or longer; am I right, Nicholas?'

'Yeah, Ma.'

'I told her she should call Pudgy's house or Jackie's house or Marty's house. They should know — their mothers should know — am I right?'

'Ma, I gotta get some warm, dry clothes on. I changed out of my uniform at the station house and put on my civvies, but I got so cold coming home, I gotta change again. Is Pa okay?'

'The same.'

'Okay. I'll be right out.'

He took a quick shower and put on a pair of woollen slacks and a flannel shirt and a sweater. He felt better that way. He went back to the living room. The old man was sitting in his favourite chair — or maybe it was just the ghost of the old man. He looked so thin and so fragile, like he would disintegrate if you touched him, like Karloff at the end of one of those creepy mummy movies.

The old lady was in the kitchen making dough. She would mix flour and water and a little lard. She would set a lump of it on the board, pound it flat with her fist, roll it with her heavy rolling pin, fold it up, and start over again. Every so often she would sprinkle it with water or flour. Train remembered watching her do it when he was a little kid. It seemed that Ma could do it for hours on end — pounding, rolling, sprinkling, folding, pounding. He never tired of watching her. It was the best show in the world.

Finally she put the dough in a bread

pan. 'There. I put in yeast — it should rise — then I'll bake it. They can't make good bread at Dugan's A&P. They make bread it's like poison in your mouth; you need bread you make at home.' She put her hands on her hips. She was wearing an apron that tied around her shoulders and around her waist. Somehow it made her look more substantial, less like a wax figure.

Train picked up the phone and called Benny's house. He got Benny's father. 'They're dragging the harbour,' Mr. Jensen told him. 'They're looking for him, Nick. He left home this morning. He had a long trip to work, you know.'

'I know, Mr. Jensen.'

'He never showed up at Staten Island. They tried to find out what happened. He used to stop for a hot dog and a cup of coffee on the ferry every night, trying to warm up and get something in his belly on his way home. Imagine, a hot dog for dinner! Not for me to judge, Nick. The vendor — they got to know each other — the vendor remembered seeing him tonight. They think he fell overboard. He fell overboard or somebody pushed him off the ferry. If he's in the harbour he's dead, Nick. Who would do such a thing? You knew Benny better than anybody — you were his best friend — that's why his mother called your house. Benny never came home. The precinct in Staten Island — I phoned the precinct and asked about him but they didn't know anything. He just never came home. Who would push a young man, a young police officer like Benny — practically a boy — who would push him off the Staten Island ferry, Nick?'

Benny's old man paused for breath. Nick Train asked, 'When you called the precinct, did they know he was missing? He worked his shift, didn't he, Mr. Jensen? He clocked out and left for home — or did he? He worked the graveyard, came home, and went to bed in the morning, didn't he? Before the next night, if he didn't show up for work, how would they know he was missing?'

Train could almost see Benny's dad shaking his head. He was a tough old Swede with iron-colored hair. 'They told me somebody called them. His sergeant told me somebody called the precinct house and told them to look for Officer Jensen, see if he ever made it home. That's when we got worried. He isn't home. If he's in the harbour he's dead, I know it. I can't find out anything. They said they're looking for him — dragging the harbour — that's all they'll tell me.' The old man stopped and made a sound, like maybe clearing his throat or maybe a sob. 'Who would do such a thing, Nicholas?'

'I don't know,' Nick said. 'I'll see if I can find out anything from my own precinct. I'll call you if I learn anything, Mr. Jensen. I'm sorry. Benny's a terrific kid; he's my best friend. I hope he's okay, Mr. Jensen.'

Nick called the precinct and got the swing shift desk sergeant. He didn't know him, but the sergeant knew Train. 'Yeah,' he told Train, 'we got word a little while ago. Maybe he jumped, Train. What do you think? Maybe he jumped. Was he having problems? Was he unhappy with his job? Graveyard ain't exactly choice duty and Staten Island is no bargain neither. I guess he didn't like it much, but nobody would kill himself over that, would he? Maybe it was something personal. I didn't know the kid, myself. Was he a drinker? Was it woman trouble? What?'

'I don't know, Sergeant. I thought he was okay. He didn't like commuting to Staten Island, but that's no reason to jump off the ferry, that's for sure.'

The sergeant didn't bother to reply.

'Jensen's father thinks somebody pushed him,' Train said.

'Why do you think that?'

'I didn't say I thought it. Benny's old man thinks he was pushed. Me, I don't know, Sergeant. There's just too much bad stuff happening. Dermott Winger getting shot, now Benny Jensen disappearing — '

'That's a stretch, Train. You're a young cop, fella. You're a kid. You gotta be a harness bull for a few years before you can play Hawkshaw. Don't try and be a detective before you're ready. Things happen every day. Doesn't prove there's a connection.'

'I don't know,' Train conceded. 'I don't like it.'

'Couldn't be an accident?'

'He wasn't drunk. Not at the end of his shift, Sergeant. Not any time, probably. I knew Benny. He wasn't much of a drinker. He wasn't drunk.'

'Okay, Train. You get any ideas, give us another call. You're on duty tomorrow, ain't you?'

'Yes.'

'Don't fall off any ferries on your way to work, Officer Train.'

★　★　★

He introduced his new partner to Susan Chen. With Charters at his elbow, Train didn't dare ask Susan what she had done with the envelope he'd lifted from Winger's body. There was no question that Susan was smart enough to know the envelope was sheer dynamite. She could have burned the envelope, but what about the money? Would she burn that, too? Would she try to spend it? That was dangerous. You didn't go around buying groceries or movie tickets with five- and ten-dollar bills with bullet holes in them, not if you didn't want somebody to notice you. She was too smart to leave the money in the safe, either. Inspector Clarke or another cop would surely look in there, and soon. She might have burned the money; either that or squirreled it away someplace safe. Where would that be?

As they left the restaurant Charters said, 'That Chinese broad is hot stuff. Anna May Wong and then some, hey? I wonder, is it true what they say about them?'

Train said, 'I wouldn't know.'

'I seen her in two or three flicks. Wong, I mean. She's really hot stuff, Nicky. You see *Limehouse Blues* or *Dangerous to Know*? Hot stuff, believe you me. I'd like to find out if that's true about — '

Train said, 'Shut up, Charters. Just do your job.'

Charters shook his head. 'You're sweet on that broad, ain't you, Train?'

Train said, 'Shut up, Charters. Just shut up.'

They found Benny Jensen's body floating in the harbour, fully clad in his uniform, brogans, and overcoat. His police officer's cap must have drifted away; little chance, if any, of its ever being recovered. There was no sign of foul play, no sign of violence, no visible trauma, no apparent cause of death except for drowning. If he fell off the Staten Island ferry he would have been left behind in seconds. If nobody saw him fall they wouldn't have heard him calling for help. If he didn't fall, but jumped or was pushed, the same thing applied.

His revolver was still strapped to his hip. Handcuffs hanging from his belt. No billy club. If he'd had it with him it had probably drifted away. His pockets contained his wallet, a five-dollar bill and two singles, eighty-five cents in change, keys, handkerchief, and a comb. One oddity: he had an empty playing card package with a picture of a heavily made-up, naked brunette on the outside clutched in his fingers.

His parents asked for his body back and arranged for a funeral. They were going to bury him out at St. Columba's. Train hadn't even known that Benny was Catholic. He sure didn't push it on his friends. There was going to be a police honour guard at the funeral and a collection for the orphans' and widows' fund taken up at Benny's precinct. Even though Benny had worked in Staten Island and Train worked in Brooklyn, he sent a contribution to the fund anyhow. Benny didn't leave a widow or orphans, but they could give the collection to his parents to buy a plot for him.

On his day off Train dressed in civvies and got ready for a subway ride into the city. Pop was still in bed. The old man tried to get up every day, at least for a little while, but he hadn't stirred when Nick came into the bedroom to see him. Train bent over and hugged the old man, and Pop opened his eyes and smiled a little. Benny gave his Mom a hug and left the apartment.

There was still slush in the streets, but the sky was clear and there were even a few buds on the trees spotted along the sidewalk. Spring wasn't here but it was definitely coming.

Train rode the BMT into Manhattan, pushed his way up the stairs, and started walking. He'd almost forgotten what it was like here in the city. The buildings were taller, the cars in the street newer and more numerous, the people on the sidewalk better dressed and faster-paced than in Brownsville. He actually managed a smile at the thought that he'd be taken for an upstate apple-knocker if he didn't watch out.

He found the Schrafft's that he and Hopkins had agreed on and pushed his way in. He spotted Hopkins sitting at a table, balding and timid-looking: a copy of the *Herald-Trib* in one hand, a cigarette in the other, a cup of coffee in front of him. He was obviously scanning newcomers, watching the front door over the top of his newspaper, ceiling lights glinting off his steel-rimmed spectacles.

Train walked over to his table and introduced himself. Hopkins stood up and shook Train's hand. He was taller than Train had expected, and even skinnier than he appeared in his photo in the *Eagle*. His steel-rimmed glasses made his eyes look huge and his face like that of an owl. He said, 'You want to go for a walk, Nick?'

Train said he was hungry. Hopkins bought him a BLT and a cup of soup. Train was surprised at his own appetite. Maybe it was being away from Brownsville, away from Brooklyn, away from his everyday surroundings and in this other world. He gobbled down the sandwich and wiped his mouth with a paper napkin.

'There's food in Brooklyn, too, you know.' Hopkins seemed to be amused by Train's performance. The newsman looked thirty, maybe thirty-five.

Train said, 'I didn't realize I was hungry.' He peered around. The place was crowded with customers. None of them looked as if they were paying any attention to Train and Hopkins. Train didn't know what to say to Hopkins, so he paid attention to his soup. It came with a little package of saltines and he crumbled them into the bowl and ate them with his spoon, waiting for Hopkins to ask him something. Hopkins finally did.

'You were Winger's partner, right?'

Train said, 'Before we talk about that, I want to know what you're going to do with this.'

Hopkins laughed. 'Print it. That's my racket.'

'I can't have my name on it.'

'Okay, I don't blame you. I'll leave it off.' Hopkins didn't have a pencil or a pad in his hands. To anyone nearby the two of them would look like a couple of friends out for a light meal.

'Okay, I was Winger's partner.'

'How long?'

'Since December.'

'Before that?'

'This is my first beat. Before that I was at the academy. And before that I was doing something else for a living.'

'I know about that. You were a plucky fighter, Nick, but you weren't very good at it.'

'I was the best middleweight at William

Seward High School.'

Hopkins barked out a single brief laugh. 'Every school has its best middleweight. Anyway, you quit the fight game and became a cop. Nice exchange.'

'Yes.'

'You were with Winger when he was shot, were you?'

'No. We were in a Chinese restaurant. He was in the back room with the owner. I was sitting at a table eating.'

'You heard the shot?'

'No. The owner is a guy named Chen. He was in the back with Winger. They were gone a long time. Finally Chen's wife went back there to see what was going on. Neither of them speak much English, but they have a son and daughter who do. The mother came out screaming and the daughter ran in to see what was going on, and she found Winger shot and came back and got me.'

'Okay. And you found Winger dead.'

'Dying.'

'He say anything before he kicked it?'

'Nothing that made sense.'

'Him and the Dutchman.' Hopkins

looked into his coffee cup and stood up. 'I need a refill. You want anything?'

'I'll have a cup.'

Hopkins left his newspaper on the table, crushed out his cigarette, and went for coffee. When he came back he asked, 'How did you figure out that this Heinz Kleinmann did the dirty deed?'

'Kleinmann? Oh, yeah, Henry Little. No, I didn't figure it out. Inspector Clarke came out; he had Horowitz and Lefcourt go over the room. They found the holes in the wall. We went over next door to the butcher shop and poor Little was standing there with a butcher's knife and a gun. He didn't fight. He was lucky nobody aced him. You know, we don't like people standing there with knives and guns in their hands.'

'Okay, okay, don't crack wise, just talk to me.'

'So Little admitted everything, but he won't say why he did it.'

Hopkins took off his glasses and stared at Train. 'You know what, Nick, you're wasting my time. You haven't told me anything I didn't already know.'

Train resisted an impulse to apologize. Instead he just sat there, waiting for Hopkins to say something else. Hopkins looked less like an owl with his glasses off and more like a tough interrogator. Even Donald Meek could play a tough guy if he had to.

'Tell me something new, Nick, or let's blow this joint. I have better things to do.'

'You don't know about the money, Mr. Hopkins.'

Hopkins grinned like the cat that drank the cream. 'Now we're getting somewhere. No, I don't know about the money. Tell me.'

'I don't know if I can.'

'Look, my young friend, you called me; I didn't call you. If you have something for me, let's have it. Otherwise, you're welcome for the meal and I'll see you in the bleachers.'

'I want you to have this, Mr. Hopkins.'

'Okay, I'll settle for Barney.'

'Barney. I mean, I can't have my name on this. I don't want what happened to Winger, or Benny Jensen, to happen to me.'

'You think Jensen's death was connected to Winger's?' Hopkins didn't ask who Jensen was. He must have heard about the body fished out of the harbour.

'I think they knew that Benny and I were pals. That wasn't hard to figure out. We went to school together, went through the academy together. That I told him things that — that I told him things. I think they wanted to stop it there, and at the same time to warn me.'

'Nick, kid, who's *they*?'

'Winger was on the take, Mister — Barney.'

'Details, Nick. That's a hell of a broad statement.'

'He was collecting every week from all the businesses on our beat. He must have known I knew about it; he didn't try very hard to hide it from me. But he never said anything to me. He must have figured I'd be too scared to say anything, or that I just wouldn't want to stir things up and cause trouble.'

'Okay.'

'And he was right, I guess. I knew what was going on.'

'You getting a taste of it yourself, kid?'

'No.'

'No money?'

'No.'

'No free pass to the local bijou? No free coffee at the local orange drink stand? No free dry cleaning? No booze on the cuff at the local saloon? No price break at the haberdasher's? No free lays from the whores?'

'Uh, I guess I get some of that. I mean, uh, not the part about the whores. But the other things. A little. I mean, the local businesses, they like to have a cop around, most of them do. Maybe not the taverns; some of their customers get nervous when they see a blue uniform. But even there, the bartenders don't mind cops; it keeps the troublemakers quiet.'

'Yeah. So tell me, what's the difference between taking a five-spot in cash and taking a five-dollar pair of shoes for free or five bucks off the price of a new suit?'

Train didn't have an answer for that one.

'Okay.' Hopkins lit another cigarette.

'You don't smoke, do you, kid?'

'No. I got in the habit when I was in training. I mean, I got in the habit of not smoking.'

'Right. You're better off. Okay, I didn't mean to be hard on you about the graft. Nobody's lily-white, I guess.' He paused and nodded as if agreeing with himself. Then he resumed, 'So Winger is on the take. The butcher kills him. You know about it and tell Jensen. Jensen conveniently falls off the Staten Island ferry. You've got the pieces of a nice little jigsaw puzzle here. What's the picture, kid? You tell me.'

'Mr. Little was one of the partners at the butcher shop. I think he was the main partner. He was making the pay-offs. And Mr. Chen was making the pay-offs for the Imperial Palace.' He stopped, uncertain as to where to go from there.

'You think Kleinmann — Little — got tired of paying off and hit Winger? That simple? Where'd he get the gun? Why did he admit it when what's-his-name — '

'Inspector Clarke?'

'Yeah, when Inspector Clarke turned up?'

'What do you think, Barney? You've been around this business longer than I have.'

'That's for sure, kid. What I think, is somebody's trying to muscle in. You don't think Winger was a lone wolf, do you? You don't think that out of every cop in the City of New York, your partner was the only one on the take?'

'Oh.' He couldn't stifle a grin — a grin directed at himself for being so naïve. 'I guess not.'

'No, you guess not. What the hell do you think Dewey and Turkus and their guys have been doing for the past — Jesus, it's been seven years now since Lehman dumped that crook Dodge and brought in Medalie and Dewey. New York still hasn't got over the crooks who rode on Jimmy Walker's coat-tails. There hasn't been a clean police commissioner in this town since Teddy Roosevelt.'

Hopkins leaned back in his chair. The lunch crowd was starting to thin and well-dressed shoppers of the female persuasion were bustling into the restaurant, shopping bags in hand, to rest their feet before heading back uptown with their newly-acquired possessions. 'So what are we gonna do, kid? Who got Heinz to knock Winger off? Who pushed Jensen into the drink? Who was running your pal Winger? And — look, I don't want you to get too upset about this, but I have to ask it — why kill Winger and Jensen, assuming that the two jobs were related, and let young Nicholas Train run around with his head up his rear end?'

Train wondered if it had been such a great idea to get in touch with Hopkins after all. He could keep walking his beat, play it straight, and let all the merchants off the hook, at least until word came down from higher up. Or he could take over for Winger, pocket the fins and sawbucks and the occasional double sawbuck. God knew that a rookie cop didn't make much of a living, and with the old man too sick to work any more and the old lady slowly fading away from work and worry, some extra money coming into the house would be a big help.

How much had Winger cleared? If there were a hundred merchants on the beat and he pulled in five or ten dollars a week from each, that meant somewhere between twenty-five and fifty grand a year. That was Train's mistake. He'd been thinking of fives and tens and he hadn't stopped to perform a little simple arithmetic.

'I think Garlington must be taking a cut.'

'Full name?' Suddenly Hopkins was all business. He'd even whipped out a little leather-covered notebook and a stub of a yellow Ticonderoga.

'I — that makes me nervous, Barney.'

'Sorry, Nick. I gotta get this down. Just ignore the toys. Pretend you're talking to your priest.'

'I'm not Catholic.'

'Never mind. Spell. And I need the full name.'

'Okay. Garlington.' He spelled the name. 'Charlie. Charles Garlington. He's our sergeant.'

'How do you know?'

'He's got stripes on his uniform.'

Hopkins pursed his lips in annoyance. 'Great. Great, Nicholas. I guess I have to spell it out for you. How — do — you — know — Garlington — is — on — the — take?'

'I've seen him huddle with Winger a few times. Winger always stayed at the station house a little while at the end of the shift on days when he'd been collecting. He disappeared with Sergeant Garlington.'

'That's all? You ever see him pass money to Garlington? Ever hear what they said to each other.'

'No.'

'That ain't much. It's something, kid. It's pretty good in fact, for what it is, but it ain't much.'

'And Lieutenant Kessler.'

Hopkins raised his eyebrows. 'Him I know. Len Kessler, right?'

'That's him.'

'A well-connected man, our Leonard is. What do you know about him?'

'I've just seen him huddling with the

sergeants, that's all.'

Hopkins grinned. 'Natural enough. He's the boss; they work for him. He's gotta talk to them sometimes. Same thing for Garlington and Winger for that matter. Who else?'

'I think Inspector Clarke suspects.'

'Why?'

'When Winger was killed, Sergeant Garlington showed up along with Clarke and a couple of uniformed officers.'

'Okay. And — ?'

'Clarke did his best to keep Garlington out of the investigation. Even when he went into the back room of the Imperial Palace, he left Garlington out in the dining room. He called me in and a couple of other cops, but not Garlington. And then when we went next door to the butcher shop he kept Garlington out of that, too.'

'Now, sonny boy, now this is starting to get interesting. Did Garlington ever make the rounds with Winger?'

'Not since I've been there.'

'No, he wouldn't. And of course Kessler wouldn't, either.'

Nick agreed with that.

'We'll have to do a little checking,' Hopkins said, 'but I'd bet a gold sawbuck if I hadn't turned 'em all in, that Garlington used to walk a beat in your precinct, most likely the very one you have now. He probably set up the collection racket, unless it was already going before he got there. Bet you a double eagle that this goes up and up, Winger to Garlington to Kessler and on up the line to — Jesus, I would never think that Valentine was dirty. I don't believe that. But somewhere along the road.'

'What are you going to do?' Train asked.

'A lot more checking before I do anything else. Then I'm going to write a story that will get me a fat bonus.'

'But what about cleaning this up?'

'Kid, you don't get it, do you? I'm not a cop. It's not my job to clean up your department. It's my job to shine a spotlight on it, maybe. That's what the *Eagle* does and the *Citizen* and the *Journal* and the *Post* and all the other papers in this town. I don't wear a badge and I don't carry a gun. I'm not a cop.'

Train let out a discouraged sigh. 'So that's it? That's it, Barney, you're not going to do anything?'

'I told you, I'm gonna do my job.'

'All right.' Train pushed his chair back from the table. 'Thanks for the sandwich. I think the mayonnaise is starting to turn, but it wasn't bad.' He turned away.

'Wait a minute.'

He turned back.

Hopkins leaned over his pad, scribbling. 'Here's a phone number. You can call it if you want to.'

Train accepted to slip of paper. All it had on it was two letters and five numbers. 'Whose is it?' But Hopkins had unfolded his copy of the *Herald-Trib* and buried his nose in it.

Train stood there for another half a minute, but Hopkins didn't look up. A woman wearing a cloth coat with a fur collar and a hat designed to mock a man's fedora bumped into him and complained that he was blocking the aisle. He left the restaurant and headed toward the subway kiosk.

5

A Lot of Smiths in the Phone Book

The afternoon was starting to turn dark, a wind had sprung up, and the sharp-edged winter air was starting to cut through Train's clothing. He descended the steps, dropped his nickel in the turnstile, and waited for an express back to Brownsville.

When he got home, the front door of the apartment was open. He pushed in and found Jocko Sullivan standing in the living room. His sister and mother were sitting together on the sofa, Marie's arms around the old lady.

Jocko said, 'Too bad you weren't here, Nicky.'

Train didn't say anything. He pushed past Sullivan, past the two women on the sofa, and into the bedroom. His father's eyes were closed in death, and even though his face was pale he looked better than he had in months. Train thought for a moment that he ought to cover the old man's face, but his mother had left it uncovered and he chose to honour her decision.

His mother had left a chair next to the bed. Train sat in it, watching his father. After a while he reached over and took the old man's cold hand in his own. He held it between his two hands, thinking thoughts for which he had no words, then laid it gently back on the bed.

In the parlour he sat down beside his mother. He put his arm around her and his sister. Marie flinched at his touch. He planted a kiss on his mother's cheek. Her skin was soft and dry and smelled of talcum powder. He couldn't tell if she'd been crying; if she had, she had stopped. He stood up and walked over to his brother-in-law.

'We called the undertaker. He's sending the wagon.'

Train said, 'Okay.'

He turned and looked back toward the bedroom. The door was still open and he could see his father — his father's body — lying on the bed. 'Poor old guy. I guess this is best. He couldn't have enjoyed his life, the past year at least. And once Mom gets over it she'll be better off.'

Jocko said, 'I guess so. You still working as a cop?'

Train said, 'Yes.'

'Where were you? You should have been here at the end.'

'I didn't know. I was in the city. I had to see a guy about a horse.'

'Well, they'll be here for the body any time now. Did the old man make any plans?'

'What do you mean?'

'I mean funeral plans.'

'I don't think he wanted any fuss. It's up to Mom, anyhow.'

Mom was pretty strong. She managed to talk without hysterics and without flooding the place with tears. She confirmed what Nick had told Jocko, that the old man had said no fuss. She wanted a simple service for him and a plain grave marker.

When the undertakers arrived to take away the body, Marie took the old lady into the kitchen and kept her occupied until everything was over. Train didn't even know that the old man had a favourite church, but he did. For some reason he liked the Lutherans and the old lady knew about it; Train relayed the information to the undertakers and they said they'd find a good cheap Lutheran church for the funeral. Why the hell did his father want to be buried at a Lutheran church? Probably because of fairy tales about the village *Kirche* his own parents — Train's faintly remembered *Grossvater und Grossmutter Zug* — had brought with them from the old country.

He went back to work the next day. He managed to ditch Tim Charters, shoveling away at a bowl of chop suey, and escort Susan Chen into the back room of the Imperial Palace. Her parents and brother were all busy running the joint. Train asked Susan if she'd had any visits since the killing. The evidence technicians had been around, she told him, to measure the back room. They took pictures of the holes that had been drilled from the Four Star Kosher Butcher Shop and took away the wood shavings from the holes. The wall was already patched up. Her father had been summoned to the precinct and a police stenographer had taken his statement. Susan had gone along to translate.

Train asked if anyone had checked the contents of the safe. Susan said they had checked, found nothing but routine business records, and let her lock it up again. Charters didn't know anything about the evidence techs' visit. It had happened while he was pounding his beat and nobody at the station house had said anything about it to him. And Sergeant Garlington had been around asking questions, too, Susan said. She didn't like that one and had given him nothing.

What about the envelope?

Susan smiled. 'I burned the envelope and mailed the money to my cousin Virginia, Virginia Wong. She lives in Los Angeles. She'll get rid of the money. Nobody knows anything about it. She'll find some way to get around the holes in the bills.'

Train shook his head. 'You could just have burned the money along with the envelope.'

'You don't understand Chinese people, Nicholas, if you think that.' She smiled at him and put her hand on his. Jesus, he didn't know what to do about this. He couldn't be falling in love with this woman. Not now. Not with his dead father not even in the ground. And not in the middle of a murder investigation. Not on a case he was involved in, and where she might become a witness. Besides, she was Chinese. He'd had his high school crushes. Who didn't? And when he was boxing, there were always women hanging around. Somehow the smell of male sweat and the sight of two bozos pounding on each other in the ring did something to them. They liked to see the sweat fly. And blood. Oh, it was worth getting a mouse over the eye sometimes just to see what it would do to certain women.

But he'd never felt this way before.

Back at the table he drank some tea and ate some spare ribs.

That night Marie and a couple of the old lady's friends from the neighbourhood kept her company. Jocko was out with some of his own pals. There was

133

plenty of food in the house; Ma's friends had provided that. They were coaxing the old lady to eat, and in fact she was actually nibbling at a sandwich. Good; she needed to build her strength back up.

Train had already changed from his duty blues to civvies. He found the note that Barney Hopkins had handed him, the one with the phone number on it. He left the apartment, walked down the street to the candy store, and used the pay phone. He dialed the number Hopkins had given him, then stuck the slip of paper back in his pocket.

He heard the phone ringing at the other end of the line. It rang for a long time. He let his eyes rove over the racks of newspapers and racing forms and pulp magazines the candy store carried. The owner, an immigrant Anatolian named Bhasmadjian, frowned at him. The phone kept ringing. He looked at his Elgin. What a fool he was. A normal business office would be closed by this time of night.

As he was about to give up and place the earpiece back on the hook he heard a click. 'Yes.' That was all. Just one word. The voice was that of a woman, Train was sure of it. There was no more information in the reply.

'Uh, I'm trying to reach a number.' He fished Hopkins's note out of his pocket again. He read the sparse contents of Hopkins's note to the female voice. 'Is this the right number?'

'Whom are you trying to reach?'

'I'm not sure. I was given this number and the person told me to call it.'

'Who was that?'

'What?'

'Who gave you this number?' The voice seemed annoyed, and not as if he had wakened its owner from an early night's sleep.

'Hopkins. Barney Hopkins. Brooklyn *Eagle* reporter.'

'Is this Mr. Hopkins?'

Was she trying to be funny? Who were those comedians that Kate Smith liked to bring on? Mom loved Kate Smith. The comedians were a pair of vaudeville veterans who did a routine about baseball players. The more the smart one tried to explain things, the more the dumb one got mixed up.

He shook his head. Enough wool-gathering. 'No, Miss. It was Mr. Hopkins who gave me this number. I'm not Mr. Hopkins.'

'All right. Whom do you wish to speak with?'

'I told you, I don't know. Mr. Hopkins told me — '

She cut him off. 'Leave your number. Someone will call you back.'

Train peered through the folding glass doors of the phone booth. There was somebody waiting to use the phone: a woman with a tired face and a tired-looking body, wearing pale powder on her cheeks and smeared lipstick. She had two bags of groceries with her. Beyond the woman, old man Bhasmadjian was glaring at Train.

'I'm at a pay phone now. Somebody else needs to use it.'

'All right. Where can we reach you during business hours?'

'That would be difficult.'

'Do you have a telephone in your

home? That number would do. You can go home now. Someone will call you there.'

He gave the woman his home number. She cut the connection without another word. He left the phone booth. The tired woman pushed past him and struggled into the booth. She gave him a dirty look as they passed each other.

Bhasmadjian brightened. 'Everything good, Officer Train? Everything all right? I didn't know you without your uniform, you know.'

'That's okay, Mr. Bhasmadjian. Good night.'

He went home. His sister, Marie, and her husband, and the old lady's neighbourhood friends had left. His mother was sitting alone in the living room with a Bible in her lap. He'd never seen her read the Bible before; didn't even know that they had one in the house. He'd never known either of his parents to show the slightest interest in religion. Death changes you. He didn't know what to say to his mother, so he went and sat with her. It was obvious that she wasn't focusing on the Bible, so he closed the book and left it in one of her hands while he held onto the other.

The telephone rang. It was the same woman he'd spoken with from Bhasmadjian's candy store. She asked, 'Are you the man who phoned here eighteen minutes ago?'

Talk about efficiency! Train admitted that he was.

'Who did you say gave you this number?'

He repeated the contact information.

'All right. Please stay on the line. Someone will be right with you.'

* * *

'What do you have to tell me?'

The new voice was male. It was an educated voice. Train had learned to listen for accents, intonations and emphases. There was nothing in this voice to suggest foreign birth. Probably a New York native, somebody with money and a college degree.

'I can't tell you anything until I know who you are.'

'Mr. Train, Officer Train, you approached Barney Hopkins at the *Eagle* and he referred you to this number. We need information, Nicholas, and it would appear that you have it.'

Train looked across the room at his mother. Her chin had fallen on her chest. 'Look, whoever this is, can you hold on for a minute? I'll be right back.' He laid down the earpiece before the man could answer. It was up to him now. Train took his mother by the elbows and half-carried, half-led her to her bedroom. He got her settled on the bed, removed her shoes and put a comforter over her. He walked silently back to the parlour, shutting the bedroom door behind him.

'All right, here I am.'

'Officer Train, we're on your side. More precisely, we and you are on the same side. You have to understand that. If we weren't, Hopkins wouldn't have sent you to us.'

'Even so.'

'All right, Nicholas, what do you want?'

'This has to be face-to-face.'

Waiting for the reaction, he shook his

head. He was going in circles. He'd gone through exactly this rigmarole with Hopkins, had got what he wanted — a meeting with Hopkins — and wound up playing the same kind of game with this new mystery man. Who's on first?

'Do you have any idea to whom you're talking, Nicholas?'

'I do not.'

There was a pause and the suggestion of a sigh. 'Nicholas, this struggle has been going on for years now. Herbert Lehman and Tom Dewey are behind me. Washington is keeping quiet right now because they think they have bigger fish to fry, what with war probably on the way, but I can tell you that Homer Cummings was in our corner and Frank Murphy is a personal friend of mine.'

Lehman and Dewey, Cummings and Murphy, the Governor and the famous racket-buster, Roosevelt's recent Attorney General and the new one just settling in — the caller was either well-connected or one hell of a liar. And with that voice, with that speech pattern, he might well share a background with the President himself.

'And who are you?'

'If you need a name you might as well call me Mr. Smith.'

'All right, Mr. Smith or whoever you are, how can we get together?'

'You don't want to be seen coming to see me, do you?'

'I do not.'

'All right. Suppose I send a car for you.'

'Make it a taxi.'

Smith let out a guffaw. 'I do like your style, Officer Train. I really do like your style. All right, a taxi cab it will be, with one of my men as the driver. Shall we say, in front of your house in ten minutes?'

'Make it outside the churchyard next to St. Columba's.'

'As you wish. Wear a white carnation, will you?'

'That's a joke, I hope.'

'You catch on quickly, Nicholas. No, we are well aware of what you look like. We'll send a Yellow Cab. The driver will say, 'Hey, bud, I think it's going to sleet.' You'll answer, 'No, I think it's going to

141

hail.' You have that, Nicholas?'

'What is this, a gangster movie or a pulp story?'

Again the guffaw. 'Please forgive the melodrama. You know, Nicholas, in any war there are spies on both sides. I don't want you going for a ride in the wrong taxi.'

'All right. I'll be there.'

He checked on his mother. She was sleeping lightly. He touched her brow, saw that a small light was burning beside the bed and left the apartment.

Mr. Smith kept his word. The cab carried him to a nondescript office building near Borough Hall. The driver had given the prescribed password and Train had given the prescribed response, feeling like a ten-year-old playing cops and robbers. After that the driver hadn't said a word, nor had Train.

The cab rolled down a ramp into a basement parking area. The driver opened Train's door and led him to an elevator. When they got upstairs, the driver escorted Train to an office door with *Mr. Smith* stenciled on the frosted glass in gilt letters. No company name. Nothing else.

Mr. Smith got up from behind his desk and shook hands with Train. He was Train's height but a few pounds lighter. He didn't have the muscles that Train had developed as a fighter and kept as a cop. He wore a double-breasted navy pinstripe suit with pointed lapels that could put your eye out, a white-on-white shirt and a plain maroon tie. His hair was going white at the temples.

'Officer Train, thank you for coming. Please sit down.'

Train complied.

'Sorry about your father, Nicholas. How is your mother taking the loss?'

'How do you know about my father?'

'It's part of my job.'

'You some kind of spy?'

Mr. Smith had lowered himself into a swivel chair behind his desk. Now he pursed his lips. 'I suppose you could call me a spy. Is it dishonourable to spy on criminals?'

Train didn't reply.

'Nicholas, I really need your help. Will you give it to me?'

Train shook his head. 'I don't know who you are and I don't know what you're up to.'

'You called me.'

'I still want to know. What's going on, Mr. Smith? If you don't want to tell me your name, you'll have to give me something else.'

'I don't think my name would mean anything to you. Smith seems to work perfectly well. It might even be real. There are a lot of Smiths in the phone book.' A muscle in his cheek jerked a small fraction of an inch. 'But if you insist on knowing, my name is Oscar Daniel McAteer. I'm on Mr. Turkus's staff. Does that help?'

'How do I know?'

McAteer, if that were his real name, opened a drawer in his desk and handed Train a business card. It had a name on it, *O.D. McAteer*; and beneath the name, in smaller letters, *Special Operations*. There was a phone number as well, not the same number that Hopkins had given Train. Train studied the card front and back, then slipped it into his pocket. Of course anybody could stroll into an office supplies store or a job printer's shop and order business cards with any name he chose. Train had always felt that he had a firm grasp on reality, but now — suddenly, surprisingly — everything was turning to sand and slipping away between his fingers.

'Sorry, Mr. McAteer, I don't have a card to give you.'

For the first time since Train's arrival, McAteer smiled. 'That's quite all right. I know how to reach you.' He leaned over and opened a heavy box, then slid it across the gleaming glass that covered his desk. The desktop was otherwise clear, save for a small brass rectangle that said, simply, *Mr. Smith*. 'Cigar, Nicholas?'

'No, thanks.'

'Oh, that's right. Clean habits, strong body, good athlete. No training on hot dogs and whiskey and cigars like Babe Ruth, eh?'

Train didn't say anything.

McAteer stood up and started to pace. A beige carpet covered the floor from wall to wall. McAteer's polished cordovan shoes made no sound as he strode. It was as if the carpet had been made to accommodate those shoes and the shoes had been made specifically to walk on that carpet. Wealth will do that for you.

'You know who Burton Turkus is.' McAteer had stopped, facing Train.

'I do.'

'Mr. Dewey and Mr. Turkus and I — I hope you won't think I'm just name-dropping, Nicholas, I really do hope that — the three of us have been watching money pour into the treasury of the mob for years. We've done our best to stop it. We've put some of the top mobsters behind bars. I'm not giving away any secret to tell you that we've got a line on Salvatore Lucania himself, and I can almost promise that we're going to get him. And soon.' He frowned. 'You don't recognize the name?'

Train shook his head.

Smith said, 'Try Lucky Luciano.'

'He's locked up.'

McAteer smiled at that. 'Living the life of Riley behind bars. Catered meals and paid companions and running the rackets as if nothing had ever happened. If all else fails, I'd like to send him back across the water.' He shook his head ruefully, electric light making the white hairs scattered among the neatly groomed dark brown look like snowflakes on a winter lawn.

'But you have to understand something about the way that money is flowing, Nicholas. Water always flows downhill, you know. I'm sure you learned that at William Seward High School. But money does a lot of strange things. Sometimes it flows uphill. It's doing that now. It's flowing from the little guys, Nicholas — from the news vendors and the candy store operators and the beauty shops and the garages — and it flows upward. It doesn't flow straight into the hands of the mob, either. That's the way Alphonse Caponi did it in Chicago, and he's rotting in a cell now.'

McAteer stood behind his desk, looking up at a painting. It wasn't the kind of painting Train would have expected to see in a government office. It looked like some kind of scene with overweight nudes and fat cherubs with wings and with strategically placed ribbons fluttering around them.

Train made a noise then and McAteer turned around. Train's expression must have been amusing because McAteer let loose that surprising guffaw of his. 'I like to look at the painting every now and then,' McAteer said. 'It takes my mind off my problems.' He thumped down into his chair once more. 'Can't I get you something, Nicholas? A cold beverage? No? Well, then, all right.' He leaned forward, elegantly covered elbows on the glass, French cuffs and what might have been ruby cufflinks showing. The stones matched the colour of his tie.

'The money flows from the little shopkeepers to the local beat cops, to the sergeants and lieutenants and captains and up the line, and it winds up in the pockets of the mob. I don't think it goes all the way up to the commissioner's office. In fact, I'm reasonably sure it doesn't. But the mob is an efficient business. It's very careful about its accounting procedures. There's a fellow named Lansky in charge of that. I'd love to put him away, but he's so careful, I can't imagine how I'm going to do that, Nicholas. Not that I've given up hope. But the mob is extremely careful to see to it that every dollar is accounted for. If they were a legitimate business, they'd be very successful.'

Train was starting to get an inkling of where he came into McAteer's picture, and of where the death of Winger and that of Jensen came into that picture. If he was right, it was just a quirk of fate that made them go after Benny and let Train live. It also meant that the killers had their eye on him.

'The mob wants what it's entitled to,' McAteer was saying. 'What the mobsters believe they're entitled to. This is nothing new, Nicholas. This has been going on for a long time. They have a nice set-up, and they intend to protect it.'

'And why did Little kill Winger, Mr. McAteer?'

The older man smiled. 'At last, the right question. The beat cops are the collectors for this shakedown racket,

Nicholas. If they don't pass the money up the way they're supposed to, Lansky will know it. He tells his pals and there's hell to pay. You see, in their eyes they're just good businessmen, that's all. Just good businessman.'

'Look, Mr. McAteer, I still don't get it. Why would Henry Little shoot Dermott Winger? And why was Benny Jensen shoved off the Staten Island ferry?'

McAteer said, 'Why do you think, Nicholas?'

Train studied the question. 'I don't know.'

McAteer steepled his fingers beneath his chin and said nothing.

Train asked, 'You want me to guess?'

'Go ahead.'

'Maybe Winger was holding back on his collections. Or maybe he was putting a reverse squeeze on — ' There was a lengthy pause. A streetcar clanged its bell in the canyon outside. A couple of voices rose in anger, then faded.

'Go on,' McAteer encouraged.

'Sergeant Garlington.'

'Very good. Any other thoughts?'

'Maybe you were talking to Winger. Winger was talking to you. Garlington found out. Or Lieutenant Kessler. Or — '

McAteer nodded. 'The world is full of maybes, isn't it, Nicholas? And you haven't even come to Officer Jensen yet.'

Maybe he wants me to do some more theorizing, Train thought, but I'm not going to do it. I'm out of ideas.

He waited for McAteer to speak.

'We want to find the answers to those questions, Nicholas. You're going to help us.'

'What do you want me to do?'

'You haven't been making collections on your beat since Winger was killed, have you?'

'No.'

'Tempted?'

Train had to think about that one. McAteer waited with no display of impatience. Finally Train said, 'Sure I was. I worked out how much Winger cleared in a year, even if he only kept half of what he collected. It made my head spin. Sure, I was tempted. But I haven't done it.'

'Why not?'

'I don't know.'

'Good answer. No homily about honesty-is-the-best-policy, honour of the force, Jesus will get me if I don't watch out, whatever.'

'No.'

'Not afraid of getting caught, were you? You get pulled in for shaking down the public; you don't just get canned, you know. You get a long vacation at the stone hotel. And the other guests don't like cops much.'

'That's not the reason, sir.'

'No, I didn't think it was. I think you're actually an honest man, Train.'

'What do you want me to do, Mr. McAteer?'

'I want you to start collecting again.'

Train stared at McAteer.

'You're going to start collecting again, Nicholas. I'm surprised nobody's talked to you about that by now. You're sure nobody's even dropped a hint? Not Garlington, not Kessler? Nobody?'

'Nobody, sir.'

'All right, you may have to drop a hint

to them, although I'll really be surprised if they don't talk to you first. When they do you'll have to decide how to react. Probably not a great idea to play dumb. If you act as if you didn't know what was going on, and you never heard of shakedowns, they'll know you're lying.'

McAteer stood up and pulled the cigar humidor toward himself. Its felt pads slid smoothly, noiselessly, across the glass. 'You're sure you won't indulge?'

'No, sir.'

'If you don't mind, I will.'

He extracted a cigar from the humidor and lit it. He blew a thin stream of blue-gray smoke toward the ceiling. He opened a desk drawer and removed a heavy cut-glass ashtray. 'A minor vice I picked up in Havana a long time ago. Cuban cigars and Cuban rum, the finest in the world.'

Train waited.

'All right,' McAteer resumed. 'You know, we have some very clever laboratory technicians. Once you've been making your collections for a few weeks, you'll mark the bills for us.'

'How?'

McAteer grinned like the cat that drank the cream. 'You'll never believe what our lab boys have done. You ever hear of an individual called Farnsworth? Philo T. Farnsworth?'

'Sounds like one of those characters on Fred Allen's radio show.'

'No, he's real.' McAteer smiled. 'He's invented a new kind of light bulb, gives off something called ultraviolet light. Black light. You can't see it, but if you shine it on certain substances, they glow. Blood, quinine, jellyfish at the aquarium, cat piss.'

'Wonderful.'

'Vitamins. The lab boys have been experimenting. You ever hear of vitamin B12?'

'Heard of it. I have no idea what it does.'

'You can get capsules at the drug store, or we can furnish them. You crush this stuff and dissolve it in water and it glows under black light. Glows bright yellow. I want you to mark those bills with vitamin B12.'

'You're joking. What a crackpot scheme!'

'It may sound crackpot to you, son, but I'm not joking. We've tried this stuff. It's completely harmless and it just screams out at you when you use it. I want you to mark those bills with a code. We'll work something out, something easy. How about *B12*, that should be easy enough. Collect your pay-offs, mark the bills, and we'll do the rest.'

Train shook his head. 'Where do I do this? I can't go marking the money at the precinct. And I don't see that I can take the bills home and bring them back.'

'Anybody you trust on your beat? I mean, any cooperative citizens?'

'There's someone.' Susan Chen was already involved. He wasn't going to mention her name to McAteer, but he knew he could do the marking in the back room at the Imperial Palace. Assuming that nobody at the Four Star Kosher Butcher Shop decided to take up where Henry Little left off.

'All right, then. I'm sure you can handle that. Good, Nicholas. You're going to be all right, I can tell.' McAteer drew once more on his cigar. A speck of ash fell onto his lapel and he brushed it off carefully. He shook his head. 'What would the missus say?' He looked back at Train. 'All right, once you're part of the system you'll share the money with your superiors as usual, and we'll be able to track it. We're not that interested in nabbing the chiselers at the precinct. They're small fry. We want to see where the money goes. Do you follow me?'

'What does this have to do with Little and Winger and Jensen?'

'That's what I want to find out, Nicholas. But if you'd like to hear a theory I'll give you one.'

'Please.'

'Very likely Dermott Winger was holding out. No honour among thieves, eh? His boss — maybe it was Sergeant Garlington and maybe it wasn't (that's one of the things I want to learn, son) — Winger's boss found out about it. Or maybe *his* boss found out about it. Somewhere along the line, the money wasn't coming in the way it was supposed to. So they enforced discipline the way they like to enforce discipline: they had Winger killed. A good object lesson to anybody else considering holding out.'

'Sounds as if you're putting me into a very nasty situation, Mr. McAteer. Are you sure Winger wasn't talking to you, and they found out and got rid of him?'

'You can walk out of here now and report back to duty, son. Pound your beat, keep your nose clean, and hope that Garlington or whoever leaves you alone. But what will you do when you get that summons into the sergeant's presence, or the lieutenant's, and they inform you that you've inherited Winger's duties as collector? What then?' He waited for Train to respond, but Train had nothing to say. In fact, he was wondering what time it was. He didn't want to look away from McAteer and study his watch. There wasn't a clock anywhere in the office — not that he could see, at least. There wasn't even a window. For all he knew it could be day or night, winter or summer in the outside world. Inside this room, nothing would change.

McAteer resumed, 'You wouldn't threaten

to call Internal Affairs, you're too smart for that. You could pretend to go along and contact IA on the sly, but you'd be no better off than you are right now. In fact, I'll let you in on a little secret, Nicholas — you'd be a lot worse off than you are right now.'

'Okay, Mr. McAteer. Why Kleinmann?'

'A nice touch, Nicholas. Who can understand the criminal mind? You'd expect them to take Officer Winger for a one-way ride. I was surprised myself, having poor little Henry Little do their dirty work. Of course that keeps it from looking like a mob killing, doesn't it? Nothing is what it seems. Or then again, maybe it is. It's all very confusing, don't you think?'

'Yeah.'

'We haven't found out why they picked Henry Little to be their assassin, or how they recruited him. Not yet, but we will. Again, here's my guess, Nicholas. Little — Kleinmann — has a big family. Aged mother, wife, crippled sister-in-law, flat full of kids. Did you know any of this?'

'No, sir.'

'We're still checking, Nicholas, but Kleinmann has a lot of debts. The Four Star Butcher Shop does. Kleinmann owes the mob money and the vigorish is mounting up.'

'How do you know?'

'Please, Nicholas. We know. Trust me.'

'All right. Now what?'

'The mob is very big on *quid-pro-quos*, son. Kleinmann's friendly lender lets him know that he's in big trouble. Of course they don't threaten his family, but Kleinmann worries. And even if they only threaten him — ' McAteer emphasized the last word ' — if Kleinmann winds up with two broken legs and can't work, Four Star can't pay its debts, the vig keeps mounting up, Kleinmann is in deeper than ever, disaster looms. Don't you see?'

'I see.'

'Well, Kleinmann's friends let him know that they need him to perform a task for them. If he does it, the past debt is forgiven. Kleinmann takes the fall. He probably won't fry, although there is a risk of that. A slight risk, but still . . . '

McAteer studied his cigar. A thin column of smoke rose from its tip. 'More likely, though, they'll furnish Mr. Kleinmann with a very good lawyer. They may even get him a kindly-hearted, sympathetic judge. He goes away for a few years, and they take good care of his family while he's gone.'

McAteer leaned back in his chair, drew on his cigar, and held the smoke while he pulled a slim watch from his pocket and checked the time. He exhaled a stream of smoke, considerately aiming it at the ceiling above his desk. It rose gracefully, swirled just under the ceiling, then disappeared. 'It is getting late. I do apologize for keeping you up like this. I don't imagine you've got much rest lately, what with your dad and all. May I offer my condolences, Nicholas, and my apologies for not doing so sooner. And we'll get you out of here very soon now.'

'What about Benny?'

'Eh?'

'Benny Jensen.'

'I see.' McAteer ran his hand around

his jaw. Despite the hour he managed to look freshly shaven, barbered, and manicured. 'I was hoping you wouldn't ask.'

'I'm asking.'

'You don't think your precinct is the only one where this is going on, do you? Or that Brooklyn is the only borough that's infected?'

'He was working for you, wasn't he?'

'I'm afraid so.'

'They found out.'

How could McAteer express an entire thought with a quick downward and upward glance?

'And if they find out I'm working for you, I'm dead. Just like Benny.'

'I'm afraid you have no choice now, son. You can be certain they're going to ask you to collect for them. If you do it and don't help me, I'll know it, and you're off the force and behind bars, believe it. I'm sorry.'

'What about Charters?'

'Young Timothy? A thug at heart, and a fool. A nasty item, but not important. We're keeping an eye on him, but just keep him from rocking the boat,

Nicholas. You can handle Charters.'

Train had another question for McAteer. He wasn't sure how to ask it. McAteer seemed to sense Train's dilemma. He said, 'You can ask me anything, Nicholas. I won't promise to answer every question. There are some things that — ' He let that one slip away, into the atmosphere. Then, 'There may be some questions that I don't find it appropriate to answer, but you may ask anything that you wish.'

'Okay. Straight out. How high does this thing go? Borough Hall? City Hall? Albany? Washington?'

McAteer laughed. 'That sounds like a railroad.'

'What's the answer?'

'I think I'll have to withhold details until another time, Nicholas. But I will say this much. Borough Hall, City Hall, and Washington all seem to be on our side.'

'You left something out.'

'Did I?'

'Albany.'

'As far as I know, Governor Lehman

and Attorney General Bennett are honour-able, honest men.'

Train stored that one away for later examination. He said, 'I think we're finished, Mr. McAteer.'

'You'll get a free cab ride home. I'll have you dropped a few blocks away from your apartment so you can arrive on foot.'

Train didn't have long to wait.

6

Honest as the Day is Long

Garlington growled at him at the end of the shift. 'Hang around, Train.' Train had already changed to civvies and was headed for the door when the sergeant clamped hard fingertips around his elbow. Garlington knew the pressure points and Train's hand went dead. Garlington laughed. 'Don't worry, it'll come back in a few minutes. Just don't try and do anything with it right now.'

'What is it, Sergeant?'

'Come on in the back, Train. Let's have a little drink.'

Garlington led Train into an interrogation room and closed the door. The sergeant was wearing civvies, too. He had a bottle and two glasses in his hand. As soon as they sat down, Garlington's jovial manner disappeared.

'Okay, kid, fork over.'

'Fork over what, Sergeant?'

'Don't play dumb, Train. Where's the cash?'

'I don't know what you're talking about, Sergeant.'

'You've got Winger's beat now. Where are the weekly contributions?'

Train wondered how long he ought to play dumb. He decided for the moment at least not to let on that he knew anything.

After a while Garlington picked up the bottle and poured drinks for them. 'Bottoms up,' he commanded. He tilted his head back and drained his glass. Train followed suit, but swallowed little more than a sip. The whiskey burned going down. He didn't recognize the label on the bottle. He wasn't sure what he'd drunk, but he guessed it was rye.

Garlington lowered his glass to the table. It made a thump as he released it. He picked up the bottle and poured himself a second drink. He looked at Train's glass. 'You're not much of a boozer, kid, are ya? Don't care for the juice, or isn't Charlie Garlington's brand good enough for you?'

'No problem with that, Sergeant. I'm just — you're right, I really don't drink much, I guess. And I'm feeling tired. It was a long shift. Mrs. Bhasmadjian had her baby today. I had to help Mr. Bhasmadjian deliver it. She had a girl.'

Garlington closed his eyes. 'Wonderful. Congratulations to the happy parents. Why the hell didn't she go to the hospital like an American woman?'

'I think the baby was early, Sergeant. I don't think she planned it this way. She seemed surprised. Her husband was pretty upset, but they were happy once it was over.'

'Well, God bless the babies of the world. Now let's talk business. Where's the money?'

He'd got about as much mileage out of the dumb act as he was going to get, Train decided. 'I haven't been collecting, Sergeant.'

Garlington jumped back. 'Nothing?'

'Nothing, Sergeant.'

'What the hell is the matter with you, kid? What are you doing on this man's police force anyhow? Don't you know how things work in this damn world?'

Train said, 'I don't think we should be talking about this here at the station house.'

'Nobody's gonna hear us.'

'Are you sure? Aren't there hidden microphones in these interrogation rooms?'

'Nobody's listening. Cripes, what's the matter with you? You think I'm trying to trap you?'

'No, Sergeant.'

'Because I'm not. Look, Train, I'm the best friend you've got around here, and the best one you'll ever have, now that Winger's dead. You'd better lace up your boots and get on the team, kid.'

Train stood up. 'I really don't feel good about this.'

'You think I'm an IA spy or something?'

'I don't think anything, Sergeant.'

Garlington stood up. He said, 'Okay, look, I'm gonna do you a big favour. I don't know why I'm doing this. Well, I guess I do. Scuttlebutt around the precinct says your old man just kicked the bucket.'

'I wouldn't put it that way, but, yes, he died.'

'All right. We still have to talk. If you won't talk to me here, how's about a nice safe place? We can get a private booth down at Walker's. Nobody's listening in there. What do you say?'

Train said okay.

They left the station house separately, ten minutes apart. Train went first. When he got to Walker's, Dinny Moran was presiding over the usual array of lushes and whores. He waved a glass at Train. Train found a booth and settled in.

A whore came over a couple of minutes later. She leaned one hip against Train's table. 'Dinny says to remind you he got no waitress service in his joint. But as a special favour, I'll take your order. What do you want?'

She leaned over. He could smell her; she gave off a mixture of loud perfume and sweat, cheap alcohol and cigarette smoke. It made him feel sick, but he felt a stirring, too. He said, 'Just a beer.'

'That's all?' She leaned in closer.

'That's all.' Train put his elbows on the

table and rested his forehead on the heels of his hands. Why the hell had he become a cop? How the hell had he got into this mess? He was sorry he'd ever phoned Hopkins, sorrier that he'd used the number Hopkins gave him and called McAteer. Now he was in up to his eyeballs and he couldn't see any way out.

The whore returned with a bottle of Piel's and a glass. 'Dinny says it's on the house.' She put the bottle and glass on the table. 'But tipping is allowed.' She pulled a church key out of her bodice and smiled at Train, opening the bottle.

Train said, 'Thanks.' While she waited he fished around in his pants pocket until he found a coin. He dropped it on the table. She picked it up.

'Thanks, you can get the next one for yourself, big shot.'

She put the church key back where she'd got it and added the coin.

The front door opened and the noise of traffic blasted in from Junius Street. Train looked up and saw Garlington roll into the saloon. He swung past the mahogany. He only had to pause for a second. Dinny

Moran had a bottle and glass ready for him. He pointed in Train's direction and Garlington nodded.

'Okay, now we talk turkey.' Garlington put the bottle and the glass on the table. There was nobody nearby. The lushes at the bar were engaged in an acrimonious exchange. Train couldn't make out their words. For all they knew they were fighting about Eleanor Roosevelt's latest speech. The whores had left the mahogany and settled at a table, a bottle in the center.

'Winger was on the take, Sergeant, I won't deny that.' Train tilted the bottle of Piel's and filled his glass halfway. He took a sip.

'You think he was on his own?' Garlington asked.

'I never thought about it.'

'Like hell you never thought about it.'

'It wasn't my money. I never asked what he did with it and he never told me anything about it.'

'Well, think now.'

'I guess he used it for his family. Cops don't make much.'

'You can say that again.'

Train didn't.

'What do you think would have happened to Winger if I'd blown the whistle on him?' Garlington raised a bushy eyebrow.

Train didn't feel like playing Garlington's game. 'Couldn't have been worse than what did happen.'

'In fact it could,' Garlington said, 'but you got a point. Too bad about Winger. I guess Little got tired of buying protection and decided to cancel his policy.'

'Is that what you call it, Charlie?' Out of uniform, out of the station house, outside the law, Train thought, he could afford to get familiar with Garlington. 'Is it? Is it an insurance policy?'

'Close enough.'

'What's the split?'

'Now you're making some sense. We've already lost two weeks' worth of income on your beat. You know something, Train?'

Train looked at Garlington over the rim of his glass. 'What?'

'I'll tell you something.' Garlington had

been alternately filling his glass and lowering its level since he sat down. 'I'll tell you something. Charters don't like you.'

'Why not? He doesn't even know me. We just walk a beat together.'

'He wants to collect,' Garlington said. 'He spotted the racket right off the bat and he wants in. But it's your turn now that Winger's dead. I told Charters nix and he got annoyed, but I told him to can it or he'd be sorry.'

'He wants the job, does he? Then why didn't you let him have it?'

'Cause I don't trust him. Guy comes up from Georgia, Alabama, wherever the hell he came from, thinks he knows it all, thinks he can start throwing his weight around. Okay, he's a few years older than most rookies — he's older than you, ain't he — but he's still a rookie as far as I'm concerned, and he hasn't even been on the force as long as you have and you're still a rookie as far as I'm concerned. That okay with you, Train?'

'I guess so.'

'You're from the neighbourhood, you're

an American, you're maybe dumb as hell, but I saw you fight and you got moxie even if you don't got much brains. I saw that Risko fight of yours; that guy was an ex-champ and you stood up to him. He beat the daylights out of you but you stood up to him. You coulda took a dive or you coulda thrown in the towel, but you stood up. I give you a lot of credit for that, Train.'

'Yeah. I remember the Risko fight.'

'I figure, as much moxie as you got, and from the neighbourhood, you're the next collector. Not Charters.'

For the second time, Train asked, 'What's the split?'

'Now you're talking!' Garlington cracked a big smile. 'Now you're talking, Train.' He reached inside his jacket and pulled out a cigar. There was a box of wooden matches on the table, and a scarred metal ashtray. He lit the cigar and blew smoke out of the corners of his mouth. He dropped the match in the ashtray and it smouldered for a while before it went out. 'Straight down the middle, kid. You get half and I get half.'

Train managed a frown. 'Seems like a lot for you for doing nothing and not so much for me for doing all the work.'

'What work? The city pays you to walk your beat. You get to eat free at the Chinese and Italian restaurants and the Hungarian's and you go to the movies free and — you got a car, kid?'

'No, I don't have a car.'

'We can maybe get you a deal on a car. Remind me, and then you can get work done on it free, I'll bet.'

'That's still a big cut for you, Charlie.'

'I don't keep it, kid. It goes up the chain. Up the chain, kid. Everybody gets his little taste. Everybody pays a little, nobody pays too much; everybody gets his taste off the tit, and nobody goes to bed hungry.'

The whores — there were four of them huddled around a bottle — were watching Garlington and Train. Garlington swung around in his seat and snarled at them. 'What the hell you watching for? Mind your business or you'll spend the night in the pokey.'

One of the girls — the bravest one, not

the one who had opened Train's beer for him — stood up, hipshot. She looked more than a little tipsy. Business must have been lousy, and the four sisters were drowning their sorrows in a shared bottle of booze. She said, 'Just try it, Charlie. Just you try it. You'll be back on the sidewalk. And no more free ones for you, Charlie. You can go home to your fat slob of a wife next time you want to get a piece.' She slumped back into her chair. The others applauded, and a couple of the lushes leaning against the mahogany joined in. It was a good show.

Garlington said, 'I need a refill, Train. You could use one, too. Go see Dinny.'

Train complied. Dinny Moran put two bottles on the bar, one a Piel's beer, the other a twin of the bottle Garlington had nearly emptied by now. Dinny opened them himself. Train made his way back to the table. The girl he'd short-tipped spat as he walked past, but she missed him. He kept going, put the bottles on the scarred wood, and took a seat.

Garlington turned back toward Train. He reached across the table and tapped on the wood with the tip of his forefinger. 'One more thing, Train. No holding out.'

'What do you mean?'

'I mean, we know how much you can take in every week. We want an honest fifty-fifty split. Don't try holding out and saying you didn't get everything this week. It ain't worth it, kid, it ain't worth it.'

'Maybe that's what happened to Winger.'

'No, don't be a wise guy. That ain't what happened to Winger. If he was holding out, they wouldn't have had that butcher shoot him. They'd have found a better way to teach him a lesson.'

'Sure.' Train had emptied his own glass and refilled it from the fresh Piel's bottle. 'How would they have done it? And who's *they* anyhow?'

'Don't ask me that, Train. Don't ask nobody that question. Not nobody, you get me? Not if you know what's good for you. Don't you dare ask me that question or ask anybody that question. You understand? You understand, Train? I don't want to tell you again, just don't ask that question.'

Train almost cringed at Garlington's vehemence. 'All right, what about the other question?' he asked. 'What would have been a better way to teach Winger a lesson?'

Garlington poured and drank and poured again, greedily, as if the amber whiskey increased his thirst instead of relieving it. He put the bottle down on the table with a thump and glared at Train, as well as he could glare out of eyes now growing bleary.

'The way they taught Benny Jensen a lesson,' Garlington said.

Train didn't say anything.

Garlington tilted the bottle over his glass, but nothing came out. 'Wouldn't you know,' he said, 'another dead soldier.' He held up the new bottle, turned toward Dinny presiding over the lushes, and said, 'Dinny, I gotta head for home. I think I'll take this one with me. Gimme the cork.' He wobbled to his feet, staggered across the room, and collected the cork from Dinny Moran. He shoved it into the neck of the whiskey bottle. Moran tossed him a paper sack, and Garlington somehow managed to catch it and slide the bottle into it.

'Might as well head for home. The old lady's gonna have my scalp as it is. Any time I'm late she thinks I'm playing away.' He leered, 'You know, Train, if I got any decent service at home I wouldn't have to go elsewhere.'

Train waited for Garlington to run down, but Garlington wasn't quite finished. 'We're already a couple of weeks behind because Winger got himself plugged. You're gonna have to squeeze the merchants for missed payments, Train. You're gonna have to catch up, even if it means turning in the whole collection instead of half for a few weeks, until you catch up. You stupid bozo, why the hell didn't you start collecting as soon as Winger caught it? There's dumb and there's dumb, but you really take the cake, you know that?'

He pushed himself upright and turned his back on Train. Train watched Garlington weave toward the door. Garlington stood peering left and right, then turned and headed toward Dumont

Avenue. Train nursed his beer until it was dead flat and lukewarm, then he headed for the door himself.

Three of the four girls were gone. Must have found johns when he wasn't looking, Train thought. The one who remained reached for him as he passed her table. She had bright red hair and a bad complexion, and she wore a peacock blue blouse scooped low in front. She leaned over. She wore a gold-colored crucifix, smothering Jesus between her breasts. 'Come on, sport. Good-looking young guy like you, you get a special price.'

Train said, 'No thanks' and kept going. When he hit the sidewalk he turned the other way, toward Linden Boulevard. He didn't want to run into Garlington. Junius Street was still pretty busy. He stopped at a drugstore. He recognized the pharmacist, a refugee named Akiva Mendelssohn. The pharmacist recognized him as well.

'So, Officer, nice to see you. Sorry to hear about your father. So sad. I hope your mother is dealing with it. Worse for those left behind than for the dead, don't you think? And what is it, what do you need tonight?'

Train bought three or four tonics and a variety of vitamins, including a bottle of B12 tablets. He didn't want to be obvious.

'Your mother, I've seen her,' Mendelssohn said. 'She needs to eat more; she needs nourishment. But tonics, vitamins, those are good, too. They should help. This B12, it's good for the blood. Very good. Come, I'll ring you up.'

The drugstore was on the pay-off list, Train knew, but since Winger's death everybody on the beat had been getting a free ride. That was about to end, but Train wasn't going to start collecting tonight. Mendelssohn made up a package. Train paid for the purchase and put the package under his arm.

'Tell your mother, please, she has my condolences,' Mendelssohn said. 'And you, Officer, you make her eat. She's like a rail, that woman. Starving herself won't bring him back, her husband. She needs to eat.'

After he left the pharmacy Train

bought a copy of the *Eagle* from a kid on the corner. Train walked home. He climbed the stairs and found his mother sitting on the sofa with a pair of his father's socks in her hands. She was repairing a hole in the toe of one of the socks. He started to say something to her, but changed his mind. She knew the old man was dead; she knew he didn't need the socks any more. If it helped her to darn her husband's socks, let her do it and feel a little better.

'Your sister called.' The old lady looked up at Train. 'She wanted to know why you weren't home. I told her you're a grown man and it's none of her business why you weren't home.'

'I guess she worries,' Train said. He started to turn on the radio, then decided that his mother might think it was disrespectful, so he left it off. He sat in his father's favourite chair and opened up the newspaper and started scanning the pages, looking for Barney Hopkins's byline.

He heard a sound. His mother was watching him and crying softly.

'I'm sorry, Ma. Shouldn't I sit in Pa's chair?'

She shook her head. 'Sit there. Sit there. Let me look at you sitting there.'

* * *

He walked his beat every day with Tim Charters, listening to Charters' comments on every kind of resident of Brownsville and every merchant on Junius Street. They stopped for lunch at a different restaurant every day. It wasn't his regular collection day yet, but he managed to maneuver Susan Chen into the back room at the Imperial Palace for a quick conference.

Her cousin Virginia Wong had disposed of the cash Susan had mailed to her with no difficulty. By now the bills with the bullet holes were circulating through Los Angeles. Probably nobody would even notice, or if anybody did they'd think the holes had been made by wiseacres showing off with cigarettes.

Train told Susan he'd need to use the back room for some very private business.

It would only be once a week and it would only take a few minutes each time. Susan put her hand on Train's arm and nodded. 'All right. You just let me know when you need it.'

'I'll need to leave a few supplies here.' He reached into his uniform pocket and came out with the bottle of vitamin B12 tablets he'd bought from Akiva Mendelssohn.

Susan's eyes widened and she looked as if she didn't know whether this was a joke or not. 'Vitamin pills?' Then her eyes narrowed. 'Or is there something else in there?'

'Just vitamin pills,' Train told her.

'All right.' She didn't demand any more information than he'd already provided. He thanked her and made his way through the clattering bead curtain and headed back to his table.

Tim Charters was munching on spare ribs. He looked up at Train. 'You got something going on with that broad?'

Train felt an impulse to commit an act of violence, but he restrained himself. 'Strictly business. Minor at that, Tim.'

Charters raised his hands in mock surrender. He still held a rib in one hand and there was a reddish brown smear on his face. 'Okay with me,' he said. 'Might not be okay down where I come from, but here in New York City I guess anything goes. Isn't that so, Nicky?'

Train sat down and ate his lunch.

After the meal he told Charters that he had an errand to run. Charters wanted to know what it was and Train was not particularly inclined to tell him, but he did so anyway to keep the peace. Charters irritated him enough as it was, and Train figured that he must be as bothersome to Charters in return.

'Going to pay a condolence call on Benny Jensen's dad.'

'Yeah. Heard of him. Must have been pretty lame at the academy to get sent out to — where the hell was it?'

'Staten Island.'

'Right. We had our lame types in Hattiesburg, sent 'em out to the sticks till they got the message and resigned. Good thing I didn't have to take the academy here.' He grinned.

184

Train asked, 'Why was that?'

'Took me as a transfer. You're lucky they didn't decide that I rank you, Nicholas baby.'

A mechanic at Jensen DeSoto told Train that the owner had knocked off early and gone home.

'Everything all right?'

'Boss hasn't been the same since his kid went into the drink. I don't blame him, poor geezer. Must be close to fifty and he loses his only kid. You know, he didn't want Benny to be a flatfoot. Whoops! Sorry, didn't mean to offend.'

'It's all right.'

'No, the old man wanted to teach his kid the car business. You know, the Depression is on the way out now. People are getting work again; once they're working we're gonna sell cars again. Just a pity. A pity.' He shook his head.

★   ★   ★

Train knocked at the Jensens' doorbell. He'd been to the house often enough during his school years, and since.

Benny's father answered the door. Train could hear the radio playing in the kitchen. He recognized the voice of one of his own mother's favourites, Mary Margaret McBride.

The elder Jensen welcomed Train, told him to sit in the living room, and asked if he'd like a beer or a cup of coffee. Train declined. Instead he asked, 'Mr. Jensen, did Benny keep any papers in the house? I mean, anything about police work?'

Jensen squinted at the ceiling, a gesture Train had seen many times before. 'Don't think so, son.'

'Documents? Notebooks? Are you sure?'

Jensen frowned. 'Nick, I've known you since you were a little boy. You and Benny together. I know you're a fine young man now, but you've got me worried. What's this all about?'

Now it was Train's turn to worry. After a minute he said, 'I'm working on a case and I really can't talk about it, Mr. Jensen. Believe me, I wish I could, but it would be a very bad idea. And I think Benny may have been working on the same matter. I just don't know. If I could look through his things I might find something.'

'You don't think Benny fell off that ferry, do you?' Jensen looked angry.

Nick Train made straight-on eye contact. 'No, sir. I do not.'

Jensen said, 'All right.' He got up and walked to the kitchen. Train heard him telling his wife that Benny's friend Nick Train was going to look for something in Benny's room. He led Train upstairs and down a hallway to a bedroom door. Train knew the way well, but he let the old man guide him. 'You go ahead, Nicholas. I'll close the door so I won't see anything I shouldn't.'

Train thanked him, waited until he heard the door click shut, and started through Benny's desk. Nothing but the usual kipple. He turned and found a bookcase. Benny had kept some of his old schoolbooks; you were supposed to turn them in at the end of the term, but hardly anybody did. There were some adventure novels, stories of pirates, cave men, jungle adventurers, voyages to other planets, detectives and gangsters. Copies of *College Humor* and *Captain Billy's Whiz-Bang*.

There was also the William Seward High School yearbook for 1938. Train opened it to the senior photo section. He couldn't resist looking at his own portrait. Had he really been that young, that recently? He shook his head and turned to Benjamin Joseph Jensen. Someone — presumably Benny himself — had sketched in a rough image of a three-dimensional box, a crude image of a naked woman on the front of it, a playing-card spade in the corner.

Benny's dresser held an assortment of civilian clothing and police uniforms. There were two smaller drawers. One was reserved for rolled-up socks. The other was full of packs of playing cards. Each package had a nude or semi-nude woman on the outside. Most of them were still sealed in cellophane. Behind them was a row of pocket notebooks, each one roughly the size of a deck of cards. Train opened one of the notebooks. Its pages were blank. Another book, same lack of results. In fact, they were all blank inside.

Train went back to the decks of playing cards. Only one box was unsealed. It was held closed by an ordinary rubber band. It felt heavy in his hand and something slid around when he shook the box. He opened the cardboard tab at the end of the package and shook out a notebook.

Inside were numbers. Train read them. They were meaningless. They could have represented anything from income tax information to batting averages. If he'd known how to break them up, they might be meaningful. Maybe they were in code, but maybe not. Maybe their meaning was right there, right there on the blue-lined pages of the dime-store notebook, if only Train knew how to read them.

One box had held a notebook, and an empty box had been found on Jensen's body in the harbor. Train slipped the cardboard box with the girly photo on the outside and the cheap notebook on the inside into his pocket. He went back downstairs, repeated his condolences to Benny's parents, thanked the elder Jensen for his hospitality, and went off to rendezvous with Tim Charters.

* * *

Collection day arrived. Train found himself following the same pattern Dermott Winger had. Garlington had warned him to keep all his records in his head. No little black books, not since the scandal that had brought down Mayor Walker of happy memory. But it was a good idea to be honest with the customers. Don't try and double-collect. Don't jack up the prices, not without consulting higher management. Don't give receipts.

Don't give receipts! What did Garlington think he was, a complete moron?

His first stop was the Junius Street Variety. Standing outside the theater, Train read the title of the current feature, a picture imported from England called *The Lady Vanishes*. There were posters in the lobby advertising a big event, a Saturday matinee showing of *Snow White and the Seven Dwarves*. The first show wouldn't be for a couple of hours, but the manager was already in the building and the slightly overweight candy girl was behind her counter, setting up for the day's and night's business.

Train left Charters talking to the candy girl. He could imagine what Charters' favourite topic would be, but the candy girl looked as if she could take care of herself. Still, Train thought, it might be a good idea to have a little talk with Charters about the dangers of getting involved with people on the beat. One of his instructors at the academy had warned the class, *Don't get your meat where you get your bread.*

Right.

The manager of the Junius Street Variety greeted Train and Charters with an uncertain smile. More than ever he resembled a nervous rodent trying to look like Adolph Menjou. Train searched his memory for the man's name and came up with Victor Tremont. The manager made some meaningless comment about it being nice to see Train again, then sighed when Train suggested a private talk in the office.

Tremont folded his hands, palm down, on his desk. The surface was cluttered with publicity folders for new movies and schedule sheets for the theater.

'I need to collect,' Train told him.

'I thought we were finished with that.'

'I'm afraid not.'

Tremont sighed again. Most of the big theaters in the cities were part of chains owned by the studios. Every section seemed to have its RKO and its Fox and its Loew's. But a scattering of independents, art theaters, and second-run houses struggled to survive in some neighborhoods. The Junius Street Variety was one of them.

'It was too bad about your partner,' Tremont said. 'What was his name, Officer Winger. A nice fellow. You'd never take him for a shakedown artist.'

'Look, he wasn't exactly a prince and neither am I. Winger didn't invent this system. Let's just keep things nice and peaceful.'

Tremont unlocked his desk, opened a drawer, and pulled out a cash box. He handed Train a bill.

Train had brought an envelope with him. He unbuttoned his tunic, slipped the cash into the envelope, and put it back in his pocket. He stood up. He said, 'Thank you.'

The manager reached into his own inside pocket and extracted a handful of theater passes. 'Some nice pictures coming up. You might want to come around some evening. Bring your girl-friend.'

Train pocketed the passes and started for the door.

Tremont called him back. 'There's another matter, Officer.'

Train waited.

'Please sit down.' Tremont gestured toward the chair Train had just vacated. Tremont ran his finger nervously along his little moustache. While Train waited he opened a desk drawer and removed a bottle and two glasses.

Train shook his head. 'No thanks, Mr. Tremont. Maybe you'd better just say your piece.'

Tremont nodded. 'Yes, I suppose I should just be direct about this.'

Train still waited.

'It's your new — your new, ah, partner.'

'Tim Charters.'

'Yes.'

'What about him?'

Tremont's Adam's apple bobbed a couple of times. Then he said, 'Officer Charters has been, ah, coming by the theater fairly often.'

'Yes?'

'He, ah, seems to be attracted to Millie. Millie the candy girl. Her full name is Millicent Sanders Johnson. She's married now. Just a few weeks, Officer Train. I wasn't so sure about keeping her on after she was married, but her husband is a medical student and they need the money, so I let her keep her job. And Officer Charters, well . . . '

He left it hanging there.

Now it was Train's turn to sigh. 'All right, I'll talk to him.'

Tremont said, 'I hope you don't — I mean — '

Train said, 'It's okay. I'll take care of it. Don't worry, Mr. Tremont.'

He left Tremont's office and pulled

Charters away from the candy counter, across the theater lobby, and into the street. 'Look,' he said, 'I want you to lay off Millie.'

He wondered, *Am I cut out for this? I could take this bum in two rounds in the ring, but talking to him on the sidewalk is another thing.*

Charters frowned. 'Who?'

'Don't play dumb, Charters. Millie the candy girl at the Variety. She's been complaining to her boss and he complained to me. Just cut it out, you understand?'

'Hey, that's my private life.' Charters jerked his arm out of Train's grasp. 'I'll do whatever I feel like in my private life.'

'She's a married woman.'

'So what, that's all the better. I won't have to break her in. Her husband is doing all the hard part.'

Train grabbed his partner by the front of his tunic. 'Don't be a wiseacre, Charters. You know that's a direct violation of department policy. Lay off her or I'll blow the gaff on you, I swear it.'

Charters laughed.

Train shook his head. 'Or I'll just deal with you myself.' He let go of Charters' tunic and moved halfway back into his ring posture.

'Good God almighty, Nicky, cool off, will you? What is it, you have something for her yourself? I'll dump Millie if it's that big a deal. Jesus, you'd think a dumb candy broad made a difference. You are really something, Nicky.'

They finished covering their beat early. Train told Charters to head back to the precinct and tell Sergeant Garlington he'd been delayed and would be along in a little while. Charters didn't like the idea but Train insisted.

Once Charters was out of sight, Train headed back to the Imperial Palace. Susan Chen let him into the back room. Before he did anything else he checked the walls. No repeat of the Winger shooting for Nicholas Train. No peephole drilled through the burlap-covered wood-work. The room was clean. He'd brought a dessert dish and a glass of warm water with him. He used a metal spoon to crush a couple of vitamin B12 tablets into powder, then dissolved them in water. He dipped a wooden chopstick in the solution and wrote *B12* in the corner of each bill he'd collected, including a ten-spot from Chen Jing-kuo, Susan's father.

The old man didn't know what was going on. Neither did his wife or son. Train would have been happier if no one knew what he was up to, including Susan, but there was no way to keep her in the dark.

The bills dried quickly. He stuffed them into an envelope and put the envelope in his tunic pocket. Grinning, he drank the unused vitamin B12 solution. What the hell, it was good for the blood. Mendelssohn had told him so.

He headed back to the station house. The building was pretty quiet. The day shift were in the locker room, showering and dressing in civvies and shooting the breeze. The swing shift duty sergeant was drinking coffee behind the desk. He spotted Train and gestured.

'Where you been, Nick? Garlington wants to talk to you. He's waiting in the back.'

Train said, 'Do me a favor. If Garlington squawks, just tell him that I'm cold and tired and my dogs are barking. I'm gonna take a shower and then I'll talk to him.'

'Okay, Officer, it's your funeral.' The sergeant took another sip of coffee. Train wondered if there was something in the coffee designed to warm the inner man.

He found Garlington waiting for him when he stepped out of the shower. Garlington said, 'Train, this is not good. I don't like to be kept waiting. Especially by a rookie patrolman.'

Train shook his head. 'Don't give me that. I've got what you want.' He pulled on his civvies, warm slacks and a plaid shirt, woolen socks and fresh shoes. The shoes were the best part of it. Warm, dry feet made him feel a hundred per cent better.

He handed Garlington the envelope. Garlington took it, looked around, and opened the flap. He counted. 'Is this all, Train?'

'I took out my half.'

'Not the way we do it. You turn in all

the kale, I count it out and give back your share. Besides, you got to make up for the weeks you missed. I told you that before.'

Train shook his head and grunted something that sounded a lot like, 'Nope.'

Garlington's eyes popped. 'Did I hear what I think I heard?'

'You did.'

Garlington swung a hard right at Train. Train blocked it with his forearm and planted a fist in Garlington's belly. Garlington doubled over, gasping.

Train didn't follow up. He helped Garlington onto a footstool. Garlington looked up at Train, his face a mixture of rage, fear, and sheer incredulity.

Once Garlington was breathing normally, Train said, 'Please, Sergeant, be more careful. You know, you're not as young as you used to be. When you slipped just now, if I hadn't caught you, you would have fallen against the locker and really hurt yourself. You might have lost some teeth or broken your nose.'

'You moron, you fool,' Garlington whispered. 'You want to hand me your badge and gun right now, or wait for a hearing?'

'Don't try and be funny, Garlington. Roscoe Arbuckle and Oliver Hardy have the fat guy role locked up.' Train smiled. 'The last thing you want is a hearing. The worst that could happen to me would be I'd lose my job. You could wind up in Dannemorra. Oh, would those cons ever love to get their mitts on a fat old cop like you.'

Garlington pushed himself to his feet. 'Okay, forget about it. This never happened. Just make sure you make an honest count and turn in your collections on schedule. We'll figure out a way to cover the missing weeks. And no skimming. You got me, you louse?'

'I'll be honest as the day is long.'

'And don't let anybody else know that you're taking your half in front. Everybody else plays by my rules. If word gets out, I'm coming after you.'

'I'll be quiet as a mouse, Sergeant Garlington. Honest as the day is long and quiet as a mouse, that what I'll be.'

Garlington was leaning against a

locker. 'Okay, Train, get the hell out of here.'

'After you, Sergeant.'

'You trouble-maker, you wise guy. I hope you don't think you have a future on this police force, Train, because you don't.'

'Honest, quiet — that's me, Sergeant. After you.'

'Not after this.' Garlington gulped for air. 'You are going to be one sorry flatfoot when I get through with you.'

7

A Municipal Lamp Post

The cab was waiting for Train a block from his house. The driver was leaning against the door, reading a copy of the Brooklyn *Citizen*. He gestured Train over with a jerk of his chin and opened the door for him, polite as a limo chauffeur.

Train said, 'Look, I have to get home and make sure my mother's all right.'

The driver said, 'Get in, she's okay.'

Train decided to take a chance.

The driver said, 'Your sister's there. You can phone from Mr. Smith's office. There's nothing to worry about.'

Train watched the streets of Brownsville roll past the cab's window. It was an unusual sight for him — not being on the street, pounding his beat: checking in on the merchants, the kids and the solid citizens, the struggling greenhorns and the known troublemakers.

He entered McAteer's office and was greeted by McAteer and Inspector Clarke. Train was not pleased. McAteer started to introduce Train and Clarke, but Train cut him off. 'I know him. We've met. I want to know what's going on.'

'Sit down, Nicholas.' McAteer was standing behind his desk. The nameplate on the desk still said, *Mr. Smith*. Clarke had been seated in a chair facing the desk; he stood up when Train entered the room.

'I'll sit down when I feel like it. I want to know what's going on. I've done exactly what you asked me to do, Mr. McAteer.' He didn't quite have the nerve to omit the *Mister*.

'Yes, you have.' A bottle of scotch stood on McAteer's desk along with two half-full glasses and an empty one. 'Sit down, Nicholas, and have a sip of whiskey. Would you like — no, I forgot, you don't smoke cigars. Never mind. But a drop of scotch will do you good.' Without waiting for a reply he poured a drink for Train, lowered the bottle, and shoved the glass to the far edge of his desk.

McAteer raised his glass, nodded to Clarke and to Train, and waited for them follow his lead. 'To the confounding of our enemies,' he said.

They drank.

Train was still chilled from his day on the beat. A single sip of the whiskey warmed him. He followed it with another, then carefully lowered his glass. 'Okay,' he said, 'I could have got that at Walker's Bar.'

'I doubt it,' McAteer grinned, 'but your point is well taken. I didn't invite you here just for a social drink.'

'You didn't invite me. You practically had me shanghaied.'

'My apologies. It seemed a good way to get you here without undue exposure.'

Clarke said, 'We heard about your set-to with Sergeant Garlington.'

'You know everything. Why do you need me?'

'Where's the money, Officer Train?'

Train looked at McAteer. 'You can speak freely, Nicholas. Inspector Clarke knows what's going on.'

'I gave half of it to Garlington. The rest is here.' He tapped his chest with his thumb.

'What are you going to do with it?'

'I haven't decided.'

McAteer said, 'You could leave it with me if you wish.'

'I don't wish.'

Clarke said, 'I think you'd better, Officer Train. You've extorted bribes from citizens and paid off your supervising sergeant with part of the proceeds. You don't want to hold onto the rest of the money.'

'Don't I?'

'You could lose your job. You could go to prison.'

'Not a chance. I'm Mr. McAteer's boy, I guess. Not that I had much choice. But I'm holding onto the money that I collect. When this case goes to court, I'll turn it in for use as evidence. I'm not putting it in any evidence room now. I know how things get lost.'

'You needn't put it in an evidence room, Nicholas. You put it in the care of my office, it will be quite secure, I can assure you.'

'No, thanks.'

'You can have a receipt if you want it. But it might be very dangerous to carry that around. Do you have a secure place to put it?'

'I'll worry about that, thank you very much. I'll just keep this money.'

'Now look here, do you know who you're talking to? Have you studied department policy, Officer?' Clarke was starting to look hot under the collar.

'Don't play good-cop-bad-cop with me! Don't you think I know how that game works?' Train got to his feet and started for the door.

'Please.' That was McAteer. That was the good cop.

Train stopped and faced the others. 'I still don't know why you got me here and unless you have something more to tell me, I'm leaving. Period.'

'Please sit down. We got off on the wrong foot. You have my apologies. We really need to talk, Nicholas.'

Train took a step toward McAteer's desk.

'Please.'

Train slid into his chair. He sat near the edge.

'Nicholas, Inspector Clarke and I are deeply concerned about your confrontation with Sergeant Garlington.'

'You already told me that. What I want to know is, how do you know about it? Is Garlington working for you? What the hell is the set-up? It sounds like *let's you and him fight* to me. The whole thing took place hardly an hour ago. But even before I get home, you have a cab waiting for me. And here you are. Don't you ever quit work, McAteer?'

He could see the tiniest suggestion of a wince twist McAteer's face when he heard his name without the title, the same kind of twitch he'd seen before. But McAteer didn't address the name issue. Instead he asked, 'You don't deny striking Sergeant Garlington, do you?'

'Of course not. Fact is — no, never mind, I'm not going to play the schoolyard game about who hit who first. I want to know how you found out about it. You didn't answer me. Is Garlington working for you or isn't he?'

Train saw McAteer shoot a glance at Clarke. Then McAteer held up his hand, his elbow on his desk, palm toward himself. Two inches of perfect white linen protruded beyond the cuff of his navy pinstripe suit. His necktie tonight was dark blue with a muted pattern of lighter specks. A gold cufflink with a matching blue stone caught the light of a ceiling fixture. McAteer spread his fingers wide.

'One hand,' he said, 'separate fingers.'

Clarke said, 'That wasn't smart, Train. You don't want to make an enemy of Garlington.'

'He's a thug. And a bully.'

'He's a crook.'

'That's no news.'

McAteer leaned forward. He had already lowered his hand, spreading both hands on his desk. If he'd just raised them and gestured hypnotically he could have conjured up a genie. He shook his head and heaved a little sigh.

'Nicholas, if we were only after Garlington, we'd have arrested him long ago. I thought you understood what you're dealing with. I must admit that I'm disappointed.'

'I don't care.'

'No, of course not. And again, I apologize. You needn't concern yourself with my emotional well-being, Nicholas. But you are now part of my team, like it or not. You've passed the point of no return. And we are out to trace this rottenness to its roots, wherever they may lie. Now I'm not going to ask you to apologize to Garlington and try to get back into his good graces. It's too late for that. But you've got to establish — should I say, *re-establish* — at least a working relationship with him, or everything you've done is worthless.'

Train stood up and said, 'I've got your number. I'll call you when I need to. And you obviously know how to reach me.'

Clarke said, 'If you keep that money you're a racketeer, Officer Train. If you turn it over to us, you're a hero.'

Holding back after that one actually made Train's teeth hurt. He told Clarke, 'Garlington has the marked bills now. You keep an eye out for those. See where they turn up. See if Lieutenant Kessler spends 'em. See if Tom Dewey uses 'em to pay for his moustache wax. You don't need my half.'

The next morning he stopped at the Kings County Citizens' and Workers' Bank. He was in uniform, officially on duty. Charters was with him. It gave Train a strange feeling of re-living moments in his life, only this time he had taken the role of Dermott Winger and Tim Charters was playing the role of Nicholas Train. He introduced Charters to the bank manager. Morris Finch was wearing the same brown suit and tie he'd worn the first time Train met him, or their twins. Finch welcomed Charters to Brownsville.

Then Train introduced Charters to the guard, Mike Calvert, the retired cop. Train wondered if Calvert had been on the take; if he was sitting on a comfortable nest egg now that he was collecting his pension from the city. If that was true, why the hell was he working as a guard in the local bank? Maybe he found retirement boring, and he did it because he was so accustomed to wearing a uniform and badge and carrying a gun that he felt uncomfortable without the tin on his blouse and the weight on his hip.

Train told Charters to go read a magazine while he made a deposit. Train stood in line at a teller window and added his half of the week's grift to his savings account. The bills were unmarked, untraceable. As he moved away from the window, carefully placing his savings book inside his uniform tunic, he sensed Mike Calvert at his side. He turned to face the bank guard, thinking how much Calvert looked like Ed Brophy, the chubby character actor who seemed to have a patent on gangster's sidekick roles in one movie after another.

'Be careful, son.'

Train frowned at Calvert. The guard had spoken softly, his words barely audible to Train. 'Careful? What's that, Mike?'

'Just watch your step, Nick. I've known you since you were a sprout, haven't I?'

'True.'

'I know your mother and your sister. I

knew your dad, God rest his poor soul. His death was a blessing. You know that, don't you? He was suffering and the end was a release. But now I'm telling you, son, just be very careful.' Calvert looked around the bank lobby. 'There are some very bad people around, Nick. Very dangerous, bad people. I'm telling you — I can't say anything more, I'm just telling you, Nick — be very, very careful.'

After that, things were quiet for a while. It wasn't a bad life. Lunch at various eating joints on his beat. Movie dates with Susan Chen. Her brother had even stopped sending Train hate-glares when he saw the two of them together. Train's mother was dealing with his father's death better than Train would have expected. She was starting to get out of the apartment, visit her friends, and eat regularly. She was taking her tonics and her vitamins, and she looked as if she was actually gaining a little weight.

Marie and her husband Jocko came over a couple of nights a week for dinner. Marie took over cooking duties those nights. Either she was putting on a little weight herself or she was pregnant. Train didn't ask. She would tell him when she was good and ready. If he asked he figured she'd be peeved with him and he didn't need any of that.

He played poker once a week with Pudgy Watterson and Jackie Goldstein and Marty Macon. The game had taken place at Benny Jensen's house in the past. Now Pudgy took it over. He and Jackie and Marty kept after Train for information about Benny's death. Were the police doing anything about it? The story had been heavily covered in the Brooklyn *Eagle* and the *Citizen* for a while, had even made the pages of the Manhattan tabloids, but the story didn't last for long. First the *Daily News* and the *Mirror* lost interest, then the story disappeared from the Brooklyn papers.

All except for Barney Hopkins' stories. Hopkins continued to contribute frequent reports to the *Eagle* and to write his weekly column in the Saturday editions. He mentioned Benny's slaying almost every week, prodding the police and the DA's office to pay some attention to this good young cop foully murdered on his way home from a long day of pounding his beat in Staten Island.

Winger's death actually got more ink, even though it had happened longer ago. It had happened right in Brownsville, and there was no question of accidental death. There was even a suspect in custody. And the papers had a field day with Henry Little, the Brownsville Butcher.

But there was no sign of progress in either case, and no gentleman of the press had managed to find any evidence of a link between the two.

Train was sitting with a pair of queens in a game of five-card draw. It wasn't much of a hand. He had a glass of beer in front of him and a half-eaten Swiss cheese and lettuce sandwich at his elbow. The game hadn't been very interesting and he hadn't even kept track of his money. He looked at the pot, looked at his pile of chips, and decided to bet the limit. Jackie Goldstein folded. Pudgy raised. Marty raised again. Train saw Marty's bet. Pudgy folded.

Macon let out a soft curse and laid

down four clubs and a spade.

Train laughed and raked in the pot.

Jackie said, 'We need to add somebody. Four players ain't enough. Not enough action, not enough gelt on the table.'

Pudgy said, 'You have anybody in mind?'

'What about Nick's new partner, what's-his-name?'

Train said, 'Tim Charters.'

'Yeah.' Pudgy said, 'You gonna finish that sandwich, Nick? I'll take it away.'

Train shook his head.

'All right.' He picked up Train's plate and took a bite of the sandwich. 'You don't know what's good, Nick. Waste not, want not, ain't that right?'

Train said, 'Yeah.'

Jackie said, 'That's a good idea. So what about that new partner of yours?'

'Not a good idea, guys. For one thing, he wouldn't like you, Jackie.'

'What do you mean?'

'What do you think?'

'The guy's a Nazi?'

'I wouldn't go that far, but he's from the South, you know. They're different down there.'

'Sure.'

Pudgy said, 'Well, try and think of somebody. Maybe somebody from the old Seward gang. Where'd everybody go? A few years ago we were falling over each other on the street, now I hardly ever see anybody.'

'We'll talk it over next week.'

Train left Pudgy Watterson's house a sawbuck lighter than he'd arrived. Most weeks he won a couple of bucks, sometimes he lost a couple, but this was the most he'd ever dropped. And it was the first time he could pay up and not hurt.

Maybe being a crook wasn't such a bad thing.

He strolled up Junius Street toward home. Somehow the night masked the ugliness of the city and gave even Brownsville an Arabian Nights feeling. He'd seen stills from the old *Thief of Baghdad* movie with Doug Fairbanks, and Victor Tremont at the Variety movie theater said there was a remake in the works. He wondered if Susan Chen would like to see it.

Even though he was off duty and wearing civvies, he kept his eyes peeled and his ears open. A couple of Seward High kids were in Mr. Bhasmadjian's store, buying ice cream cones. Train felt a sudden pang of longing for the old days. Was it really less than three years since he'd been a Seward kid, palling around with Pudgy and Jackie and Benny and Marty, chasing girls, trying to buy beer even though they were underage?

The Four Star Kosher Butcher Shop was closed. The Imperial Palace was still open. He caught a glimpse of Susan Chen. She was running the cash register, making change for a customer. Train didn't catch her eye, so he kept walking. He spotted a streetwalker leaning against an iron lamppost. Why didn't she join the line in Walker's Bar where it was warm on a cold night and relatively safe? Train stopped and showed the girl his tin. She looked incredibly young and undernourished, and she could definitely use a good hot bath.

When she saw Train's badge she jumped. Most whores he knew were totally blasé when it came to dealing with cops, but this one looked as if she were going to cry. Train said, 'Miss, you ought to get to a settlement house. You don't belong out here. This is a lousy way to make a living. I know you can do better.'

Then she actually did start to cry. She pleaded with Train not to arrest her. He asked her name and where she lived, and she said she was Agnes Anne Amato from the Bronx and she was working Brownsville because she didn't want her family to know.

Cursing himself for six kinds of fool, Train took her to the Imperial Palace. He grabbed Lawrence Chen and handed him a fin. 'Give her a good meal and send her home, Lawrence. Make sure she goes. She comes from the Bronx. Ride up there with her if you have to, you got me?'

Chen looked too startled to answer.

'Do it,' Train told him. Then he added, 'Please, as a favour.'

He left the girl sitting at a table, crying into a linen napkin.

Train started for home once again. As he passed the iron streetlamp where he'd found the streetwalker a woman screamed. He turned and felt an impact that threw him sideways. He crashed to the sidewalk, trying to break his fall with his hands. Two brilliant disks roared at him like twin suns in a Buster Crabbe serial. He felt a sharp pain in his left arm, a powerful pain that momentarily filled his being with a searing orange-red. He felt a second impact on his back and thudded again against the sidewalk while an immense crash filled his ears. Everything went out of focus.

As soon as the weight was off his back he was able to push himself upright using his right hand. His left arm continued to send waves of pain through him.

There were hands on him, voices around him. People were rushing toward him, or so it seemed until he realized that he was a secondary event.

A car had crashed against the lamppost. Steam was rising from beneath the crumpled hood. The windshield had popped out and shattered, spraying daggers of glass for yards in front of the car.

The driver had been propelled forward by the impact. His skull must have been the missile that blew the windshield out. Train managed to stagger to the car. He bent and peered at the face that lay sideways on the dashboard. The top of the skull was flattened and the nose was crushed, but otherwise the face was intact and Train recognized it.

Who the hell was the swing shift patrolman on this beat? Train's brain was numb. The woman who screamed and the person who had hit him like a football lineman had saved his life. No question about that. He would have been pinned against the lamppost by the onrushing car. He knew the dead man. Who was the cop on the beat? Where was he?

He heard a siren. People were scurrying around, coming and going. His arm felt as if it were on fire, but when he looked at it there were no flames. Both his hands were bloody, but that looked like nothing more than scrapes from hitting the sidewalk. His face felt the way it did after he'd taken a beating in the ring; he decided that could be from hitting the sidewalk, too. His only serious injury, it looked like, was to his arm. And there wasn't much question, the arm was broken.

Who was on the beat?

A bluecoat pushed through the crowd, police officer's cap and badge showing. Who the hell was it?

'Train?'

'Yeah, yeah. You're — ' The name wouldn't come.

'Paulson. You know me? Wally Paulson. Train, you okay?'

'I know you, sure. Paulson. Right. I just — for a minute — I just — '

'It's okay. You gotta see a doc. Ambulance coming, we'll get you to the hospital.'

'Okay. I'm okay.'

'Like hell you are. C'mere.' Paulson commandeered the services of a couple of civilians. 'Get him over there. Make him sit down.'

'Wait,' Train managed, 'Wait a minute. The guy in the car.'

'Yeah?'

'The guy in the car.'

'Yeah, Train, the guy in the car, what about the guy in the car?'

'He tried to kill me.'

'Maybe he did, we'll see.'

'He's dead.'

'Okay, don't worry about that.'

'He's Jake Lefcourt.'

'He's — ' Paulson turned and ran the few steps back to the car. Train could see him. Train was sitting on the sidewalk, his back against a dirty tile storefront. The ambulance siren was coming closer. His arm was on fire. He was staring at the car. He was trying to identify its nameplate. He thought it was a Ford. An old one at that. What the hell did they call them, a Model A. That was it. A Ford Model A.

Paulson bent over the steaming hood, peering into the tonneau, staring at the dead driver. He pushed his way back through the crowd. He squatted on the sidewalk next to Train. 'It's Lefcourt okay, Train, but he wouldn't have tried to kill you. It was an accident. He must have lost control. He was going too fast, anyhow. You can't drive like that on Junius Street. He must have been driving like he was on a highway. Now he's dead.'

The ambulance pulled to the curb and a couple of white-uniformed attendants came running toward Train with a rolled-up stretcher. They opened it and laid it on the sidewalk. They took Train by the elbows and he screamed. The attendant who had taken his broken arm muttered, 'Sorry, buddy, sorry, didn't know, sorry.'

They got Train onto the stretcher. He felt them lift him from the sidewalk and slide the stretcher into the back of the ambulance. He heard the siren wailing and felt the ambulance lurch into motion. Every time it rounded a corner or braked or accelerated, his arm sent up waves of pain.

When they got to the hospital he wanted to walk in, but they made him stay on the stretcher until they transferred him to a gurney. They wheeled him through the hallway. He was on his back. The ambulance attendants wheeling the gurney looked like giants. The ceiling lights passed overhead like the sun, like he was living the same day over and over, his world consisting of the ceiling suns and the white-coated giants and the red pain pouring from his arm and flooding the rest of his body. For a moment he thought he was boxing again, and he'd taken a thumping from somebody stronger and tougher than he was — somebody with more ring-smarts than he had or would ever have. Somebody like Tony Zale.

He'd been punched out and knocked his head on the turnbuckle and slammed onto the mat so hard they'd had to carry him out of the ring on a stretcher and take him away in an ambulance and he was in the hospital. But that didn't seem right either. He was woozy and there was a ringing in his ears. He shook his head to try and clear his mind but the pain that brought on made him stop.

A voice said, 'Just lie still, you'll be all right.' It was a woman's voice and he managed to get his eyes open and see a white figure, a woman in a white nurse's uniform, pacing along beside him. He closed his eyes and everything went away.

8

A Monstrous Throbbing

Train opened his eyes in a strange room and tried to figure out what had happened. He hadn't lost a bout to Tony Zale. He been walking on Junius Street and a woman screamed, a man slammed into him with his shoulder and a car's headlights had loomed; and the next thing he knew he'd been riding a gurney under a row of ceiling lights.

He couldn't remember right. He had a vision of a funeral service: a coffin; the old man lying in a box, pale, his face painted by the undertaker to look like a healthy man asleep — but this was a sleep from which no one ever awoke.

The ride to the cemetery. Riding in a limousine. He'd never ridden in a limousine in his life. The priest delivering a eulogy, reading from a worn, leather-bound breviary. Was that Father Dempsey from St. Columba's? Was that possible? Train's mother standing at the grave between her son and daughter, tears running down her face and falling from her chin. The sound of crunching gravel as the hearse purred away from the gravesite. It had delivered its burden, there was no need to remain there any longer.

In the small group standing around the grave, a handful of Train's buddies from Seward High. A couple of cops. Garlington. What the hell was Charlie Garlington doing there? And Lieutenant Kessler in dress blues. And Dinny Moran? Why was there a bartender at a funeral? And a tall, distinguished-looking man, every hair carefully trimmed and in place.

Gray sky, a chilly breeze. The sun broke through the clouds and glinted for a moment off the tall man's golden cufflink. He had worn a fedora that probably cost him as much as a cop's weekly earnings. An honest cop's earnings. He held the fedora in his carefully manicured, immaculate hands.

Train opened his eyes. He was lying in

a hospital bed. Sunlight had illuminated the room, glinting off a water pitcher that stood on a bedside stand.

Train let his eyes slide closed again. He was back at the cemetery, reliving his father's funeral. The priest was talking about heaven and angels, something about angels singing thee to thy rest. And Train could hear one, could hear one angel singing. He could hear every word. 'Suddenly, the setting is strange, I can see water and moonlight beaming.' Was there water and moonlight in heaven? A woman — a woman's voice — an angel's voice. 'Through it all the face that I adore.'

A voice. A face. Dark hair, emerald green eyes, red lips, a silken dress. Was this the face of the singing angel? Or was it the face of a living woman? Of Susan Chen?

A trumpet, a voice. Train opened his eyes, tried to push himself upright in his bed, and felt agony lance through his shoulder. He was able to turn his head, to see the stand near his bedside. An envelope leaned against the pitcher.

By moving gingerly, Train was able to

reach it with his uninjured arm and work the card out of the envelope. The card said, *Sorry to learn of your mishap. Of course all expenses have been taken care of. Please come and see me when you recover. I believe in you and what you are doing.* The signature was a simple, elegant capital *S.*

I believe in you and what you are doing. That's what it was about. That's what his life was about. That's what he got for joining the police force and going to work for Mr. Smith. Sure, he could have kept on boxing and losing but if he'd done that, nobody would ever have run over him with a car. The man who had tried to kill him had paid with his own life. But the *real* criminals who had ordered it were still out there. These people had also killed his friend Benny. They had to be stopped.

And Benny had left him the one thing that might make that possible: the clue of the playing cards. He owed it to Benny and to Susan to see this thing through.

He knew what he had to do. He would get well, get back on the force and finish the job. It would be difficult, but he could do it.

He was a rookie no more.

★   ★   ★

The doctor holding his chart swayed back and forth a few times, slowly changing from a blurred image to a human being. A white-uniformed nurse was cranking the hospital bed and Train found himself sitting up. The waves of pain were no longer coming from his arm; they had faded into a monstrous throbbing that echoed in his ears. His head felt fuzzy and he found it hard to formulate his thoughts.

'You can probably go home tomorrow unless there's an unpleasant surprise waiting to jump out and bite us.'

Train looked around, gathering his wits. 'This is the hospital, right?'

'That's right,' the doctor told him.

'Why — what time is it?'

The doctor pointed at a huge wall clock. Train had to blink and then squeeze his eyes to bring the clock into focus. 'One thirty,' Train muttered. 'A.m. or p.m.?'

'A.m.,' the doctor laughed. 'You've been here for five hours.'

Train turned his head carefully. Now that his mind was coming back into clarity, or starting to anyway, he was feeling more uncomfortable. His injured arm — it was broken, nobody had to tell him that — looked like something that a stranger had attached to him. The throbbing increased and decreased in intensity, never completely disappearing. First it was like a huge bass drum, then it was a kid banging a pot with a spoon, then the drum started in again. But at least this discomfort was less acute than the searing agony of the fresh break.

There was a window on one wall of the room. Through it he could see the Brooklyn sky and the Manhattan skyline beyond. He turned back to the doctor. 'What's the score?'

The doctor smiled, apparently pleased that Train was not only conscious but reasonably coherent. 'You can guess that your right arm is fractured. It's a compound fracture involving both the ulna and radius. We took X-rays and there's not much other damage. We set the arm while you were out. You'll be in a cast for three or four weeks at the least. If you're lucky, all you'll have to show for it is a nasty scar.'

Train asked, 'Is that all?'

'You suffered a mild concussion when you smacked your forehead on the sidewalk. Other than that, there's nothing but the classic contusions and abrasions — bruises and scrapes, in plain English.'

Something made him ask, 'Can I go back to work?'

Frown lines appeared between the doctor's eyes. Then he said, 'You'll have to avoid any sudden moves or strenuous activity for a few days. Your arm is in a cast.'

'So I noticed.'

'You'll have to come back here so we can remove the cast. Until then you'll need a sling as well. The contusions will take care of themselves. We've bandaged the abrasions. You'll need to keep those clean until they heal. Not a difficult task.

I understand you're a police officer, Mr. Train.'

'Yes.'

'I've dealt with the police before. I'll certify you for light duty when you leave here. You can do deskwork. I'd avoid any strenuous physical action until that concussion clears. The skull is pretty strong, the forehead especially. That's to protect the brain. But yours got a good shaking up, and your brain needs to settle down before you get back into action. Otherwise, it could be really bad. If the brain swells or if you manage to break a blood vessel up there, you could very well find yourself in a precarious spot.'

Train didn't see the doctor or the nurse leave. He didn't realize he was falling asleep, but the next thing he knew sunlight was pouring through the window and there was a tray of food waiting for him beside the bed. He tried to get some nourishment down, but he had no appetite. When he tried to swallow some scrambled eggs all he did was gag. The wall clock said it was seven o'clock. This time he knew it was morning.

There was even a copy of the Brooklyn *Citizen* on the tray. Train leafed through it and found a three-paragraph story about the car crash. The story described the crash as an accident and went on for a couple of sentences about the tragic death of Officer Lefcourt. The last paragraph was one sentence long and said that a second police officer received minor injuries in the accident. The whole thing was treated as a tragic irony.

He was ready to put the paper aside when another item caught his eye. A patrolman had fallen from a subway platform in the Bronx and been crushed beneath an onrushing express. The officer's name was Morris Hurley. Train had never heard of him, but there were thousands of cops in New York City. How many cops were getting killed, Train wondered, and what was the connection? Odd that the story was even covered in a Brooklyn daily, he thought.

Also, where the hell were his clothes, and how was he going to get dressed with his right arm in a cast?

With a token knock on the door,

Inspector Clarke entered Train's room. He closed the door behind him and pulled a chair for himself to Train's bedside.

'Sorry to hear about your accident, Officer Train. The department extends its best wishes for your rapid and total recovery. You'll stay on full pay for the time being. I talked to your doctor and he says you'll be cleared for light duty in short order and regular duty after a few weeks. There'll be plenty of work for you at the precinct in the meanwhile, so don't worry about being idle.'

Train said, 'Good morning, Inspector. Nice of you to come and see me.'

'Damned pity about Lefcourt, though.' Clarke looked at Train's meal tray. 'You ought to eat your breakfast, Train. Don't waste good food. What have you got there? Scrambled eggs, half a grapefruit, toast, marmalade. Huh! Better than I get at my house. Don't tell the missus I said that.' He laughed.

'How are we going to handle the — ' Train hesitated ' — special project, Inspector? I think I can get out and make the collections next week, anyway.'

'Don't worry about it, Train. That's all taken care of.'

Train pushed himself upright. 'What do you mean?'

'Do you mind?' Clarke tipped his head toward Train's meal tray. 'You're sure you're not going to eat that? Think of the starving Armenians, Train. Didn't your mother ever tell you?'

'What about my mother?'

'Nothing to worry about.' Clarke made himself a scrambled-egg sandwich and started in on it. 'A patrolman from the precinct went to your apartment last night and assured her that you were all right.'

'I'm surprised she didn't come here.'

'We told her no visitors. She wasn't happy but she bought it. She'll be home when you get there today. Bet she treats you like a baby. Enjoy it, Train. You won't get pampered much once you're married.' He finished his sandwich and chased it with a juicy grapefruit section. 'How the hell were you supposed to eat that anyhow with one hand? Take it from me,

Train, I know all about being married.'

'What about the collections, Inspector?'

'Train, Mr. Smith has asked me to convey his thanks for your good work.'

'What does that mean?'

'You'll probably get a commendation for this. You're on your way, young man. You have a bright career ahead of you.'

'What are you telling me, Inspector?' Train used his left arm and hand as a lever and shifted himself so his legs dangled off the side of the mattress. The bed was high and his feet failed to reach the floor. 'What are you telling me?' he repeated.

'I'm telling you that Mr. Smith and I appreciate your good work, and you are to report for duty at the station house as soon as you're able.'

'You mean I'm off the case.'

'Exactly.' Clarke pushed his chair away from Train's bed and rose to his feet.

'Like hell I am!' Train pushed himself off the bed. He felt himself falling freely for a fraction of a second. Then his feet hit the floor. That was a mistake. He felt the impact all the way up his spine and back down into his injured arm. He had intended to grab Clarke by the lapels of his well-pressed suit and go at him face-to-face, but he was shockingly weak and wound up instead grabbing Clarke to keep from collapsing onto the cold floor.

'Hey, you belong in bed, Train. You're not ready to go anywhere, son.' Clarke helped Train back onto the bed. It was humiliating.

'I'm not off the case,' Train managed.

'That's not for you to say, Officer.'

'God damn it, they killed my partner, they killed my pal Benny Jensen, and it looks to me as if Jake Lefcourt bought the farm trying to kill me. If a couple of good citizens hadn't acted fast I would have been pinned against that light pole and that would have been the end of Officer Train.'

Clarke stared at him silently. After an uncomfortable interval he picked up a spoon and ate some more grapefruit. 'People complain about hospital food, Nick, but they haven't eaten my wife's cooking.'

'I'm not quitting, Inspector. I'm in this thing to stay.'

'Where's the money, Train?'

'I gave it to Garlington like a good little grifter.'

'The rest of it, bub.' Clarke could be mean when he wanted to, that was certain.

'None of your business.'

'We'll find it. If you get out of line you're going to suffer.'

'I'll risk it.'

'All right, then. You just report back to duty as soon as you're able. You'll take orders from the desk sergeant or from Sergeant Garlington or Lieutenant Kessler. You'll be on light duty until you're certified to return to your beat. They'll work around you until then.'

Clarke held up the spoon he'd used to eat Train's grapefruit, polished it on a napkin, and slipped it into his suit pocket. He crossed the room and pulled the heavy hospital room door open. He turned back to face Train. 'Don't do anything stupid, Officer. Give me a call. You've got my number.'

'I have that,' Train said.

Who should show up next but Train's favorite brother-in-law, Jocko Sullivan. 'Aren't you supposed to be on the docks?' Train asked.

'Took a day off to bring you home, brother.'

Train was surprised. 'Nice of you, Jocko. I thought I could just get up and walk out of here, but it turns out I'm still a little wobbly.'

'Jesus, Nick, what's this all about?'

What to tell him? 'I got lucky.'

'Sure, you look it.'

'I mean it, Jocko. I nearly got squashed between a car and a lamppost. Couple of civilians saved my life. Woman screamed and then a fullback hit me with a tackle that would put Bronko Nagurski on his ass.'

Sullivan laughed at that one. 'Okay, brother-in-law, can you get into your clothes yourself? No? All right, I'll lend a hand, then we'll deal with the office and get you out of here. And don't thank me too much. I'd never hear the end of it from Marie if I didn't help out.'

239

An hour later Train was home, sitting in his father's favorite chair, a bowl of soup on the table next to him. The old lady had tried to get him to go to bed, but he wouldn't hear of it. At least his cast left his fingers free and he could use them to handle small implements, but he couldn't hold a newspaper and feed himself at the same time.

His mother had retreated to the kitchen. Train put down his spoon and switched on the radio. It gave out with a sound of sirens and gunfire, screeching tires and snarling voices. He clicked the radio off. He managed to get most of the soup down, drag himself into the kitchen, and give his mother a goodnight kiss. He crawled into his bed and tried to do some serious thinking, but instead he passed out and slept until mid-morning.

A couple of days later he reported for work. Sergeant Garlington put him at a desk with a stack of reports to read through and file. It took him about five minutes to become bored with the work, but he stuck to it. In the middle of the afternoon Garlington invited him into an interrogation room for a private meeting. Train hoped that Garlington wasn't going to let him have it with a billy club or with his fists. Garlington couldn't have forgotten their encounter in the locker room, or the humiliation Train had inflicted on him.

'Things ain't going so great since you fell down that flight of stairs, Train. I been sending Horowitz out with your friend Charters, and I hear they don't get along so great.'

Train said that didn't surprise him and Garlington asked why he said that.

'Charters is a hater, Sergeant. He hates black folk especially. That's no surprise. Where did he grow up? Hattiesburg, Mississippi. They never got over the Civil War down there. If blacks are number one on his hate list, Jews have to run a strong second. Charters hates everybody who's not like him, that's all. He's bound to hate Horowitz.'

'Well, he's a cop and he has to do his job.'

Train was aching to ask Garlington why Charters had left Mississippi and how he'd wound up in New York City and on the police force to boot, but he didn't say anything. Not now. Not when there were more urgent matters to pursue.

'Who's collecting the money?'

'We're taking care of that, Train.'

'Really? When do I get my share?'

Garlington leaned back and let out a single guffaw. 'Your share? Your share, Train? You mean the collector's share, don't you? Sure you do. Whoever collects the money gets to keep his share, that's all. Right now nobody's collecting on your beat. Horowitz has a stiff rod up his spine; I wouldn't trust him to take on the job. And as for Charters, I think you're right about that guy. There's something wrong there. I don't trust him, either. So the citizens will just have to wait to make their contributions when you get back on the beat. When will that be? Or are you gonna tell me you like sitting at a desk better?'

'Oh, no.' Train shook his head. 'The sooner I can get back on the street, the happier I'll be.'

'Okay, Train.' Garlington slapped him

on the shoulder. A wave of pain unlike any he'd felt since the night he hit the sidewalk rolled up his arm and through his body. He felt nauseous and he saw points of light before returning to normal. By that time Garlington had left the room. Train made his way back to his borrowed desk and resumed his paper-work.

When he got home he found his mother sitting on the living room sofa, crouched over a photograph album. She looked up and he saw tear streaks on her face. She wore an apron over her dress, a costume Train had seen a thousand times over the years. When she saw him looking at her she picked up a corner of her apron and dabbed at her eyes.

Train asked what she was doing.

His mother said she was just looking at some old pictures.

Train went to his room and put on a pair of warm slippers in place of his heavy brogans. When he came back to the living room his mother was still poring over the album. Its pages were made of a peculiar black paper. The crinkle-edged prints were held in place by gummed paper corners. Train sat next to his mother.

His mother said, 'Look at this.' She pointed to a photo of the entire family, his parents and his sister and himself. They were all impossibly young. His father had dark hair. His mother was positively beautiful. His sister couldn't have been more than nine or ten years old, wearing a short dress and pigtails, and grinning. And Train himself would have been five or six. He was wearing short pants and a striped shirt. Each of them was holding up a fish.

'That was at Sheepshead Bay,' his mother said. 'Do you remember? Your father loved fishing.'

'That was a long time ago.'

'Of course it was.' She put a hand forward and touched the picture as if she could somehow touch the past.

There were other pictures taken on fishing expeditions, snapshots of children's birthday parties, of sightseeing expeditions. There was a photo of them on the Staten Island ferry, with the towers of Wall Street behind them. His mother turned the pages back. Train saw himself revert to a toddler, then an infant, then disappear as his sister, Marie, followed his example. The album ended — began — with his parents' wedding portrait.

His mother handed Train the book. 'Go ahead, look through it.' First he looked at her. She was smiling and crying at the same time. He found pictures of himself with his gang from Seward High. Then he found one that stopped him. It was out of sequence; it must have fallen out of the book and been re-attached in the wrong place. It was a picture of a mounted police officer in the uniform of ten or twenty years ago. The officer was holding a little boy in front of him on the saddle. The officer looked delighted. The child looked as if he were about to burst into tears.

Train felt his mother's hand on his uninjured arm. She leaned over the book. 'That was you, Nicholas. Your sister was at a party and you couldn't understand why you couldn't go to the party, so your father and I took you to Prospect Park. You were two years old. I held you up to pet the horse and he frightened you and you started to scream, so the policeman picked you up and you stopped screaming.'

'I'm not sure I remember that.'

'After that you became a favorite with that policeman. He used to take you for rides on his horse. Don't you remember?'

'I guess I do.'

'He was Officer Calvert. I don't know what became of him.'

Train said, 'I do. He works at the Citizens' and Workers' Bank.'

His mother reached across Train's arm and turned the pages of the book. She stopped when she got back to her wedding portrait. She said, 'Nicholas, you should get married.'

He didn't say anything.

'Don't you have a girlfriend any more? You used to have girlfriends when you were in high school.'

He said, 'Well, I sort of have a girlfriend.'

'Do I know her?'

'I'm not sure. She lives in the neighbourhood.'

'You could invite her to dinner here. I want to have a little family gathering. I'll invite your sister and her husband. You can invite your girlfriend.'

'Are you sure, Ma?'

'Of course. Why wouldn't I be sure?'

'Just — well, all right, I'll invite her. When do you want to do this?'

She shrugged. 'Sunday. Sunday would be nice. We always used to have company on Sundays when your father was alive. When he was healthy. When we were both young and healthy.'

Train wasn't sure she could handle a family dinner plus Susan Chen — Chen Shu — but he was willing to try. 'All right, Ma. I'll invite her.'

'What is her name, Nicholas?'

'Susan.'

She frowned and put her hand to her hair. It was gray and dull-looking. She took a wisp between two fingers and tucked it behind her ear. 'I thought I knew everyone in the neighbourhood. I can't think of any Susan, though. I don't think I know her.'

'I'll invite her, Ma. Don't worry. I don't

know if she can make it but I'll ask her.'

'Why couldn't she make it, Nicholas?'

'She might have to work.'

'Oh, she has a job? Would she still work after she's married?'

'To me, you mean?'

'I didn't — ' she looked flustered.

'Well, I don't know, and I have no plans to ask her anyway.'

'You don't like her that much?'

'I like her fine. I just — we've never talked about anything like that. Ma, leave it, please. What's for dinner?'

She told him brisket with noodles. He offered to help her but she told him to rest. He turned on the radio and listened to the news. Europe seemed to be on the brink of war and nobody was doing anything to keep it from happening. At least the weather report at the end of the news wasn't too nasty.

*   *   *

It was strange; he couldn't tell what Garlington was thinking. Garlington kept a close watch on Train at the station house. Train reported to work every morning, settled in at his borrowed desk, and spent the day playing clerk. The work was easy enough, but as boring as shelling peas for eight hours at a stretch.

His father's medical expenses had strained the family finances, and a burial plot and casket and funeral were another blow. Now, with Train's salary the only support for himself and his mother, he had to trim expenses. He started carrying lunch to work with him instead of eating at restaurants. Sometimes cops ate free, but you couldn't count on it.

The money that he'd put into the Citizens' and Workers' Bank didn't amount to very much. He'd only been collecting for a few weeks before his accident. Even so, it would have been a help.

He considered heading to the bank on his lunch break and taking out some cash, but that would have been dangerous. McAteer and Clarke could have found out easily if he'd deposited the money in his savings account, but they couldn't get into his safety deposit box without his key. Not unless they got a court order, and if they did that their whole cloak-and-dagger operation would be exposed. No, the money was safe enough where it was.

Even so, he knew that he was skating on thin ice. He was in serious peril if the rake-off investigation foundered, worse yet if McAteer and Clarke decided they needed a sacrificial lamb and elected him to play the role.

It struck him that Inspector Clarke was either amazingly dull or was playing a game. He'd pushed Train to tell him where he kept his share of the money he collected from Brownsville merchants, and Train had refused to tell him. Hadn't Clarke checked with the Citizens' and Workers' Bank? Was that so obvious a place for Train to put the money that Clarke had dismissed it out of hand? Or had the point of his question been to make Train admit, in so many words, what he had done with the cash?

If Train pulled money out of the box and started spending it, Clarke could pounce. Getting caught with a pocket full of cash that he couldn't account for would put him right in Clarke's crosshairs. He'd turned in only marked bills. The ones in his box were clean, at least he was safe on that score. But even so, when a cop suddenly started flashing mazuma in front of his higher-ups it was as good as waving a red flag at a pissed-off bull.

But as long as the cash sat in the vault at the Kings County Citizens' and Workers', Train might be able to turn the tables and use it as evidence that he was working for McAteer. It wasn't much, but it was all he had. McAteer hadn't given him any paper to show what he was doing, and there had never been any witnesses to his conversations with McAteer or Clarke. Not as they concerned the investigation, anyway.

★   ★   ★

As soon as the docs removed the cast and cleared him to go back to active duty, he collared Garlington and demanded reinstatement. For once Garlington was cooperative. Who was doing the collection work while Train was out of action? Garlington had said not to worry about that. Maybe Garlington was collecting in person, Train thought. Or maybe Garlington was letting all the local merchants pile up past-due payments. He knew he'd find out as soon as he got back on the beat.

His arm felt tender and weak, but he was still happy to be rid of the cast. *This must be the way a chick feels, fresh out of the egg-shell*, he thought. And at least the injured arm was the left one. Train was a righty, and if he needed to draw his sidearm and use it, it was on the side of his uninjured arm.

The merchants on Junius Street didn't seem so happy. Everybody knew what had happened, and Train was not personally unpopular. But his return meant that they had to pony up for missed collections, and now it would be back to the regular system. There was an unpleasant part to it, though. He found himself spending eight hours a day with Officer Timothy Charters, late of Hattiesburg, Mississippi. Charters said he was glad to see Train back on the job. 'Walking the beat with Horowitz gave me the squirmies, Train. At least you're a white man. You know what they say about them, Train? Turn one inside out and — '

'Cut it,' Train said, 'I don't want to know. Change the record.'

Charters said, 'Okay, okay. I guess that accident really shook you up, didn't it?'

'I'm still me,' Train said.

He didn't know how much Charters had learned about the rake-offs going on in Brownsville. Brownsville and everywhere else in the city, in all likelihood. McAteer would surely know, and probably Clarke, but they had both cut him off. When he tried to phone McAteer, he got a polite receptionist who said there was no Mr. McAteer at that office, Mr. Smith was in charge of operations, and she would be happy to take a message for Mr. Smith and ask Mr. Smith to return his call at his earliest opportunity. Which was never. Nor was there any sign of the taxicab that had picked him up for meetings with McAteer.

He could have gone around McAteer

and called Inspector Clarke directly. Clarke had as much as invited him to do that. And with Clarke's help he might leapfrog over McAteer to — to whom? Who was McAteer's boss? Tom Dewey? J. Edgar Hoover? He considered trying that tack, but after the last exchange in Train's hospital room he couldn't bring himself to approach Clarke.

Train was sure he could find the building where McAteer had his office, the businesslike office with *Mr. Smith* neatly lettered on the door. He considered going there and confronting McAteer, but he wasn't ready to try that yet, either. Besides, he had a feeling that he'd be stonewalled if he tried it. He could just imagine himself going up against an attractive secretary who would inform him that her boss was in a meeting, or out of town, or had called in sick for the day. He'd sit in the outer office and wait for McAteer to leave, and then he'd collar him when he started for home. But knowing McAteer, there would be a second exit, and Train would be left cooling his heels until the secretary politely informed him that there was nobody left in the office and she had to shoo him out and lock up for the night.

That whole sequence of ideas led nowhere.

9

Half-Defiant, Half-Terrified

Outside Mendelssohn's pharmacy, Charters took a copy of the New York *Journal-American* from a newsboy. He didn't bother to pay for it. Train reached into his pocket for a nickel. He tossed it to the kid and told him to keep the change. 'Charters, what's so interesting in the newspaper?'

'Look at this.' Charters folded the paper and pointed to a photo on the front page. It showed a sea of white-hooded figures, their leader standing with his arms outstretched. A tall cross rose behind the leader, enveloped in flames.

Train nodded and grunted.

'You know what that is, Nicky? It's a Klan meeting. Don't know how they got the photo. Meetings are supposed to be secret. Don't know how the sheriff let a photographer in there, unless he didn't have any deputies available, 'cause they were all wearing their regalia and carrying torches.'

'You like the Klan, Charters?'

'Like it? Why, I really couldn't say. I wouldn't know much about it, myself.' He gave Train a grin and a wink.

'That wouldn't be why you left Hattiesburg, would it?'

'Would what?'

'The Klan lynches people, doesn't it? Hardly anybody ever gets arrested, and when they do they're always acquitted, isn't that true?'

'You're saying it, brother, not me.'

'You wouldn't have been involved in something like that, would you? And even if you got away with it, somebody told you it would be a good idea to leave town, put a lot of miles between you and Mississippi? Is that why you moved to Brooklyn?'

Charters folded the newspaper and stuffed it into his overcoat pocket. 'Say, I'm afraid there's a disturbance over there at Walker's Bar and Grille, Officer Train. Don't you think we'd better go make sure that the peace isn't being disturbed?'

At the end of the shift Train told Charters to report in at the station house; he had to make a brief stop. He'd made the week's collections, a triple pick-up because of his weeks of desk duty. The local merchants were unhappy about that. They'd made their peace with the system as it existed — the bite on each establishment was small enough to cause only an acceptable amount of pain — but it was more noticeable when they were relieved of the payoffs for a while and then had to catch up.

Now Train pushed open the door of the Imperial Palace, taking in the appetizing odors of Chinese food, garlic and peppers and soy sauce, pork and chicken and fish. He nodded to Susan Chen and made his way with her to the back room. She left him there. He checked the walls again to make sure there were no holes in them. He was seeing ghosts in the dark and assassins under his bed, he knew, but he didn't want to wind up like Winger. Or Lefcourt. Or his old pal Benny Jensen.

Who had sent Lefcourt after him? The

two patrolmen knew each other around the station house; everybody in the precinct knew everybody else, at least casually. They'd never had anything to do with each other except in the line of duty, however, and even that had been minimal. Train couldn't believe that Lefcourt had tried to run him down for personal reasons. No, it had to be connected with the rake-offs and McAteer's investigation.

Dermott Winger dead, Benny Jensen dead, Jacob Lefcourt dead. That patrolman in the Bronx — what was his name? Martin? No, Morris Hurley. Dead. Four cops dead. Hurley's death might or might not have been connected with the others, but Train doubted that it was a coincidence.

As he pushed his way through the bead curtain at the Imperial Palace, he stopped in his tracks. A thought had just occurred to him. He got an image of the would-be street-walker he'd sent home to the Bronx. What was her name? He remembered her initials, A.A.A. Agnes something. Yes, Agnes Anne Amato. What the hell was a junior hooker from the Bronx doing in Brownsville? She'd told a story about not wanting to shame her parents. Possible, possible . . . but the more you thought about it, the more far-fetched it became.

Train sends Agnes Amato back to the Bronx under the protection of Lawrence Chen, and the next thing you know Officer Morris Hurley has a dizzy spell as he stands on the IND subway platform and falls into the path of an oncoming train. Amato and Hurley couldn't possibly have been connected — or could they? Come to think of it, was the little hooker's name really Agnes Anne Amato? Train hadn't seen any ID and there wasn't even an entry in the precinct daybook. As far as records were concerned, the incident had never occurred; Agnes Anne Amato had never existed. Train made a mental note to look into the connection, if any, starting with the Amatos in the Bronx phone book. Or — better yet — put a call through to some precinct stations in the Bronx.

For now, he divided the collection

money in half, marked one half with the solution of vitamin B12, and waved the bills in the air until they were dry. There was no visible trace of the marking. He put the marked bills in one envelope, the unmarked bills in another. He left the envelope of unmarked bills in the desk. He could pick them up the next day and deposit them at the Citizens' and Workers' Bank. He didn't want to carry them with him when he returned to the station house.

Garlington was waiting for him, and Train handed him the envelope with the marked bills. Garlington opened the envelope and counted the money, grinning. 'Nice work, Train. By the way, don't think I forgave you for that cheap shot you took at me; I ain't. You'll pay for that someday, you will. But you're doing good work. This is very nice work.' He fanned the bills in the air, then returned them to the envelope and slipped the envelope into his own pocket.

'I hope you're not going to keep all that for yourself, Garling.' Train managed a grin.

'*Sergeant* Garlington, Officer Train. And don't start playing dumb all of a sudden; you know damned well how the system works. If you don't like it, get the hell off this man's police force. And it wouldn't be a bad idea to get the hell out of this town altogether.'

Train started to turn away but Garlington wasn't quite finished.

'Don't go sticking your nose in where it don't belong, Train. You already got it busted once, didn't you? Some guys just don't learn, you know that?'

★   ★   ★

Sunday dinner, a longtime family tradition. Train remembered the days when the old man would spend Sunday morning with his feet on a hassock, the radio playing and the newspaper on his lap. He'd always turn to the funnies and read them with the kids while the old lady worked in the kitchen, preparing ingredients for the big afternoon meal.

Most weeks it was roast chicken with noodles and peas; sometimes it was brisket with potatoes and carrots. There was a turkey at Thanksgiving, and maybe once or twice a year a gigantic rib roast of beef or leg of lamb. Sometimes the old man drank a bottle of beer with his meal. Once in a while they shared a bottle of wine. As the kids grew older the Sunday meals became less regular. Once Marie was married and out of the apartment, they became rarities. When the old man got sick and had to stop work, the old lady's energies went into caring for him, and family dinners became haphazard affairs at best. Train could see the old lady slowly wearing down as she helped her husband through his last months.

But now with the old man gone, the old lady was visibly regaining lost weight and energy. When Train came home from work, she announced that she was planning dinner for Sunday. Marie and Jocko were coming over, and she wanted Train to invite his girlfriend to join them.

Next day he planned to have lunch at the Imperial Palace. He left Charters at their table and managed to draw Susan Chen aside for a private conversation. He told her about his mother's plan and asked if she'd join the family for the meal. He was amazed when she accepted without consulting her parents. Even her brother Lawrence seemed to be softening toward Train in these days.

Once they left the restaurant Charters said, 'That Chinese food is good, you know? They're okay, though I wouldn't want my sister to marry one — but they can really cook.' He laughed.

Junius Street was peaceful today and spring was in the air. They were half a block from St. Columba's when they spotted a man running from the church. Train didn't have a chance to answer Charters. Pedestrians were screaming. Train got a better look at the man. There was blood on his face and hands and he was waving a carving knife around his head.

Train and Charters sprinted toward him. Pedestrians scattered left and right, but one woman didn't get out of the way quickly enough and the man grabbed her hair in a bloody fist and held the knife to her chest, his arm over her shoulder. The woman screamed once and the man gave her head a violent shake. He shouted at her. She stopped screaming and began to sob, her breath coming in gasps between gusts of sobbing.

By now Train and Charters were ten yards from the couple. Train hoped that Charters would remember his training. They moved apart, Charters to the left and Train to the right. Train sent a glance to Charters and drew his service revolver. Charters mirrored his action.

'Come on, now, let the lady go.'

The man with the knife was wild-eyed, emitting incoherent roars. Train didn't want to panic him any more than he already was, or he would surely use that knife on the woman. 'She's another one. They're all the same. Look at her!' The man with the knife shook the helpless woman the way a terrier shakes a rat. At this rate he could break her neck.

'Just let her go, fellow. Let's talk about this.'

'Talk about it? You're nuts! There's nothing to talk about.'

Train said, 'We can help you. Just tell

us what you want.'

'Look, they all do it. They're all no good. I'm gonna kill her and then I'm gonna kill myself.'

'No, no.' Train was trying to calm the man down. Was his revolver adding to the man's stress? Would it be better to put the revolver away? Would the man be more likely to surrender his own weapon or less so, more likely to stab the woman or to release her?

'I'll tell you what.' That seemed to get the man's attention, at least. 'I'll tell you what, just put the knife on the ground and we can talk. How about that? Does that sound good to you? Tell me your name. Mine is Nicholas. Nicholas. Like the saint, eh? Like Santa Claus? You can call me Nick. Is that okay? What's your name?'

The man's face changed. He seemed to be coming back into focus.

'Nick? Santa Claus? What?'

'You know, Jolly Old St. Nick?'

The man blinked a couple of times. Tim Charters had circled around to his other side. The man said, 'St. Nick? St.

Nicholas? Oh, I get it.' He grinned and lowered his knife a few inches. The woman's life still hung in the balance, but Train felt that he was getting somewhere with the man.

Charters's round was perfectly aimed. It blasted into the man's head just above his ear. The man's head exploded like a jack-o'-lantern dropped from an apartment roof when it hits the sidewalk. Red splattered onto the woman, onto the sidewalk. The man's knife hand shot up and the knife flew over the heads of the onlookers. It landed in the middle of Junius Street. The man's other hand, the one clutching the woman's hair, jerked away from his body, the fingers opening, hurling the woman onto a couple of teenaged girls. The girls screamed. The woman bounced off them and landed on the sidewalk in a sitting posture. She put her hands to her face and started to moan, softly at first, then louder, until she was giving out a horrifying wail. One of the teenaged girls dropped to her knees and put her arms around the woman, cradling her head to her shoulder. The woman stopped wailing and reverted to sobbing.

Train stepped over the man who had wielded the knife. There was no question that he was dead. Train looked at Charters. Charters was grinning happily. Train wanted to say something to him, wanted to thump him on the side of the head with his own heavy revolver. He realized that he was still holding the weapon. He slipped it back into its holster and knelt beside the dead man. He looked around. The nearest call box was forty or fifty yards down Junius Street. He yelled at Charters to call the station house and get a squad car and some officers. They'd need an ambulance for the woman. They would need a meat wagon too, he realized, but that could wait.

It was strange that nobody had followed the knife-man from the church. Train felt as if he needed to be three or four individuals at once: one to stay with the knife-man, one to tend to the woman, one to head for St. Columba's and see what was going on there, whether there were any other victims.

Charters came pounding back from the call box. 'Talked to Sergeant Garlington. He's sending a squad car, couple officers, ambulance.'

Train left Charters in charge of the crime scene and quick-timed it to St. Columba's. The illumination inside the church was dim, softened and tinted by stained glass windows. It took his eyes a little time to grow accustomed to the low light. There was a smell of incense in the air, and of something else. Then he spotted a misshapen mound lying in front of the altar.

He ran up the aisle and halted when he realized what he'd seen. There were two bodies lying on the floor. He couldn't see any movement, but there was sound coming from one of the bodies. He dropped to one knee. He could see a woman lying face-up, with a man spread-eagled face-down across her. There were bloodstains on the back of the man's coat, dark blood still seeping slowly from several apparent knife wounds, as if the man had thrown himself across the woman's body to

269

protect her from the knife-wielder.

Train grasped the man's shoulder and rolled him off the woman. There was a gash in the woman's throat and another in her chest. Blood had gouted from her wounds, but he could see no further blood flow. Hoping against hope to find signs of life, Train managed to turn the man onto his back. His face and chest were covered with blood. The man moaned and stirred feebly. Damn, he was alive after all!

Train turned his attention back to the woman. She lay still and silent. Train pressed his fingers to her throat, searching for a pulse, but found none. He turned back to the man. The man's eyes were slitted, two miniature stained-glass images of Jesus carrying a lamb on his shoulders reflected from them. The man wore a black priest's shirt and dog collar. A large crucifix hung from a chain. It lay on his chest, reddened. Train said, 'Father Dempsey?'

The priest moaned again, a little more loudly, but there were no words.

'Just hang on, Father, help is coming.'

He ran to the front steps of the church. The squad car had arrived from the station house, although the ambulance was nowhere in sight. Officers from the precinct were milling around, talking with civilians and jotting notes. Train dropped to one knee and rattled his billy club on the slate walkway that led from the sidewalk to the door of St. Columba's. That produced the desired reaction among the newly arrived officers. Two of them broke away from the crowd and responded to Train's urgent signal, running toward the church.

The officers followed Train back up the aisle. Train recognized them both: a pale Scandinavian named Stig Torkelson and a sallow-skinned Armenian named Kaloosh Yerounian. Pending the arrival of any higher-up, Train was in charge of the scene. That was the lucky break of the first officer present. He sent Torkelson to search the building and Yerounian to the rectory behind the church. Train stayed with the priest, trying to remember his first-aid training, trying to think of something to do for murderous stab wounds. He feared that they had punctured the man's lungs or heart. Could the priest live more than a few minutes with a knife-wound to his heart?

Torkelson pounded back and reported that he'd found nothing. Yerounian returned after five or ten minutes — Train's time sense was running in alternate sprints and sudden stops — with two terrified kids. One was struggling to escape but Yerounian had him by the scruff of the neck, and the more the kid fought him the tighter Yerounian held on. The other was bawling his eyes out. The first kid was wearing a sweatshirt, rough trousers, and sneakers. The second wore a stained shirt that might once have been white, and a pair of corduroy knickers.

Father Dempsey opened his eyes. 'Billy, Frederick.'

Yerounian released the two kids and they ran to the priest. They both fell to the floor next to him. That only lasted a second. The tough kid, Billy, jerked as if somebody had stuck him with a branding iron. He stumbled over the priest and threw himself on the dead woman, shaking her by the shoulders, apparently trying to get her to respond.

Train tried to pull the kid off the woman but he didn't want to let go and Train had to pry his fingers loose. He was finally able to drag the kid away from the woman. 'Who is she, son?'

'She's my mom.' Now Billy, too, started bawling.

The priest was moving one hand feebly and trying to say something. Train released the kid and bent over him. The priest pointed at the two kids, or tried to. He managed a few words. All Train could get from him was, 'Sorry. So sorry. Not their fault.' He managed to turn his head toward the boys. He emitted another low moan, actually more of a sigh. Jesus and the lamb disappeared from his eyes.

Billy was trying to get back to his mother but Yerounian was holding him back. The other kid, Frederick, was tugging at Yerounian's sleeve, tears rolling down his cheeks as he pled with the cop. 'Don't tell him, don't tell my pop. He'll kill me if he finds out. I couldn't help it and he'll kill me.'

Without being told, Torkelson was trying to secure the scene and at the same time to search for a weapon. Train told him, 'I don't think there's a weapon here, Torkelson. Did you see the perpetrator outside? Charters is there. I'm pretty sure he's dead. The perp. Charters should have recovered the weapon, anyhow.'

Sergeant Garlington came clumping into the church. A couple more officers trailed in his wake. He stopped and surveyed the scene. 'Jesus, Train, what the hell are you, some kind of Typhoid Mary? How many killings under your nose? How long you been on the beat, and how many killings under your nose?'

Train didn't have to answer.

Garlington said, 'That poor lush in Walker's, then your partner Winger, now these.' He leaned over the corpses. 'Jesus. Jesus, Joseph, and Mary! Who killed the priest? It's Pat Dempsey. Jesus. We play poker and drink whiskey together every week. Jesus. And who's the twist?' He bent over the dead woman. 'Who's the twist?' he asked again. Train saw him reach down and take a handful of the woman's hair. It was astonishing; there was such obvious tenderness in the gesture.

'Kerry,' Garlington said. 'Kerry Casey. Jesus Christ almighty, what in hell was Kerry Casey doing in the church with Pat Dempsey? And now they're dead. Who done it? That must be him outside. Jesus. I'll bet it's Casey himself. Joe Casey. Oh, Jesus God, what's this about?' He raised his face and Train was again amazed to see actual tears falling from Garlington's eyes.

Seemingly for the first time, Garlington paid attention to the two boys. 'What are you kids doing here? Don't you know this is a church?' Then, as if he finally noticed that they were crying and distraught, he asked, 'What's the matter?' He shook his head. 'Train, what the hell is going on? What are these kids doing here?'

'Yerounian brought 'em in. He found them in the rectory.'

'They were drinking wine.' Yerounian was an older cop, whatever color had once been in his hair and face now faded to a neutral gray-brown. He had many more years on the force than Train, Train knew that, but he was shying away from the dead woman and the dead or dying priest. 'Sitting in the rectory drinking wine and smoking cigarettes, Sergeant.'

Garlington knelt beside the priest again, bending over his face. He felt for a pulse in his neck. He peered into the priest's slitted eyes, muttered something, and pushed himself to his feet, struggling for breath. He pointed a trembling finger at one of the cops who had followed him into the church. 'Get out of here. Where in hell is that ambulance, didn't anybody call for an ambulance? Get an ambulance and get it here fast. Father Dempsey's still alive. We gotta get him to the hospital; maybe they can save him.' The cop sprinted out of the church.

Garlington grabbed the two boys by their collars. Billy Casey was still leaning over the dead woman and Garlington lifted him bodily and set him on his feet. The other kid, Frederick, was pleading with Yerounian. Garlington tugged violently on the back of Frederick's shirt and peeled him away from Yerounian. The man was overweight and out of condition, but he was still strong. Train had gone up against that type a couple of times in the ring. He knew that they lacked stamina but they could be tough customers if they got to you in the early rounds.

It was strange, too, that some kind of bond had formed between Garlington and Train. Maybe it was the fact that Train had stood up to Garlington when the sergeant seemed able to bully everybody else he came in contact with. Maybe it was even the one-punch decision that Train had scored over Garlington in the precinct locker room. You couldn't call it friendship, not by any stretch, but there was a kind of respect there, and a grudging trust.

A wailing siren announced the approach of the ambulance. White-coated men bustled into the church carrying the familiar rolled-up stretcher. Train was getting used to the sight and he didn't like it. The ambulance attendants dropped to their knees beside the now-silent priest. They started undoing the buckles that held the canvas stretcher closed. As they worked, one of them bent over the priest, studying his face. He repeated Garlington's move, feeling for a pulse. Then he turned to look up at Garlington.

'This guy looks pretty bad, Sergeant.'

'Shut up.'

'I don't know if he's a customer for us. He should be headed for the morgue, not the hospital.'

'He's alive. I checked him. He's in bad shape but you're no doc and neither am I. Don't play big shot, you're just an ambulance driver. Give the poor guy a chance.'

'Okay, okay.' They lifted Dempsey onto the stretcher. A couple of minutes later the ambulance pulled away from the curb, its siren wailing again.

Yerounian said, 'What do you want to do with these kids, Sergeant Garlington?'

Garlington shook his head. 'What was going on, boys? You was just goofing off in the rectory, right? Smoking cigarettes and drinking wine? You come here all the time?'

The kids hung their heads. Neither of them had anything to say. They were both sniveling copiously by now.

'Billy, what was going on? Look, kid, this is bad stuff, this is very bad stuff; we're not talking about stealing Hershey bars from candy stores. Two people, probably three people are dead.'

Billy Casey didn't answer. He just hung from Garlington's beefy fist like a sack of flour.

'What about you, kid?' Garlington shifted his attention to the other boy. 'Frederick, what's your last name, kid? I thought I knew everybody in this precinct. 'What's your name?'

'Korb.'

'Frederick Korb. What's your old man do? Where do you live?'

'Right around the corner. I know Billy from school. My old man is a printer. He works in Garden City.'

'You just move to Brownsville?'

'Nah. I lived here all my life.'

'What's going on?'

'Nothin.' Waddaya mean?'

'Don't gimme a hard time, Frederick. You better level with me, kid. You and your little pal here are in trouble. You could wind up in reform school.'

'I got friends there, it's okay.'

Garlington let go of Billy Casey and smacked Frederick Korb with his open hand. The kid swung back and caught Garlington a right on the beezer. Train had a hard time not laughing. Garlington's expression wasn't one of pain. The kid's punch looked sharp but it couldn't have done more damage than a light jab. Train had thrown hundreds of those and caught more than he ever landed. They could sting but it would take a lot of them to do serious harm. No, Garlington's expression was one of shocked disbelief. He'd punched plenty of citizens, but they'd known enough not to hit back; that just invited more abuse. But this kid — Train covered his mouth with his hand to hide his grin.

Garlington's nose began to gush crimson. Using his free hand he produced a huge bandana and used it to stanch the flow of blood. Frederick Korb made a break for the street, but Stig Torkelson brought him down with a tackle half way to the church's door. He dragged the kid back.

Train said, 'Sergeant, this other kid, Billy.'

Talking through his bandana, Garlington said, 'Yeah?'

Train leaned in and spoke quietly. He hoped the kid wouldn't hear what he said. 'Sergeant, look, the kid's father killed his mother and stabbed Father Dempsey, and Officer Charters' — he used his partner's title — 'Officer Charters was forced to fire at Mr. Casey to save an innocent hostage. What's going to happen to this boy?'

Garlington muttered something incoherent. Train didn't ask him to repeat it. Garlington resumed, 'I better call for a matron. They'll have to put the kid up in an orphanage or something. Jesus, who'd ever of thought something like this could happen? What's this town coming to?' He shook his head. 'Okay, let's get these two kids back to the station house.'

He glared at Frederick Korb. 'You know what you get for assaulting a police officer and attempting to flee the scene of a crime?'

The kid looked half-defiant, half-terrified. He didn't say anything. He just shook his head.

'You want to go home?' Garlington asked.

The kid nodded.

'I want to hear it.'

'Yeah.'

'Try yes.'

'Yeah. Yes.'

'Yes, sir.'

'Yes, sir.'

The kid started bawling again.

'Go on,' Garlington told him. 'Torkelson, take the kid home. Turn him over to his father if he's there, or to his mother. Make sure an adult gets him.'

'They'll kill me, Sergeant.'

'No they won't.'

'You don't know my people.'

'Take him home, Torkelson.'

10

The Smile of the Wolf

Once Torkelson and young Frederick Korb were gone, Garlington said, 'The evidence guys will have to work this place over, and we'll need the meat wagon for Casey and his missus. Yerounian, you and Charters will be in charge of the crime scene. No, wait a minute.' He stopped himself. 'That won't work. Charters did the shooting. He'll have to come back to the station house. Okay, you.' He pointed at one of the other cops who'd arrived with him. 'You and Yerounian here, you're in charge of the crime scene. You stay here until the corpses are gone and the evidence bozos have done their work.' He was still holding onto Billy Casey. With his free hand he clapped Train on the shoulder. 'Soon as we get back to the station house we'll need a full report from you and a shooting statement from your partner out there.'

★   ★   ★

When Train got home there was an *Out of Service* sign on the elevator; the walk up to the apartment felt like crawling up a mountain. The climb left him feeling exhausted and depressed. He met his sister and brother-in-law coming out the front door. They went back in with him. The old lady was still standing in the doorway. He could see the lighted dial on the living room radio behind her and hear a voice murmuring from the speaker, but he couldn't make out what it was saying.

Jocko Sullivan shook his head at Train, an expression of mixed pity and contempt on his face. Train felt like taking a poke at him, but instead he stood there with his hands at his sides. After a minute he turned away from his brother-in-law and put his arms around his mother and said, 'I'm sorry, Ma. We had an awful mess today. Awful. I just got off work.'

Jocko said, 'We heard, Nick. Awful ain't the word for it.'

Marie said, 'What happened, Nick? They was talking about it on the radio, but they sounded pretty confused.'

The three of them stepped into the living room. Jocko closed the door to the stairwell. The dinner table had been cleared. The old lady disappeared briefly, then brought in a tray with a pot of coffee and four cups and half a sponge cake. They sat around, Marie and Jocko and the old lady waiting for Train to furnish information. Train held his coffee cup in both hands. He felt chilled and the warm cup was a big help. He looked at the others.

'You know Joe Casey?'

Marie said she did.

'He came out of St. Columba's waving a bloody knife. He grabbed a woman in the street. He said he was gonna kill her and himself. It was like a movie. My partner shot him.'

'But why?' The old lady had been crying, that was obvious. 'Why would he shoot Mr. Casey? What was he doing waving a knife?'

'That's where it gets worse.' Train was wearing a heavy jacket, a sweater, and a flannel shirt. He was starting to warm up. The jacket had a zipper front. He opened it and let some house air inside. 'That's where it gets worse,' he repeated. 'I think Charters — my partner, Tim Charters — I think he didn't need to shoot. Maybe we could have got Casey to put down the knife. I don't know, maybe he was right. Charters. Maybe Casey was dangerous. No, not maybe, he was dangerous. There was blood on the knife. But I still think we might have got him to surrender. Charters and me. I was talking to him; I think he was listening. I might have got him to put it down. I don't know. I never saw anything like that before. Charters used to be a cop in Mississippi; maybe he dealt with something like that before. I don't know.'

Jocko said, 'Slow down, Nicky. You're running off at the mouth.'

'Yeah. I feel like I'm on a coffee jag, only no coffee. I guess I need some of that.' Train took a sip of steaming coffee, then lowered his cup. 'You got any food,

Ma? I haven't had anything since lunch. I didn't realize I was hungry. You guys all had dinner, right? I'm sorry I missed dinner. Anything left? I'll take a sandwich, whatever we have.'

The old lady got up and disappeared into the kitchen. Train said, 'Let me get it, Ma.'

She stuck her head around the corner. 'No, Nick. I'll get it. You go ahead. Talk loud. I can hear.' Jocko got up and turned off the radio.

'He was coming out of St. Columba's,' Train repeated. 'I ran in and I found Father Dempsey and Mrs. Casey, Kerry Casey. She was lying on the floor; he was on top of her. I think he tried to protect her. Tried to shield her from Joe. He stabbed them both. Joe Casey. Mrs. Casey was dead. Father Dempsey, I don't know, they took him to the hospital. I don't know if he's alive. He looked in bad shape. Joe Casey stabbed his wife in the chest and the belly and Father Dempsey in the back.'

Marie looked horrified. 'What are you saying, Nick?'

'What do you mean?'

'Was Mrs. Casey involved — you know, involved — with Father Dempsey?' She blushed.

'I don't know.'

'Sure sounds like it to me.' Jocko was rotating his right fist in the palm of his left hand as if he wanted to hit somebody.

'Is that all?' The old lady had returned from the kitchen. She carried a plate with a sandwich on it. She put it in front of Train. 'The radio was mixed up. I mean, I was mixed up when I heard the radio. Was that all? I mean, that's enough, that's bad enough, isn't it? But was there anything else, Nick? Eat your sandwich. It's good pot roast. Good pot roast on that nice homemade rye bread you always liked, remember? You always liked that rye bread. You used to call it whiskey bread because you heard of rye whiskey and you thought the bread was made out of whiskey.'

'I remember, Ma.' He took a bite. It really was good. The old lady must have made the pot roast for dinner. He wished he'd been there to share the meal with his mother and his sister. He could tolerate Jocko if he had to, and Marie had always been there. She was older than Nick and she'd always been there. He chewed and swallowed and washed the sandwich down with hot coffee.

Jocko said, 'Yeah, what else? That radio guy was stammering and double-talking. Bad enough that this Casey killed his wife and the priest. Was there more?'

Train took a deep breath. 'When Casey came out of the church waving his knife he grabbed another woman and looked like he was going to kill her too. At least she escaped. But there were a couple of kids in the rectory.'

'So what?'

'Yerounian — you wouldn't know him; a good cop, not really very bright but a good cop — he went out and checked the rectory and he found these two kids there smoking cigarettes and drinking wine.'

Jocko laughed. 'Ain't that something! Cigarettes and wine. How old were the kids?'

'I'm not sure. I think about ten or twelve. Maybe a couple years younger.'

'Twelve-year-old kids drinking wine and smoking cigarettes. Come on, Nicky boy, don't tell me you never tried that when you was that age.'

'One of 'em was Billy Casey.'

Marie said, 'Oh, my God.'

It took Jocko a little longer to put that together. 'His mother. His mother and the priest. And his father killed them, killed Mrs. Casey and the priest. And your partner, Choppers, what's his name?'

'Charters,' Train muttered.

'Charters killed the father. Killed Joe Casey.'

'That's what it looks like. I shouldn't have said all of this. I'm screwing up. I'm supposed to leave this at work, leave it all to go through channels. I shouldn't have said anything.'

The old lady said, 'Where is the child now?'

'I don't know. I think they sent him to the hospital to be checked. I don't think there's anything wrong with him, but I think they want him to be checked.'

'And then? I know the Caseys. They

live near the church.'

Jocko said, 'That figures.'

'And what will they do with Billy?' the old lady asked.

'I don't know, Ma. I guess . . . I don't know. I think they have a policy. There are police matrons to take care of kids. Then they'll probably send him to some kind of boys' home until they can sort things out. An orphanage. I don't know. Does he have any other relatives? Would you know, Ma? Do the Caseys have anybody else who could take him?'

'I don't think so. It was just Mrs. Casey and her husband and Billy.'

Marie asked, 'Who was the other child?'

'Frederick Korb. Another neighborhood kid. Sergeant Garlington sent him home with a police escort.' Train managed a feeble grin.

'It's lousy.' Jocko Sullivan pulled a dark green pack of Luckys out of his shirt pocket, shook one out of the pack, and lit up. 'You can't like it, Nicky. Be honest. Why don't you get the hell out of that bag and get an honest job?'

'Thanks, Jocko. I'll stay on the force.'

'Okay, brother. It's your funeral.'

Jocko stuck his cigarette in the corner of his mouth and stood up. 'Come on, Marie, I have to get up early. I got an honest job.'

After they had left, the old lady sat at the dining room table with Train and cried a little. 'You weren't here for the news, Nicholas. I don't know why they didn't tell you. They told me all about it but you weren't here.'

'What news, Ma?'

'Your sister is going to have a baby.'

'That's great, Ma. Yeah, I would have liked to hear that from her. I guess she didn't want to talk about it in front of Jocko.'

The old lady didn't say anything.

Train added, 'I don't think Jocko likes me much, anyhow.'

'I don't know, Nicholas. Anyway, I hope you'll like being an uncle.'

Train didn't say anything.

The old lady stood up and started to clear away the dishes and coffee cups. She halted in the doorway and turned back to face Train. 'We need to talk, Nicholas.'

He rubbed his temples with his fingertips. 'Sure, Ma. Let me help you.' When the work was done they sat in the living room.

The old lady said, 'Now that your father is gone . . . ' She stopped talking and held up her hands, studying her fingertips as if the words were written there. 'Everything.' She stopped, then tried again. 'It was very hard, Nicholas.'

'I know, Ma. You were terrific. You did everything you could. You were a real trouper, Ma.'

She nodded. 'Now we have to go on living, Nicholas. Marie and Jocko are having a baby. And you.'

'What about me, Ma?'

'You were going to introduce me to your girlfriend.'

'Yeah.'

'Maybe I know her already, Nicholas. I've lived in this neighborhood for forty years. More.' She counted on her fingers, adding up numbers. 'I was born right here in Brooklyn. Your father and I moved into this apartment when we were married. We lived here all our lives. I know this neighborhood. I know everybody.'

'Maybe.'

'Please invite her for dinner. I want to meet her.'

'Okay, Ma.' He pushed himself to his feet. 'I'm worn out, Ma. This killing, this was too much for me. We're supposed to be professional, you know. Detached. That's what they teach at the academy. But you didn't see what I saw today. You wouldn't want to. I wouldn't want you to.'

'You need to rest.'

'Yeah.' He leaned over and kissed her on the top of her head. He made his way to his room and crawled into bed, feeling like a little boy.

The next day he was due to collect bribes from the merchants on his beat. Word was out that Charters was suspended pending investigation of the shooting. Everybody knew it was routine; nobody was going to say anything against him. Train didn't think he would have been so quick to shoot Joe Casey, but it was a judgment call. Maybe Charters was right. Maybe Casey would have killed the woman he was holding or maybe gone nuts and attacked some bystander because he didn't look at him right or because he was wearing the wrong kind of hat or because she looked like Casey's wife and Casey thought she was a ghost coming to get revenge.

So Charters shot Joe Casey and that was that.

That would be the end of that.

★　★　★

Susan Chen accompanied Train when he headed for the back room at the Imperial Palace to mark the dirty money he'd collected. He ground the vitamin pills to a fine powder and mixed them with water to make the marking compound. He marked half the bills, as he did each week.

When Susan Chen asked him about the shooting and stabbings at St. Columba's, he didn't have much to tell her. The facts were straightforward and ugly. Their meaning was uglier. He changed the subject. 'Ma wants you to come to dinner.

Saturday. Okay?'

'I can do that.'

'Okay. I'll come by for you. You'll be upstairs?'

She said she'd be upstairs.

He put the marked bills in one envelope and the unmarked bills in another, as he did each week. He walked to the Citizens' and Workers' Bank and stowed the unmarked bills in his safety deposit box. It would have been nice to add them to his feeble savings account, but there was too much danger in that. He didn't want McAteer or Clarke to find out where he was keeping his half of the graft.

When he got back to the precinct, Sergeant Garlington was waiting for him. 'Come on.' He turned and led Train to their usual rendezvous. They sat facing each other across a battered wooden desk in the interrogation room. Train pulled the envelope from his pocket. Garlington took the envelope and shook the money out, fanning the bills onto the scratched wooden surface. He stood up and moved two switches simultaneously, one a bead chain hanging from the ceiling and the other a little toggle switch on a lamp on the desk. The green-shaded light bulb hanging from the ceiling went dark. The dark blue, almost black bulb in the desk lamp glowed. The letters B12 flared a bright yellow on the bribe money.

Train sat there, stunned. He was still wearing his uniform, cap on head, service revolver on hip. For one fleeting moment he almost reached for the revolver, then he realized that drawing his weapon would be the worst thing he could possibly do.

Garlington's expression could be described as a smile, if it were possible to smile without including one iota of good will. This was the smile of the wolf when it realizes that its prey is hopelessly trapped. 'You want to tell me about this, Train?' With one stubby fingertip he tapped the bills. The markings couldn't have flared more brightly, but to Train it seemed that they did.

Train didn't say a word.

'You're a clever kid,' Garlington said. 'I thought you were just a crooked cop. At first, that's what I thought. Then I found out you were working for McAteer.' He shook his head, heavy forehead and bushy eyebrows shading his eyes.

Train's own eyes had grown accustomed to the dim blue-black light. What had McAteer called it? Ultraviolet. He tried to concentrate but his mind was too confused by the shock. He could hardly think. It was bad enough when he was working for McAteer and Clarke, but then Clarke had cut him adrift, fired him from the investigation. He had his personal treasury in his box at the Citizens' and Workers'. He was still working the grift with Garlington, the racket that he'd inherited from Dermott Winger, trying to get the goods on Sergeant Garlington and Garlington's contacts — and now the sergeant had got the goods on him.

'I don't know what you're talking about, Garlington. I collect the way I'm supposed to and I turn in half of what I collect. Every cent of it.' Right, he told himself, there's honour among thieves. 'Why are the bills glowing like that? Is this some kind of Houdini trick, or what?'

Garlington raised his hand as if he were going to backhand Train. Train brought up his forearm. His ring instincts were still with him. Garlington's eyes opened wide. Clearly, he'd thought he was going to get in a quick shot — one not designed to do serious damage to the other man, but one that would set his ears ringing and humiliate him. It hadn't worked.

'You didn't think of this yourself, Train. You're not smart enough; you haven't been around long enough. Who are you working for?'

'I'm a sworn officer of the Police Department of the City of New York, Sergeant. I'm working for the people of this city.'

'Who, Train?' Garlington was back to tapping on the bills with his forefinger.

Train realized that not drawing his revolver was probably the smartest thing he'd done in his life. If he'd drawn, there were any number of things that might have happened next, all of them bad.

Garlington said, 'I can sit here all night, Train, if I have to. I suppose you could, too. So let's save us both some time, okay? I want to go home and eat my dinner and maybe get laid if my old lady's in a good mood.'

'Your move, then, Garlington.' Train resisted the temptation to look at his watch. That would be a sign of weakness.

'Okay, kid.' Garlington straightened the glowing bills on the desktop, tapped their edges to line them up, and slipped them back into the envelope they'd come from. He thrust the envelope into his tunic and stood up. He turned the overhead light back on and the black light desk lamp off. 'Clarke is playing both sides of the game,' he said. 'I guess you're too dumb to realize that, Train.' He grinned again, this time with a little less of the wolf in his expression. 'Clarke is working for McAteer. And he's working for the mob.'

A low moan escaped Train's lips. He put his hands to his face.

Garlington said, 'Golly, kid, you do look surprised, you know?'

Train shook his head, waiting for Garlington to go on. Instead, Garlington plopped himself into the chair opposite

Train. After a while he said, 'You want to go downstairs and change, kid? Want to head over to Walker's for a snort?'

'No.'

'Well, kid, we can't leave it like this, can we?'

'Who are you working for, Garlington?'

'Me? Hey, Officer Train, I'm just like you. I'm a sworn officer of the law. I work for the city, same as you do.'

'Who's your boss?'

'Fella name of Oscar Daniel McAteer. I've known him since France. He was a light colonel over there. You never knew when you were going to see him. He was always around the next corner, behind the next door. We called him On Duty McAteer. O.D. McAteer, you get it, kid? O.D. McAteer. On Duty.'

'I get it.' He thought about that. 'What about Inspector Clarke? You said he was part of the mob.'

'Not part of it. Just too chummy with the big boys. When things get too hot they toss a few soldiers to Clarke, Clarke turns 'em over to McAteer, and everybody's happy.'

'Then what's this investigation about?'

'Look, kid, I may look like an overweight slob to you, but I'm not as dumb as I look. I know about you and Clarke and McAteer.'

'Do you know about Benny Jensen?'

'Sure.'

'Do you know who killed him?'

'A couple of mob soldiers. Thugs trying to make their bones.'

'And Hurley?'

'Who?'

'Morris Hurley. The cop who fell in front of a subway train up in the Bronx.'

'Oh, yeah. More of the same.' Garlington opened his mouth as if he were going to keep talking, but Train interrupted with another question.

'What about Agnes Amato?'

Garlington's eyes looked as if they were going to pop out of his head. 'Agnes who?'

'Agnes Anne Amato. Underage hooker from the Bronx. Or so she said.'

'Why are you talking about her?' For the first time, Garlington looked genuinely puzzled.

'I picked her up looking for johns on my beat. She was so pitiful, I bought her a meal, got a citizen — Larry Chen, from the Imperial Palace — to take her home. Didn't write it up. Then Hurley had his accident.'

'Oh, my God. What if my old lady found out about her? Oh, my God.'

Train said, 'Garlington, who's Agnes Amato? Was she involved in Hurley's death? Jesus, Garlington, what the hell is going on around here?'

Garlington opened a desk drawer and pulled out a bottle and two glasses. He filled both glasses and downed the contents of one.

Train waited.

Garlington said, 'No? Okay.' He emptied the second glass, put the bottle and empty glasses back in the drawer. 'Good Christ, Train, I needed that. Now let's go over to Walker's.'

★ ★ ★

They got a booth and bottle at Walker's, and Garlington mumbled a couple of sentences' worth of nonsense, then looked up and said, 'Look, how naïve are you, Train? Do you have any idea how big this thing is? How high it goes?'

Train shook his head. 'You tell me, Garlington. And while you're at it, tell me where you fit in.'

'You think I'm dirty, don't you, Train? You think I take half the grift that comes through this precinct? Wouldn't that be great! No, it goes up to Lieutenant Kessler. And from there it goes to Captain Kober. And from there — I don't know the path, kid, and if I did it would be dumb of me to talk about it. But believe me, it's big. There are millions in this.'

He rolled his lips over his teeth as if he were deciding what to say next. Train didn't wait.

'Why did Henry Little kill Dermott Winger?'

'Winger was skimming.'

'That's all?'

'What do you mean, that's all? That's everything. This system has to be watertight from top to bottom. It has to be. That's why I gave you such a hard time about splitting before you turn in your take instead of letting me work the split. Jesus, kid, you realize that you were risking your life when you did that? And I went to bat for you. I risked mine.'

'Of course. Because you like me.'

Garlington made a noise that sounded like a combination curse and Bronx cheer. 'Don't deceive yourself. Because you're working for McAteer and Clarke. If you weren't, if you were just a soldier, you'd be dead by now. You nearly were, anyhow. When Jake Lefcourt was trying to hit you and he kissed that lamppost instead, Train. You know that, don't you?'

Train knew it. He grunted. 'Who told Lefcourt to run me down? He didn't do it on his own, no way he'd do that, no reason for him to do it.'

'He was following orders, Train. You never been in the army, have you? You get orders, you follow them. You don't ask for reasons.'

Jesus, what a mess. Train sat there watching Garlington watching him watching Garlington watching ... *Can that!*

But why the hell had he ever joined the force? Mainly, he told himself, because it looked like steady work that would bring in a check every month. His old man was already sick when Train took the exam to get into the academy. He hadn't wanted to admit it to himself, but somewhere in his belly he already knew that the old man was dying.

And was there some crazy notion that he was doing a noble thing, putting on a uniform and picking up a gun and defending the decent citizens of the Borough of Brooklyn against crooks, like a doughboy marching off to war against the Hun? Maybe. Maybe. He really wasn't sure about that.

When he learned that Winger was on the take he hadn't really been shocked; he might have been innocent, but he wasn't totally naïve. But he hadn't expected to take over Winger's customers, and he'd been amazed when McAteer recruited him as a double agent. And when Garlington made his own revelations . . .

Train's head was spinning.

'Hey! Kid! Wake up, what are you

doing, passing out on me? You going into a trance?'

Shaking his head, Train said, 'What do you want me to do, Garlington? Whose side are you on?'

'Side? What the hell are you talking about, Train?'

'I think the question is clear enough.'

'No it ain't. Look, you're not a schoolboy no more. And this ain't no football game. There's no sides, see, no Dodgers and no Giants, no Columbia and no Fordham.'

Train rubbed his eyes, waiting for Garlington to go on.

Garlington said, 'I'm on my side, see? Me, my own side. I got a house and a family. I ain't no John D. Rockefeller and I got no yacht and no stable of racehorses; I don't drive a Packard. But I like my life and I want to keep living it. I don't want to wind up in the stone hotel with all of those saps what Dewey put there, and I really don't want to wind up with Winger and Jensen and Lefcourt and Hurley. Too many stiffs, kid, and I don't want to become another.'

Garlington stood up and circled the room. Train watched Garlington do his inspection of the saloon. He caught Dinny Moran's eye and exchanged nods. Garlington stopped at the mahogany and picked up another bottle. Then he came back to the booth.

'Nobody snooping on us, as far as I can tell.' He slumped onto the worn wooden seat, studied his wristwatch for a moment, and shook his head. 'I gotta get the hell out of here. You living with a broad or what, Train?'

'I live with my mother.'

'Oh, Christ. You ain't a pansy, are you?'

'No.'

'You ought to get laid, Train. You'd be happier.'

'I'm sure.'

'Okay, look, I want you to make like this never happened, okay, kid? Just stay on your beat, keep a lasso on Charters. Christ, I don't know why the department ever took that moron on. If he couldn't get along in a hick town like Hattiesburg, Mississippi, how the hell does he expect to make it in Brownsville?'

Train shrugged.

'Never mind, I wasn't really asking.' Garlington ran his square fingers through his graying hair. 'Here's what I want you to do. Just keep on doing your job. Walk your beat, hold your mommy's hand, for God's sake get yourself a girlfriend and get laid, or at least snag a free sample from one of Dinny's girls. And keep collecting from the customers and turning in the gelt. Keep marking it, too. Just keep going. I'll talk to you again soon and we'll figure out what comes next. Maybe we'll find a livelier place to hold our conference than this joint.'

Garlington stood up. He picked up the nearly full bottle and stuffed it into his pocket. He started to move away from the booth, but Train grabbed his wrist and pulled him back. Garlington looked at Train, surprised.

'What? What do you want now, Train?'

'You didn't answer my question.'

Garlington frowned. 'What question?'

'Who is Agnes Anne Amato?'

'Never mind, Train. I don't got to

answer your lousy questions. But I'm drunk. Okay? Can you see, I'm drunk? Or I wouldn't tell you if they beat me with a rubber hose. But I'm drunk, okay? She's my kid.'

11

She Wouldn't Discuss It

A rookie cop doesn't get to pick his shifts, but Train was lucky enough to get one day off each weekend. He worked Monday through Saturday with Sunday and Wednesday off. It wasn't the greatest schedule, but it could have been a lot worse. This Saturday he headed home from work and put on a suit and tie. This was going to be the big night. Marie and Jocko were coming for dinner, and Train was going to pick up Susan Chen at the apartment above the Imperial Palace. His mother had asked him his girlfriend's name and he'd told her it was Susan. He hadn't told the old lady that her last name was Chen.

He bypassed the restaurant and made his way upstairs. When he knocked at the apartment door, Susan's father, Chen Jing-kuo, answered. He knew Train from the Imperial Palace. He'd been paying off for a long time, long before Winger was shot and Nick Train took over his collecting job. Chen had always been quiet and diffident when Train came to collect, and relied on other members of his family to translate for him.

But now the relationship had changed. And suddenly, astonishingly, Chen Jing-kuo was perfectly fluent in English. 'My son, Chen Long, is running the restaurant right now. I'm not happy that Chen Shu is seeing a European, especially at night. Children nowadays have no respect for propriety. They are disobedient. No good will come of this, Officer Train, mark my words.' He paused and then demanded, 'How do you plan to treat my daughter?'

Train assured the old man that he would treat Susan with respect. He made no comment on Chen's sudden acquisition of perfect English. Maybe the old man had been going to night school.

'She must be home early,' Chen asserted.

'Yes, sir.'

The old man frowned but said nothing more.

Susan appeared wearing a blue beret, a navy-blue pleated skirt, and a blue and white striped jacket. She was just pulling on a long woolen coat with fox-fur trim on the collar and pockets. She clutched the coat over her chest with dark-coloured cloth gloves.

Train and Susan walked toward the Trains' apartment house. Winter was making a last effort to fight back the arrival of spring. A late snow was falling. Their breath made clouds in front of their faces in the cold air. The thoroughfare was lighted by orange streetlamps, red and green traffic lights, and store and restaurant windows, with glaring neon signs inviting passersby inside.

They paused beneath the marquee of the Junius Street Variety Theater. There were posters for the current feature, a John Ford Western, and for the big forthcoming attraction, *Gone with the Wind*. Train recognized the cashier. She was the same girl who worked at the candy counter: Millicent Sanders, now

Millicent Johnson. He wondered if this were a promotion. The girl recognized him as he passed with Susan and waved a greeting.

He looked down at Susan Chen. There was something different about her. He felt as if his lungs were expanding with each breath. He saw Susan raise her hands in front of her, and he reached and took them in his own. He realized with a shock that she was wearing vivid lipstick and eye makeup. He'd never seen her like this before. He couldn't think of anything to say. She smiled up at him and he inhaled her scent. It was dizzying. Train was wearing his best suit and a hand-painted tie. He'd polished his wingtips and he was wearing a fedora that had belonged to his father. Compared to Susan, he still felt shabby.

They walked on. When they reached the apartment, his sister and brother-in-law were already present. The place was warm, the living room radiator hissing as steam rose from the basement boiler. His mother came bustling from the kitchen. He introduced Susan to her and to Marie and Jocko. For the first time, Train decided that Marie was visibly pregnant.

Train's mother embraced Susan. Susan said, 'I was so sorry to hear about your husband.' Train's mother managed a wan smile. Marie shook Susan's hand. Jocko Sullivan stood watching.

The old lady went all out. She served leg of lamb with mint sauce and roasted baby potatoes and carrots. There was a green salad and fresh rolls. For dessert she'd baked a chocolate cake. The meal was great but the conversation was a disaster. Marie was full of talk of her coming baby, but Jocko couldn't get over the fact that Susan was Chinese. Train couldn't decide whether Jocko was being deliberately annoying or just stupid. When Jocko asked still again how she liked working in a Chinese restaurant, Susan looked at her wristwatch and announced that she had to get home.

Train got Susan's coat and hat for her. He didn't wait to reach the street to apologize. He started as soon as the apartment door closed behind them, as they stood, waiting for the ancient elevator to creak up from the lobby. He'd known that Jocko Sullivan was hostile to people unlike himself, but he hadn't expected anything like the steady stream of needling that his brother-in-law had administered.

Once inside the elevator, Susan Chen said, 'I shouldn't have gone to your house. I should have known better. Your mother was nice enough and I think your sister will be a good mother in her turn. But her husband made me sick.'

'I'm sorry. I should have called him on it the first time he said anything.'

The elevator swayed to a stop and the door rolled back.

Susan said, 'Maybe not. It was my mistake.'

'No, it wasn't. I should have socked him one. Don't quit me because of that moron, Susan, please.'

Patches of ice made the sidewalk dangerous. Susan took Train's elbow. Probably to keep from falling. Her pumps were hardly suited for navigating slippery territory. The tension between them was thick, almost palpable, and almost visibly dark. It was like a curtain of dark red, nearly black, between them. It was like being in the ring, trying to get a bead on his opponent after a series of hard jabs had opened both Train's eyebrows and blood ran into his eyes.

He said, 'Please, Susan, let's stop somewhere. Let's — how about a drink? We can stop somewhere warm and have a drink and try and fix this. It isn't too late to fix it, is it?'

'Maybe it's too soon.'

Still, she seemed willing to listen, if not to agree.

'How about Walker's?'

'I don't like that place. I don't like the atmosphere.'

A chilly wind swept some loose flakes off the ledges and awnings of adjacent buildings. Chunks of snow sped through the air. Train felt them sting his face and he saw Susan wince as they struck her cheeks and her eyes.

'There's the Brocklyn van der Zee,' she said.

They headed for the old building on Junius Street. The cocktail lounge hadn't been refurbished since Wilson was in the White House. It had somehow survived Prohibition; Train didn't know whether it had shut down for those years or functioned as a blind pig, but it had been back up and running since FDR killed the Volstead Act. Bob Corona, the Stan Laurel of the Corona brothers, was presiding. The clientele seemed to consist entirely of couples cowering in dark booths. Well, not quite. There was a gentleman in a dark suit perched on a barstool, hunched over a highball. He was wearing a black homburg. If the room had been any darker he would have been invisible.

Train and Susan Chen found a booth. Susan folded her coat and laid it on the leather seat. She kept her beret on her head. Train asked what she wanted to drink. She told him and he headed back to the bar. At least she wasn't sticking to coffee this time. Train hoped that was a good sign.

Corona recognized him and asked how the cop business was going.

Train told him, 'Martini and a Manhattan.'

Corona stirred the drinks, added an olive to one, a Maraschino cherry to the other, put them on a tray, and slid it to Train. 'On the house,' he said.

As Train started away, Corona gestured him back. 'Lovely companion you have, Officer. Night manager's running the desk in the hotel; you can have a house room if you want.'

Train said, 'I don't think so.'

'Okay by me. If you change your mind, though . . . '

Sitting with Susan, Train started to apologize again for Jocko Sullivan's conduct at the apartment.

Susan Chen lifted her glass and held it to her lips. Train looked at her, studying her features as he never had before. He'd had girlfriends since he was in the eighth grade and plenty of women in the hot, sweaty world of boxing, but he'd never known anyone like Susan. Glimpsed through the reddish-brown liquid in her glass, her mouth swam like a dream seen through an ocean of red-gold. Train felt as if he were going to explode.

'Aren't you going to drink?' she asked.

He felt as if he'd been awakened from a trance. He lifted his glass and they sipped. There was a jukebox in the corner. Some love-smitten swain had left his date to drop a nickel in the slot and play 'The Way You Look Tonight.' Train found himself smiling like a goof.

'What was that about, Nick?'

'What?'

Susan said, 'When you got our drinks. The bartender called you back and he said something to you.'

Train looked at his watch. 'It's getting late.'

'It's not so late.'

'I don't want to get you in trouble. Your father said you had to be home early.'

'He's an old-fashioned Chinese father.'

'Yes.'

'I'm a modern American girl.'

Train didn't know how to respond.

'You haven't answered my question.' She picked the Maraschino cherry from her drink and popped it into her mouth. After she'd chewed and swallowed she repeated, 'What did the bartender ask you?'

'Well, he's the brother of the hotel manager. He said — '

'What?'

Train was actually blushing; he could feel the blood rising into his face. 'He said we could have a room if we wanted.'

'And what did you say?'

The record ended and another began. The swain must have dropped two nickels in the slot. A big spender. The juke box played 'That Old Feeling.'

'I wouldn't want to get you in trouble.'

'You're so damned considerate, Nick. You don't mind extorting money from my family and you don't mind dragging me into some crazy scheme that has to involve mobsters, even if you won't tell me what it's all about. What the hell are you doing with those vitamin pills? What are you doing with your graft money? Who the hell do you think you are, Meyer Lansky?'

'What do you know about Meyer Lansky?'

'Nothing.' She picked up her Martini and drained it. 'He's Lucky Luciano's brains. What does anybody know about him? He could be FDR's Secretary of the Treasury if he wanted to, but the mob pays better.'

Her Martini glass was empty. She held it up and said, 'I want another one of these.' She pushed the empty glass at him. He'd never seen her so angry. He'd apologized for Jocko's crude conduct and Susan had seemed to accept his apology. Now her face was a mask of fury. He couldn't figure out what he'd done wrong.

He stood up and crossed to the bar, then ordered another round from Skinny Bob Corona. Corona refilled the glasses. Train reached for his wallet and started to throw a bill on the mahogany, but Corona shook his head. 'Your money's no good here, Officer Train.'

Train picked up the glasses. They were on the tray, its cork lining damp from prior drinks.

Corona said, 'Offer's still good.'

Train turned away and started back to the table. He could feel his face reddening.

Susan Chen said, 'I'm sick of all the

mystery around here. You think you know everything because you're a cop and nobody else knows anything because we're all citizens. You're wrong and you're wrong. You don't know everything. I can see it in your face. You walk around wondering what the hell is going on. If you knew you wouldn't look that way. And don't think the citizens are so damned ignorant. Brownsville is nothing but a small town and Junius Street is Main Street. Everybody knows everybody. Everybody knows everything.'

Train was stunned. He'd found himself becoming fond of Susan, wondering what future they might have. When they were together he'd forget she was Chinese until they passed another couple on the street, or loiterers standing under a lamp-post, or walked into a restaurant and asked for a table. Then they'd get the look.

What's the white guy doing with the likes of her? That's what the look said.

Train felt dizzy. He lowered the tray to the table before he could drop it, then he sat down. He said, 'Here's your drink.'

Susan repeated, 'What did the bartender say to you?'

'His brother's the hotel manager.'

'Is that what he said?'

'No. I already knew that.'

She stared at him.

'He said we could have a room. They're brothers, the Corona brothers, Alf and Bobby.'

'What did he say?'

'I just told you. He said we could have a room if we wanted one.'

'Okay, what did you say?'

'I just ordered us drinks.'

'Get the room.'

Train counted to five. 'Are you sure?'

She stared straight ahead. She didn't say anything.

He said, 'All right, finish your drink.'

★   ★   ★

The room was stuffy, so he opened the window enough to let in a blast of cold, moist air. It didn't look as if the rug had been vacuumed since McKinley was president. There was a rickety dresser and a cracked mirror. Water dripped in the sink; it must have been dripping for a long time because there was an orange stain leading from the faucet to the drain.

A wooden coat-tree stood beside the room's only window. A single light bulb hung from the ceiling. He turned it on long enough for them both to get their bearings in the room, then turned it off again. There was enough light from outside to let them see what they were doing. Susan Chen hung her heavy coat on the wooden coat-tree and placed her blue beret carefully on top of the tree. She had to stand on her toes to reach it. She removed her shoes, then her jacket, and hung it in the room's single closet. She stood beside the bed, unzipped her skirt and stood facing Train, wearing only her slip and a white lace brassiere.

She said, 'Well?'

His ears were ringing as if he'd tried to duck under a hard right hook and caught it on the side of his skull. He lowered himself to the edge of the bed and bent to undo his shoelaces. He heard the whispery sound of Susan's slip as she pulled it over her head.

★　★　★

When Susan Chen woke him up in the morning Train looked at his watch and cursed. 'I won't have time to go home. I've got to get to the precinct for shape-up.'

She had already slid from the bed and was drawing on her clothing. She grunted something that he didn't catch and he didn't want to ask her to repeat it. He said, 'Will you be all right? I should take you home but I'm going to be late.'

She said, 'It's all right.'

He couldn't tell whether she snarled or merely growled. He wanted to ask if she were still angry, but he suspected there was no need to ask. He tried again to apologize for what had happened at dinner but she wouldn't discuss it. All she would say was, 'It was my mistake. I shouldn't have gone to your house.'

'But you should. I mean, I'm sorry. Jocko is such a moron. I don't think he even meant any harm; he's just stupid. The smarter he tries to act, the stupider he gets.'

'He's family. Are you ready to go?'

She had dressed in the same outfit she wore for dinner. Of course, she had no other clothing with her. She was standing in front of the low dresser. The mirror was mounted on gimbals and she tilted it up so she could see her face. She had put on lipstick and was brushing her hair with a small brush she'd extracted from her purse.

Train hadn't shaved. He hadn't expected this to happen. He hadn't brought a razor. He tried to remember if he'd left one in his locker at the station house. He thought he had, but he doubted that he'd have time to use it before reporting for duty.

When he and Susan Chen passed through the lobby of the Brocklyn van der Zee the desk was manned by Alf Corona, the Hardy of the Laurel-and-Hardy Corona brothers. Corona bulged under a tan suit and a tie with a Hawaiian dancer on it. Train realized that Corona looked even more like Fat Stuff, the character in the comics who kept popping buttons off his shirt into the mouth of a hungry chicken.

On the sidewalk Susan Chen turned left and Nick Train turned right. He'd started to reach for her, to deliver a quick embrace and a peck on the cheek, but she was already on her way, high heels tapping angrily on the sidewalk.

* * *

Sergeant Garlington inspected the patrol officers before sending them to their day's work. He signaled to Train. 'You stay here.' He told Train's partner, Tim Charters, to hit the bricks. 'You can handle it alone, Hattiesburg. You know the beat now. If you need any help get to a call box quick and call the station house.'

Once in his sometime office, Garlington motioned Train to the visitor's chair. He produced a bottle of whiskey and two glasses. 'Snort, kid.'

Train picked up one of the glasses. Garlington looked surprised but he poured for them both, hoisted his glass, and threw back the whiskey. Train took a sip and managed to get it down. Barely.

'What is it, Sergeant?'

Garlington was watching him. Watching, not speaking. 'I don't know, Train.'

'Know what?'

'Know if I can trust you.'

'Cripes, Charlie, let's not start playing that game again. If you don't trust me just say so. I'll hit the sidewalk and do my job. You want to get another collector for my beat? Ask Charters. He'd love to start shoving people around, squeezing as many extra bucks out of them as he can.'

'And what would you do then?'

'What do you mean?'

Garlington raised a fist and slammed it down on the desk. 'Don't mess with me, Train. You know damned well what I mean. You're in with McAteer and Clarke. You're thick as thieves, you and those rotten lice.'

Train kept quiet. He didn't know where Garlington was going with this, but he knew he was on dangerous ground. Previously, Garlington had said that he was working for McAteer and Clarke. And that Clarke was playing a double game, himself. Now Garlington spoke of them as enemies.

The door opened behind Train. He heard the mechanism turning and he heard a couple of quick steps behind him. He saw Garlington looking startled, then pushing himself to his feet and frantically sweeping the nearly empty liquor bottle from the desk into a drawer. Train whirled, recognized the new arrival, and jumped to attention.

Lieutenant Leonard Kessler shut the door behind him. He wore a neatly trimmed moustache. He was tall and slim. He could have passed for Warren William at a costume party. His hair was combed straight back from a widow's peak. He wore a dark woolen suit, a shirt with a collegiate-looking button-down collar, and a tie printed in a futuristic geometric pattern.

Garlington made an inarticulate sound. Kessler frowned at Garlington. 'I think you'd better relieve Ralston on the desk, Sergeant.' Garlington shoved the drawer closed, shot a warning look at Train, and headed out of the office.

Kessler shook his head. 'Train, how are things going? I've hardly seen you since you joined the precinct.'

Train said things were going fine.

'No problems? Lot of rookies get discouraged after a few months. They want some excitement and police work can be boring sometimes.'

'Understand, sir.'

'Okay.' Kessler turned his back and reached for the doorknob. He grasped it and twisted, then released it and turned back to face Train. 'Come and see me. I want you to come and see me any time you feel the need, Train.'

'There's the chain of command, sir.'

'I know that, son. I've been a police officer for a long time. How old are you, Officer Train?'

'I'm twenty-one, sir.'

Kessler smiled. 'That's wonderful, young man. Enjoy it while you can.' He reached for the doorknob again. 'I want you to come see me in ten minutes. In my office. Do you understand me, Officer?'

Train said he did. Kessler left.

Train was tempted to open the drawer and swallow another swig of Garlington's booze. What the hell did Kessler want from him? Was Kessler part of the racket with Winger and Garlington? Did he have any idea what Train had been doing? Or was Kessler part of the operation set up by Tom Dewey and Burton Turkus? Did Kessler know all about McAteer and Clarke? Was he working with them or against them, or was Turkus playing Kessler against McAteer? It made Train's head spin.

He checked his watch, pulled a comb out of his uniform trousers and ran it through his hair. He couldn't find a mirror in the interrogation room, nor was there even a window. Just plaster walls, ancient and stained by water leaking from a cracked roof. His mind flashed back to the image of Susan Chen leaning over the mirror on the dresser in their room at the Brocklyn van der Zee. How long ago had that been? A couple of hours at most and it seemed like forever. Susan would have been back at the restaurant by now, would have confronted her parents and her brother.

Somehow it was the brother who seemed most likely to cause trouble. Susan could handle her father, the old-fashioned Chinese man, and her quiet, passive mother. She was a modern American girl. But Chen Long, Lawrence Chen, he was more of a puzzle. And he might be more of a threat.

Train slipped the comb back in his pocket and went to face Kessler. On his way to the lieutenant's office he passed the duty desk. Sergeant Garlington was holding a telephone to his ear with one hand and scratching words onto an official form with the other. He looked up at Train and nodded and grunted.

Train threw his shoulders back, knocked on Kessler's door, waited to be summoned, and marched in. Kessler was seated behind a glass-covered desk. Train halted and saluted like a soldier reporting to his commanding officer. That was they way they taught it at the academy.

Kessler said, 'Sit down, Nick.' Every

time Kessler switched between calling him Officer, Train, or Nick, he had to shift gears. He sat down. 'What do you think of Sergeant Garlington, Nick?' Kessler's expression was neutral. Train had no idea how to respond, so he kept it simple.

'He's a good policeman.'

'He's been here a long time,' Kessler said.

'Yes, sir.'

'That can be a good thing. He knows the neighborhood. I could turn him loose at three in the morning, blindfolded, and he could find his way around.' Kessler turned sideways, leaned his elbows on the arms of his swivel chair, and steepled his fingers beneath his chin. Train sat still, waiting for Kessler to go on.

'Charlie knows everybody in the station house, everybody on Junius Street, just about everybody in Brownsville.' He nodded agreement with himself. 'A good, solid cop.'

Train said, 'Yes, sir.'

'But you keep a man on one job for a long time, bad things can happen, too.'

Kessler was waxing philosophical. 'He forgets that he's here to do a job. He turns into a homesteader. He starts to think that he owns his beat.' Kessler dropped his hands to his lap and swung to face Train, leaning forward across his desk, his forearms flat against the glass, his hands toward Train. 'You know, Officer, you've become something of a mystery man around this precinct.'

'I didn't know that, sir.'

'You've got some surprising friends in high places. You told me that you understand the chain of command.'

'Yes, sir.'

'But you don't seem to mind holding little *tete a tetes* with some very powerful people.'

'Who would that be, sir?'

Kessler shook his head. 'There was white at his temples and his fingernails looked as if they'd been manicured that morning. 'Don't bullshit me, Officer. Don't bullshit me.'

12

That's a Trunk Line Number

Train settled into his father's one-time favorite easy chair. His mother was in the kitchen. No matter how many times he tried to lure her out, she migrated back there, making flour, turning chuck into hamburger meat in the hand-cranked grinder, washing dishes, preparing meals. She had the radio on to a music show called *The Cavalcade of America*. There were brief news reports every half hour, portentous voices warning of war in Europe in a few years, a few months, a few days.

Nick Train sat with Benny Jensen's notebook, trying for the hundredth time to make sense of the numbers that flowed from page to page to page until the book was filled. They had to mean something, and that something probably — almost certainly — had to do with Benny

Jensen's death and the shakedown racket that Train found himself in, getting in deeper and deeper. But what did they mean?

It came to him in the middle of the night. Not the answer to the puzzle, but a way to find the answer. It wasn't exactly a dream. Train opened his eyes and stared at the ceiling. There was an elm tree outside his bedroom window and a streetlamp below it. The elm's branches were waving back and forth in the wind and the light from the streetlamp made patterns that wove and danced above him. His mind wandered. He remembered his dead friend, Benny Jensen, and the night of the poker game when Jackie Goldstein had knocked over the beer and ruined the deck of cards. Jackie Goldstein, the numbers wizard of William Seward High. Jackie Goldstein, the kid with the gift. He couldn't throw a basketball through a hoop, not if his life depended on it. But anything to do with numbers, anything to do with numbers, Jackie could handle.

Train sat up and clicked on a lamp. He

found a scrap of paper and wrote himself a note. This was one midnight inspiration that would not evaporate with the dawn's early light. He turned the lamp off and pulled the quilt up to his chin and fell sound asleep.

He phoned the Goldstein house before he left for work in the morning. Jackie answered. They exchanged a couple of sentences of small talk. Jackie knew all about Benny Jensen, but this was the first time he'd talked about Benny's death with Nick. Nick said, 'Jackie, are you still the numbers whiz?'

Jackie said, 'I dunno. I guess so. I'm doing okay with my accounting courses and they seem pretty happy with me at the phone company.'

Nick Train described the book he'd found in Benny Jensen's dresser drawer, but he didn't tell Jackie Goldstein where he'd got it. Jackie seemed interested, but he said he couldn't really tell anything about the book without seeing it.

'Okay,' Nick told him. 'Will you be home tonight?'

'I have classes during the day. I'm on

the swing shift at the phone company. I get home around eleven.'

'Is it okay if I bring the book over then?'

There was a pause. 'My parents will be in bed. They don't like a lot of noise, especially late at night.'

'Would you rather come here, then?'

'I guess not. If you're quiet, we can look at it here. I might want to look some things up.'

Train got through a routine day on the beat. Charlie Garlington — Sergeant Garlington — didn't raise any issues at the shape-up, and nothing worse happened during the day than a couple of bullies trying to steal a younger kid's bicycle. Train took the junior gangsters by the scruff of their necks, shook them like a mother cat with a troublesome kitten, and sent them on their way. By then their would-be victim had hopped on his two-wheeler and headed in the opposite direction.

After work, Train avoided Garlington and headed for home. Marie and Jocko were over for dinner. Marie was really starting to bulge, but she helped her mother in the kitchen while Jocko ragged Train about his job. Several times, Train was on the edge of raising the issue of Jocko's conduct with Susan Chen, but he held back. What was the point? When Jocko and Marie finally left, Train helped his mother clean up, then spent the rest of the evening in the easy chair, trying unsuccessfully to get into a pulp magazine novel.

By half-past ten his mother had gone to bed. Train had pulled on a pair of woolen slacks and a flannel shirt when he got home from work. Now he changed his socks, climbed into a mackinaw and a knitted hat, and made his way to the lobby. He could see the street outside, elms swaying in the late-night wind. No one in sight. Was that a good sign or bad? He had his badge with him, and his service revolver in his mackinaw pocket, along with Benny Jensen's notebook. He started toward Jackie Goldstein's house and arrived without incident.

Goldstein answered the door wearing a Seward High sweatshirt, dungarees, and bedroom slippers. He greeted Train. 'Glad you're here. I was about to give up and climb into the sack.'

Train was all business. 'Where can we sit down and take a look at this thing?'

Jackie led the way downstairs. The Goldstein basement contained a ping-pong table, a couple of wooden chairs, an ancient sofa, and a dark wooden desk.

'How's here?'

Train said okay.

Goldstein said, 'It's chilly down here. I'm gonna get myself a cup of hot cocoa. You want some? Cocoa with marshmallows, you can't beat it on a cold night.'

Train grunted something positive and waited while Goldstein padded upstairs. When he returned they sat side-by-side at the desk. Train had Benny Jensen's notebook in his pocket. He took it out of his pocket and held it toward Jackie Goldstein. 'This goes with me when I leave here, Jackie, understand? You can copy anything you want out of it, but you might not want to. It could be dangerous.'

Jackie Goldstein grinned. 'Cut the Secret Agent X-9 stuff, Nick. Let me see the book, and you tell me what you want me to do.'

Once he had the book, Goldstein scanned page after page. Finally he laid the book on the desktop. 'Okay, Nick, what gives?'

Train said, 'You remember how we used to rib Benny about the girly cards he used in our poker games?'

Goldstein did.

'Okay,' Train went on. 'When they fished him out of the harbor he had one of those packs in his pocket. Not the cards, just the box they came in.'

Goldstein said, 'I don't get it. So what?'

'I didn't either.' Train tapped the miniature notebook with one fingertip. 'But that just didn't seem right.' He paused and sipped at his hot chocolate. It helped. 'Jackie, I'm telling you things that I shouldn't tell anyone, certainly no one outside the department. You'll keep your mouth shut about this. For your own good, Jackie.'

'Okay. What? What didn't seem right?'

'That deck of cards. Or, rather, the empty box. I don't know where the cards went. But why did Benny have that box in his hand? You ever read one of those mystery stories where the murder victim leaves a dying message for the detective, to tell him who the murderer was? I guess this is something like a dying message. The box. What was Benny trying to tell us?'

Goldstein waited for Nick Train to continue.

'So I went to Benny's house. His father let me see his room, all his things. I found another girly card box.' He put his fingertip on the box. 'This was in it.'

'So now we're missing two decks of girly cards.' Goldstein raised an eyebrow quizzically.

'I don't think we'll ever find the cards, and if we do they probably won't mean anything. I think Benny was keeping records in those little notebooks. I had a hunch he'd finished one notebook, filled it up, and started another book. He had that with him when he got on the ferry in Staten Island. Whoever pushed him off the boat got hold of the box and got the book out of it. There must have been two of them, at least. They hoisted Benny over the railing, but he managed to reach back and grab the empty box as he went over. He hung onto it until he was fished out of the harbor.'

'Holy smoke!' Goldstein took his glasses off, squeezed the bridge of his nose between thumb and forefinger, put his glasses back on, and reached for the notebook. 'And this is the notebook? How did you get it back from the bad guys?'

'No, Jackie. Close but not quite. The notebook they got when they murdered Benny wasn't the first volume. I guessed there was more. I went to Benny's house and I found this book in a girly card box. I wondered how many books I'd find in Benny's drawer, but there was only one. This one.'

Goldstein rocked back and forth in his chair. 'You think I can tell you what all these numbers mean.'

Train said, 'I hope you can.'

Goldstein said, 'Okay.' He picked up the notebook and opened it to the first page. From there on, as far as Train could tell, he was in trance. His eyes moved as he scanned the numbers and his fingers moved as he turned the pages, and other than that he could have been a million miles away.

Train was starting to doze off, holding his cup, sipping at the hot chocolate, when Goldstein said, 'Okay, this is simple. Look, Nick.' He spread the notebook on the desk. 'The first couple of pages are a directory. You see? If you read every seven digits you get a phone number. We think of exchanges as letters — you know, Havermyer, Flushing, Butterfield, whatever. But that's just for convenience; it's easier to remember Flatbush 3-9103, but to the switching equipment the eff-ell looks like three-five. The switches see that number as 3539103. The first three numbers are the exchange, the other four are the individual line. So all I had to do was go through the book and look for repeated runs of three numbers, and they were exchanges.'

Train grunted. 'Is that all?'

'No, not quite. Sometimes there are extra digits. Instead of a number being seven digits long it will be ten.'

'What does that mean?'

'The extra digits — here, look at this run of numbers — that's a trunk line number. When you call long distance you use a trunk line.'

'But how do you know whose number it is?'

'You ever hear of a reverse directory? No? We use them at the phone company all the time. When you call information, you give them a name and address and the operator gives you a number. When somebody inside the company has a phone number and doesn't know whose it is, we use the reverse directory and look up the subscriber.'

'So this whole notebook is just a list of telephone numbers?'

'I said, not quite. After the first few pages it switches. The seven-digit or ten-digit pattern stops. Instead there are other numbers.'

'Digits? What other digits? Jackie, I was never much good at math. Remember at Seward, trying to figure out the value of *pi*? I'd still be at it if old whatsizname hadn't explained about irrational numbers.'

'Right. You can't get an exact value for *pi*. It just keeps on going and going. I'm not sure what the numbers in this book mean, but they seem to be simpler than the phone numbers. There will just be a digit, one, two, three, whatever, separated by an asterisk, then some more digits, another asterisk, and so on, then a double asterisk, sometimes a triple asterisk.'

'You're losing me, Jackie.'

'Hang on, Nick. We're almost at the finish line. I think this book is somebody's financial records. Maybe Benny's, maybe not. The smaller numbers are individual transactions. I think one represents five dollars, two would be ten dollars, and so on. I'll have to do a little math, but I think an asterisk represents a subtotal. A double asterisk represents a total, and three asterisks are a grand total. They keep building and growing, like an upside-down pyramid. It isn't really a very complicated code. Benny wasn't a mathematician.'

Train whistled. 'No wonder they

wanted the book back. They must have found out he was keeping records. If it had been found on Benny it would have been dynamite.' Train put his empty cup down carefully and took the book back from Goldstein. 'Next job is to find out whose numbers these are.'

'Nick, that's what I was telling you. The reverse directory. I can get those for you in a breeze.'

'How about the out of town numbers — those trunk lines you were talking about?'

'That'll be a little more work, but not much. I can look those up, easy.'

Train stood up and put the notebook in his pocket. 'Watch yourself, Jackie. I'm afraid I've got you mixed up in something very nasty. I'll get this book back to you tomorrow. What time do you go to work at the phone company?'

Goldstein told him.

'Okay. Look, do me a favour, take a look outside. Right now, I mean. Don't turn on a light, just pull the curtain back a crack and let me know if you see anybody watching your house.'

Goldstein came back in a few minutes. 'I'm not sure. There's a car parked outside. Somebody's in it. Could be just a drunk pulled over to sleep it off, or a couple of high school kids necking.'

'You have a back door?'

'Yes. Leads to the alley.'

'Don't worry about anything, Jackie. Keep the front door locked. Lock the back door after me. I'll see you tomorrow.'

★   ★   ★

Making his way home from Jackie Goldstein's house, Train was struck by the irony of his being taken for a burglar and collared by one of his colleagues. It could happen. Either that, or taken out by a shadowy enemy. Who would have taken Jake Lefcourt for an assassin, primed to run down a brother cop?

But it didn't happen. Nothing happened. The streets of Brownsville were still and dark at this hour of the night. There was little evidence of the bustle of Brownsville's days, or of the corruption that lurked beneath the surface of the community.

Train got a few hours of sleep, shared coffee and eggs with his mother, and headed to the precinct. Sergeant Garlington presided in his usual manner. There was some discussion of the violence at St. Columba's. The diocese had sent in a replacement priest for Father Dempsey, and Bishop Riordan was using every tactic available to keep the story out of the local papers. Lieutenant Kessler had invited the new priest to come in and introduce himself at the precinct. He was an Italian-American instead of an Irishman: Santo Stametti, barrel-shaped and balding, an easy twin for Two-Ton Tony Galento, born and raised in Five Points. Train thought he'd regard Brooklyn the way a Russian regarded Siberia, but he would doubtlessly be primed to address the Dempsey affair and urge his parishioners to avoid gossip and prevent scandal. Oh, the Church shuddered at the prospect of scandal!

As for the two kids, Billy Casey was in a foster home, while Frederick Korb had been returned to his parents' tender care. Train had a feeling that either of them would envy the other.

The shift was pretty ordinary. Train and Charters grabbed a bowl of goulash at the Hungarian restaurant, rousted a kid for shoplifting Baby Ruth bars from Mendelssohn's drug store, broke up a fight outside Walker's Saloon, and headed back to the precinct to check out for the day.

Marie and Jocko were over for dinner. Marie spent most of the evening discussing pregnancy with her mother. Jocko wanted to talk politics. The situation in Europe was looking more and more dangerous. At least Jocko had everything solved. 'It's the limeys and the frogs, they don't know how to run a country. Every time you turn around there's a different king or president or prime minister. Now you look at the krauts, Nickie-boy. Or the eye-ties. Or even the russkies, for God's sake. They put somebody in charge and he stays in charge. Hitler, Musso, Stalin — that's the way you run a country. Somebody supports you, you take care of 'em. Somebody squawks too loud and the next day he's gone. Believe you me, brother-in-law, we'll have something like that in this country one of these days. Then we'll really go places!'

Train said, 'I want to check on Mom and Marie. How's she doing at home? Not too much morning sickness?'

'She's doing great, Nickie. Just great. One thing I can say about the Train family, they know how to handle a muffin in the oven without complaining too much.'

★ ★ ★

Train bundled up and made his way to the phone company to meet Jackie Goldstein at the end of his shift. He carried his badge and wore his revolver under his mackinaw. There was a spring mist in the air. It formed a nimbus around each streetlamp and traffic light. He stood outside the dirty red-brick building and watched shift workers pour out the doors and disperse toward their homes.

He spotted Jackie Goldstein. They

exchanged nods and headed toward a corner of the building. Goldstein gave Train a smile. 'Don't even ask, Nick. I've got the trunk information. It's pretty amazing. These guys are all over the place. Albany, Boston, Philadelphia, Chicago. A lot of them were Washington numbers. And overseas, too. There are numbers in Havana, London, Berlin, Paris.'

'You have it written down?'

'Right here.' Goldstein was wearing a heavy jacket against the late night chill. He tapped himself on the chest.

'Then let's get out of here,' Train said. 'We need to go someplace where we'll have some privacy.'

They headed for the Imperial Palace. The last customers had left and the restaurant was closing for the night, but Train rapped on the door and Susan Chen let him and Jackie Goldstein in.

'I don't know if there's any food left.' She stepped aside and locked the door behind them. 'Do you want me to ask Lee Hop to put something together for you?'

Train said no, this was strictly business.

'Something to do with vitamin pills?'

Train frowned. Goldstein didn't know anything about the marked money and Susan Chen's question might sound peculiar to him. Train decided that the best tactic would be to ignore the question. Instead, he introduced Goldstein. 'We're old school chums. We need a place where we can talk in private. I was hoping you'd help us out.'

Susan Chen said, 'Sure,' and nodded toward the bead curtain. Before they settled in the back room, Train checked carefully for holes in the wall covering. There were none. He gestured Goldstein to a chair, pulled one up beside him, and spread the notebook and Goldstein's worksheets on the table.

'It wasn't too tough,' Goldstein said. 'The phone numbers themselves were the easiest part, once you knew what you were looking at. The trunk lines for other cities were a little bit more difficult, but once I figured out Benny's system they weren't too bad. And the overseas lines — those were pretty weird. If you didn't know what they were, they seemed to be completely meaningless. But once I saw the pattern — it's all a matter of seeing patterns, Nick, believe me — once I saw the pattern, all it took was a little back-tracking into the circuits.'

'So this is everything?'

'Everything.'

'Then what we have to do is get you home safely and get this paperwork to a safe place. You're a pip, Jackie. I don't think we appreciated you at Seward. Thanks!'

13

The Longest Shift He'd Ever Worked

The problem was, who were the good guys and who were the bad guys? Train spent the rest of the night trudging up one street and down the next. He'd got Goldstein home safely. The kid had done marvelous work, but there was no need to place him at risk — at further risk — by asking him to hold onto Benny Jensen's notebook and his own, Goldstein's, decoding of its contents.

He didn't want to leave the material at the Imperial Palace. There had been no further trouble from the Four Star Kosher Butcher Shop, but Train didn't want to take any chances there. And he certainly didn't want to take the dangerous materials home with him. He watched the sun come up — a misty, peaceful event that belied what he held in the pockets of his mackinaw.

He made his way to the precinct. He kept an extra uniform and a set of civvies in his locker so he could change at the station or at home as necessity dictated. He shaved and combed his hair and put on his uniform. He was still early for the morning shape-up, so he found a telephone and dialed Barney Hopkins' home number. The *Eagle* reporter could be difficult, but as far as Train could determine he was honest and reliable. Everybody else — McAteer, Clarke, Kessler, Garlington, Charters — was either dirty or, at best, questionable.

Hopkins sounded sleepy and grouchy and not at all pleased to be roused at this hour of the morning. But when Train identified himself, Hopkins agreed to meet the next day. 'No, not today, damn it. I got too much to do. Tomorrow, kid, tomorrow.' Train would have liked it sooner, but he settled. Hopkins suggested Keen's Steak House in Manhattan. They'd have a nice, leisurely meal. Train said he didn't know the place. Hopkins gave him an address on the West Side on Thirty-Sixth Street. 'You'll love it, kid.

The best-stocked bar in New York. And I can't wait to enjoy one of their spreads on the swindle sheet.'

Next question: Was the notebook and accompanying paperwork safer in Train's locker or in his pocket? He decided on the latter.

It was the longest shift he'd ever worked, but eventually quitting time came. He showered and changed at the precinct, walked home, and sat in his father's favorite chair reading the Brooklyn *Eagle*, listening with half an ear to Stan Lomax on WOR. Lomax was an old-time newshawk, had been one of the great sportswriters before switching over to radio work. Listening to him was a lot pleasanter than listening to political news, war talk, and speculation about whether Roosevelt and Garner were going to go for a third term in the 1940 election.

When his mother called him to the dinner table, he felt too tired to do more than pick at his meatballs and spaghetti in marinara sauce. But after a couple of bites he perked up and downed three servings. He drank a beer and skipped coffee so he could sleep better, but it didn't do much good. After a couple of restless hours he got up and went back to the kitchen. He opened Benny Jensen's notebook and Jackie Goldstein's worksheets on the table and stayed up until midnight studying them.

Finally he took a pair of scissors and carefully removed one page from the notebook and a page from one of Jackie Goldstein's worksheets. He folded them up and sealed them in a letter-size envelope. Then he put the notebook and the rest of Goldstein's worksheets in a larger envelope, one with a string-clasp, and closed it, wrapping the string around two pasteboard disks.

Once he climbed in bed he had a hard time falling asleep, but he managed it at last and didn't wake up until almost ten o'clock the next morning. It was Wednesday, his day off. He showered and shaved, dressed in a suit and tie, drank a glass of juice, and waited for the elevator. It was a good thing Hopkins had suggested a day's delay before their meeting. This way he didn't have to attract attention from

Garlington or Kessler by calling in sick.

He took the subway into the city, got off at Grand Central, and walked across town until he came to a bank. The sign over the door read *Broadway Savings and Trust Company*. Train had never heard of it, and it was a safe bet that nobody at the bank had ever heard of him. Good.

He went in and rented a safety deposit box using his father's first name and his mother's maiden name. He put the manila envelope containing Benny Jensen's notebook and Jackie Mendelssohn's worksheets in the long gray tray and slipped it back into its place in the bank vault. A bank clerk slammed the door shut on the box like a morgue attendant closing the door on a cold storage vault containing a fresh corpse.

Train left the bank and walked down to Thirty-Sixth Street. He found Keen's. There was actually a doorman outside and one of those guys you see in the movies about fancy restaurants and nightclubs, standing inside behind a wooden lectern with a little electric light on it. And wearing a tuxedo and a bow tie. A hat check girl gave Train the once-over, then got a sour look when she saw there was no business there for her.

Train asked the guy in the tuxedo if he had a table for Mr. Hopkins and the guy said, 'Right this way, sir,' and led Train to a table where the newsman was sitting with a shot glass of amber fluid in front of him.

The first thing Hopkins said was, 'You drink single malt, kid?'

Train shook his head.

Hopkins said, 'An acquired taste. First sip of lowland could pass for liquid dirt but it's ambrosia once you learn your way around it.'

He lifted his glass, growled, 'Strike a blow for freedom,' and downed half of his scotch. 'Take a load off, kid.' With a nod he indicated an empty chair.

Train realized that the tuxedo guy was still there, waiting to hold his chair for him when he sat down. Then the tuxedo guy disappeared as if he'd never been there. Train reached for his pocket and said, 'Mr. Hopkins — '

'Barney.'

' — you need to see this.'

Hopkins made a slicing gesture with one hand. 'Later, later. You should really have a drink before lunch, but if you're voting dry this year I guess we can look at the menu.' He waved his hand and a white-coated waiter produced menus the size of billboards. 'Lamb chops for me, kid.' Hopkins barely glanced at the menu. 'Baked potato, sliced tomatoes. Have it every time I come here, which ain't as often as I'd like, but what the hell, kid, what the hell. Have anything you like.'

Train ordered a Caesar salad. After they'd eaten, Hopkins said, 'Okay, I can tell you're itching to show me some French postcards.'

'No, I — oh, you're joking.'

'You catch on fast, kid. What have we got?'

Train used a polished silver knife to slit the envelope containing the page he'd removed from Benny Jensen's notebook and the page he'd lifted from Jackie Mendelssohn's worksheet. He spread them on the white linen between Hopkins and himself.

The newsman stared at the two sheets of paper, then looked up and shook his head. 'As old Casca once said, it's all Greek to me.'

Now Train was puzzled.

'Shakespeare, Nicholas, Shakespeare. Sorry about that. Every so often my eddie kayshun sneaks one over on me. But I don't get it.' He tapped the two pages, first the little notebook page, then the larger worksheet. 'You gotta tell me what this means.'

'My friend Benny Jensen made this.' He indicated the notebook page. It was marked with narrow blue lines. Jensen's handwriting was cramped but legible. 'We went to school together, we went to the academy together, he got shoved off the Staten Island ferry on his way home from work.'

'Yeah, I know about that. But what about all the numbers?'

'My other friend — I don't think I better say his name — my other friend works for the phone company. I have a whole notebook of Benny's figures. My other friend took the book down to the phone company and turned all of Benny's work into names and phone numbers and dollars and dates. Look at this.'

He traced a line on Jackie Goldstein's worksheet.

Barney Hopkins leaned over the paper, turning his head slowly as he followed Nick Train's finger. When Train came to a phone number, Hopkins nodded. When Train came to the dollar amount, Hopkins hummed. When Train came to the name, Hopkins exploded.

'Holy cow! Holy cow, kid, do you know what you've got here?'

Before Train could answer, Hopkins grabbed the two sheets of paper and turned them face down on the tablecloth. He waved to a waiter. As the waiter approached, Hopkins lifted his shot glass and snapped, 'Bring the bottle.' The waiter nodded and reversed course.

Hopkins shook his head. 'Kid, it don't make sense to fly on one wing. Not at a time like this.' The waiter left the bottle on their table. Hopkins refilled his shot glass, nodded the waiter away, and turned the papers face-up once more. 'Nicky, do you know who these guys are?' He nodded toward Goldstein's worksheet.

Train said, 'I've looked through all the sheets. I recognized some of the names. People in Brooklyn, in Borough Hall, in City Hall, in Albany, even a couple in Washington. Most of 'em, I don't know.'

Hopkins held his shot glass under his nose, his hand warming the glass so fumes rose from the whiskey. He inhaled slowly, sipped at the whiskey, then lowered the glass to the tablecloth. 'You say you have a whole book of this stuff? Both these Jensen pages and the other worksheets?'

'Yes. I'm sure there was another book, that Benny had with him when he was murdered. They probably got it from him. If they didn't it's in the harbor and nobody is ever likely to find it. But I do have a whole book. Except for this one page.'

'I gotta see it. I gotta see everything. Where's the rest of the paper?'

'It's all in a safe place.'

'Train, I don't think you better go back to Brooklyn now. Not to work and not to your house.'

'Why not?'

'They don't know you have this but they've got their eyes on you, they're probably watching your house and they've got people in the precinct. You start acting suspicious and anything could happen. They tried to kill you once, didn't they?'

Train grunted.

'They'll try again. They probably don't know you're here; you're lucky, but don't push it.'

Train shook his head. 'What do you want me to do, then? I can't just disappear. My mom, my job . . . '

'Can you give me the rest of the paper?'

Train hesitated. He trusted Hopkins, or thought he did, anyway. But still he hesitated. 'Do you have a plan, Barney? How long is it going to take? Barney, look, I'm just a beat cop. I'm no Melvin Purvis. I wish I'd never got mixed up in this thing.'

Hopkins grabbed Train's shoulder and shook him. 'I don't blame you, kid, but you're in it now. You're in it up to your *tuchus*. You can't pretend it never happened. There are too many corpses now, too much gelt involved, and too many big shots.'

Train slid his hand across his face, starting at the forehead and ending at the chin. He took a couple of deep breaths, waiting for Hopkins to say something more, but Hopkins didn't speak. Finally Train said, 'Okay, Barney. Here's what we can do. You go back to your office. We'll get together again tonight.'

Hopkins's eyebrows shot up. 'When? Where?'

Train said, 'Never mind. I know what I'm doing.' He could almost hear Hopkins grinding his teeth, but finally Hopkins signaled for their check. While Hopkins settled up, Train left the table, left the restaurant, and disappeared into the midday, midtown crowds. He walked over to Herald Square, mingled with shoppers and sightseers for a while to make sure Hopkins hadn't followed him, then headed up Broadway. He trusted the news hawk but he didn't want to take any chances.

He stopped at a news stand and bought

a couple of adventure pulps, then went back to the bank and removed the manila envelope from his safety deposit box. He walked up to Forty-Third Street, ducked through the street entrance into the Plantation Bar, left the bar through a connecting door into the lobby of the Hotel Dixie, and registered for a room. He used the same name he'd used at the Broadway Savings and Trust.

Before taking the elevator to his floor he crossed the lobby to a pay phone and called Hopkins's office number. When he heard Hopkins's voice he said, 'Barney, seven o'clock, Plantation Bar, Forty-Third Street.' He hung up before Hopkins had time to respond. Then he called his mother in Brownsville and told her he wouldn't be home that night, maybe not for a few nights, but not to worry about him. If the precinct called she didn't know where he was.

Next, he took the elevator to his floor and headed for his room. The desk clerk in the lobby hadn't seemed surprised by a guest checking in with no luggage, but he'd insisted on payment in advance and

Train paid with cash. Once in his room he sat at the writing desk and opened the manila envelope. Everything was there, safe and sound. He put the papers back in the envelope and closed it up again. He loosened his tie, took off his shoes and put his feet up on his bed, and closed his eyes; but he couldn't fall asleep, so instead he opened one of the pulp magazines and read a couple of stories. One was about an ex-drunkard sailing around the South Seas looking for lost treasures. The other was about a humble bootblack who had a secret identity as a crime-busting scientific genius. Right. That was what the world needed, more crime-busting scientific geniuses.

He must have dozed off after all, because the next time he looked out the window night had fallen and the Times Square area was illuminated by a million bright lights. He could hear car horns honking from the street below. After looking at his watch, he headed for the bathroom to slap some water on his face, straightened his tie, put on his shoes and his jacket, and headed for the elevator.

Then he left the Hotel Dixie by the street entrance, walked once around the block, and entered the Plantation Bar. He spotted Barney Hopkins seated at a table, a half-empty shot glass in front of him.

Hopkins looked up at him. 'What's with the Mata Hari stuff, kid?'

Train said he was just being careful.

Hopkins said they needed to talk. If Train was that worried about being spied on, maybe they should find a private place. Train agreed and they headed for his room. One they were there, Hopkins asked if Train had Jensen's notebook and his mysterious other friend's worksheets. Train undid the string-seal on the big envelope and spread the worksheets on his writing desk. He held onto Benny Jensen's notebook.

'That's the original, hey?' Hopkins tipped his head toward the notebook.

'It is.'

'All right.' Hopkins started through the many pages of worksheets. He'd pulled a notebook from his own suit coat and he began jotting names and numbers. He didn't say anything for almost an hour, and Train sat watching him, waiting for him to finish going through the worksheets. Finally Hopkins stood up, rubbing his neck with both hands, then his temples, then his eyes. 'I suppose you know what you've got here, Nicholas.'

'I think so.'

'The sample you showed me at Keen's was impressive, but compared to the sample, this — this — is like Big Bertha compared to one of them Red Ryder BB guns.' He shook his head, stood up, and walked into the bathroom. He came back carrying two water glasses. He reached into his pocket and came out with a leather-covered hip flask. 'Never quite got over Prohibition, kid.' He put the glasses on the desk.

Train hastily gathered the worksheets and slid them back into their envelope along with Jensen's notebook.

'Smart move,' Hopkins said.

Train slipped the envelope into his suit coat pocket. Hopkins poured a stiff drink for himself, a smaller one for Train. 'Come on, kid. This is the big time. Strike another blow for freedom.' He lifted his glass and drank. Train followed suit. He'd been exposed to plenty of booze back on the fight circuit, not to mention the saloons on his beat in Brownsville, but he'd never developed a big fondness for whiskey and he'd never experienced anything quite like this stuff in his life.

'You're right, Barney. Definitely tastes like liquid dirt.'

Hopkins grinned. 'You'll change your mind. Now, let's get down to business.'

Train asked what Hopkins wanted to do.

'I couldn't do much after you showed me that sample at Keen's, kid. Those names made my ears ring, but I couldn't talk to anybody about it until I saw the rest of what you've got. What if I tipped off somebody on the list, you see?'

Train said he did.

'You know who Billy Bray is?' Hopkins asked.

'Sure. Big-time Tammany pol.'

'Right. City bosses wanted him for governor. Roosevelt wouldn't hear of it. Crooks is crooks, but Bully Billy was more than Franklin could take. Roosevelt and Jim Farley pushed Lehman onto the ticket back in, what was it, '32, and they tossed a bone to Tammany by letting them put Billy in as lieutenant gov.'

'Lehman dumped him in '38,' Train said.

'Right. The guy was too crooked to stomach. Besides, he was getting to be an embarrassment to Roosevelt and Farley. They got bigger chickens to stew. And Lehman wants to move up, too. So now we got Honest Charlie Poletti in there, in case Lehman resigns. Johnny Bennett is attorney general, another straight shooter. And Bray is shaking in his boots.'

Train had followed Hopkins's rant as far as he could. 'And Bray is in Jensen's notebook.'

'Along with half of the politicians in this city. And an honour roll stretching from Albany to Washington, London, Berlin, and all the ships at sea. They're all mixed together. There are agents and double agents and triple agents. Your pal McAteer is a straight arrow, as far as I can tell. His pal Clarke looks clean, but he's in it up to his ears according to your friend's worksheets. Unless he's playing both sides against the middle. Your pal Charlie Garlington I'm pretty sure is a good guy posing as a bad guy posing as a good guy.'

Train had walked to the window. He stood, looking out at the traffic below and the city skyline beyond. 'Where does that leave us, Barney?'

'It leaves us — ' He paused and looked at his wristwatch. 'It leaves us making some phone calls. A lot of people aren't going to like hearing from me at home, at night, but this can't wait.'

Train said, 'You can use the room phone.'

'No.' Hopkins shook his head. 'I'm not going through no hotel operator. Did you call me from here earlier?'

'I used a pay phone.'

Hopkins snorted happily. 'See that? You ain't just a dumb flatfoot after all. Let's get out of here.'

'What about — ' Train tapped his bulging pocket.

Hopkins said, 'Right.'

'What about the hotel safe?'

'Come on, kid. Don't make me take it back, what I just said about your not just being a dumb flatfoot.'

Train pursed his lips. 'I see what you mean. I guess.'

Hopkins said, 'Okay. I'll take care of this. You sit tight. Don't let nobody in. You hungry?'

Train shook his head.

'Good. I see you got entertainment.' He jabbed a thumb at Train's pulp magazines. 'Read yourself to sleep. Don't let nobody in, don't go out, don't make no phone calls. Your phone rings, pick it up but don't say nothing. Wait for the other person to speak first. If it's anybody but me, just hang up. If it's me, I'll tell you what to do.'

14

Like One Big Prospect Park

'Okay, Nicky, it's me. Anybody else call? Any visitors, anything?'

'No.'

'Good. Now listen, I gotta talk to you. I'm in the lobby right now. I'm coming up to your room. You decent? All right, just hold on, I'll be right there.'

While he waited for Hopkins, Train stood at the open window, breathing the clean air, the bright sunlight, and the morning vitality of the City that Never Sleeps. Brooklyn was home — always had been — but this was the real New York, the engine of color and sound and energy that made Train's world go around.

Five minutes later, Hopkins was knocking on Train's door. Train had showered and freshened up as best he could. The Dixie provided its guests with complimentary razors and toothbrushes, shaving cream and shampoo. But he was still wearing last night's clothing.

Train had never seen Hopkins as animated as he was this morning. He paced the hotel room's beige carpet, chattering like Winchell. 'I called John Bennett last night. His wife answered the phone. Didn't want to put him on. Said he was reading a bedtime story to the kiddies. Said he was never home, always at the office, in the field, traveling, working. His own kids barely knew him, so she wasn't going to bust in when he was actually home, reading them bedtime stories. I couldn't blame her. I know Bennett — he's a good man — but I wasn't going to let this go, so I waited till he finished 'Goldilocks and the Three Bears' or whatever the heck he was reading to the kids and then he picked up the phone.'

Train had taken a seat to hear Hopkins's story. Now Hopkins strode to the window and looked down into the midtown street, smiling and nodding like Joe McCarthy after DiMaggio put one in the bleachers to win another game for Ruffing or Gomez. If only the Dodgers had that kind of talent . . .

'Kid, I gave Johnny Bennett an earful and he couldn't get enough. I gave him those names and he went bonkers. He's been trying to get this kind of stuff for years. Dewey and Turkus barely scratched the surface. The feds ain't worth the powder to blow 'em to hell. Hoover don't believe the syndicate even exists. He loves to chase gangsters like Dillinger and Baby Face Nelson and Creepy Karpis and get his mug on the front page when he catches 'em, but he's a greedy glory hog in my book and I know Johnny ain't had no help from him.'

Train shook his head. 'I hear you, Barney. But these guys — Bennett, Dewey, Turkus, Hoover for heaven's sake — they're so far above my head — Barney, I'm just a harness bull. My partner got murdered and now I feel as if I'm fighting way the hell out of my class. I wish I'd never even got involved with this whole thing.'

'Yeah, but you did, and you're in it now and you're either gonna be a hero or a corpse. Believe me, kid, hero is better.' Hopkins had stopped pacing and was peering down into Forty-Second Street. 'Will ya look at that. Will ya just look at that!'

Train got up and stood at Hopkins's elbow. 'Look at what?'

'Just look at the parade of gorgeous women down there.' Hopkins turned from the window. 'Nicky, you ain't had breakfast, have you?'

Train hadn't.

'Come on. *Eagle* buys.'

They went to a Childs Restaurant on Forty-Sixth Street. Train had bacon and eggs and an English muffin and a glass of orange juice. Hopkins drank coffee and started on a Danish. He didn't have much to say about what he did last night after he left Train at the Dixie, and less about his plans for today.

Train said, 'I'm supposed to report for duty this morning. The precinct must have called my house by now.' He peered up at an oversized Sunoco Gasoline clock. 'I'm on the book as absent without leave.'

'Nicky, don't worry about that.' Hopkins bit off a chunk of Danish and washed it down with coffee. 'That's the least of your problems, believe me.' Another bite, another gulp of coffee. 'Besides, you've got friends in high places. Remember that.' Bite. Gulp. Then Hopkins said, 'Finish your grub and let's beat it out of here.'

Once they were in the street, businessmen and secretaries and shoppers and out-of-town tourists rushing past on every side, Hopkins said, 'Here's the thing. I gave Johnny Bennett everything you gave me. It's a good thing he trusts me. We're like this — we're like David and Jonathan, Pyramus and Thisbe — '

'Who?'

'Never mind, more Shakespeare. Bennett trusts me. He knows I've never fed him bad dope and he knows I can keep quiet when he needs me to. He was up all night on the phone. He's working with everybody he can that he trusts, and he told me that the flag is going up first thing Monday morning.'

'Right.' Train frowned. 'But this is Thursday.'

'Exactly. So here's the thing. You got

any greenbacks with you, kid?'

'Not many.'

'That's all right, I've got a drawing account on the *Eagle*. We'll go to my bank and I'll take an advance and I'll front you what you need. Nobody in Manhattan knows your mug. You're not using your right name at the Dixie, are you?'

Train said he wasn't.

'All right. You've gotta lie low for the next three days. You can call home and tell your mother you're okay, but don't tell her where you are or what you're doing, you understand? I'm damned serious about this. If anybody asks her, the safest thing for her is not to know.'

A cabby hit his brakes for a red light and didn't quite stop in time to miss the bumper of a sedan. The drivers got out and started yelling at each other. A cop strode up and Hopkins and Train moved away from the scene.

'What you gotta do, kid, is mingle with the crowds. Act like some apple-knocker in town to stare at the tall buildings. Take a subway ride down to Klein's and buy some cheap union suits and socks and a couple of shirts. Take in some movies. Eat in cheap restaurants. Buy yourself some more of them pulp magazines and enjoy yourself. Stay out of saloons and keep away from whores. You got me? You okay with that?'

They went to Hopkins's bank and he fronted Train the money he'd need. 'Okay, you've got my home phone number. If you need me and I ain't at the office, call me at home. My sweet little helpmeet knows how to take a message.'

Train hadn't even known that Hopkins was married.

'I'll pick you up at the Dixie on Sunday. We'll have a nice little Sunday drive up to Albany. Monday morning, bright and early, we go see Johnny Bennett.'

★ ★ ★

A uniformed attendant brought Hopkins's Lafayette sedan up from the Hotel Dixie's basement garage. Hopkins tossed the man a coin, then he and Train climbed into the car. Hopkins piloted the car skillfully through Manhattan traffic, past the new apartment buildings of the prosperous Bronx and Yonkers. As they sped through the Hudson Valley past Peekskill and Poughkeepsie, Hyde Park and Kinderhook, Train observed the rolling hills and lush estates. He shook his head.

Hopkins said, 'Ever been out of the city before, kid?'

'Never been north of Manhattan.'

Hopkins laughed. 'What do you think of it?'

'I've never seen anything like it except in pictures. I never believed it was real.'

'Hah! You thought they just made that all up?'

'Well, maybe in Europe. The paintings. They had them in my school. Copies, I guess. Or prints. All those scenes of trees and flowing streams. But I've always lived in Brooklyn. This,' he waved at the passing countryside, 'it's like — like one big Prospect Park.'

Hopkins said, 'Okay. Enough of ain't-nature-wonderful. We gotta talk a little business.' With one thumb he tapped his suit jacket over his heart. 'I got my version of your friend's facts right here. You brought the originals, I hope.'

'Everything.' Train had purchased a cheap valise. He'd put his precious manila envelope with Benny Jensen's notebook and Jackie Goldstein's worksheets in it, along with his accumulation of new clothing. The valise was safely locked in the trunk of Hopkins's Lafayette.

Hopkins said, 'When we see Bennett we gotta show him those originals. I told you the flag goes up tomorrow bright and early. I spoke with Johnny today. I caught him as he was leaving the house with his missus and the sprouts to go to mass. I told you, kid, he's a straight arrow. Brooklyn boy, just like you and me. Church every Sunday. Everything is set. Tomorrow, Nicky, tomorrow you're a hero.' He didn't remind Train of the alternative.

They checked into a nondescript, lower-middle-class hotel in Albany. Ate dinner in a steakhouse. Shared a room like a couple of business travelers or lobbyists in town for the State Assembly session. Hopkins climbed into bed and was snoring before his head hit the pillow. Train read a story about a love-smitten ranch hand and an innocent schoolmarm. When that failed to put him to sleep, he tried one about a maniacal dwarf transferring the brain of a gorgeous virgin into the skull of a giant ape. That did the trick.

★ ★ ★

The Office of the Attorney General of the State of New York was located in a gothic structure that would have fit into one of Nicholas Train's pulp magazines, but inside it was modern and reasonably comfortable. The Attorney General, John J. Bennett, Junior, greeted Barney Hopkins like an old school chum. When Hopkins introduced Train, Bennett shook his hand warmly. 'To paraphrase the late President Lincoln when he met Mrs. Stowe, 'So you're the little policeman who started this great big crackdown'.'

Train had no reply for that.

They were in Bennett's outer office. A middle-aged secretary pounded away at a Remington typewriter. A row of file cabinets stood against the wall, and a threadbare carpet covered the floor. The main decoration in the room was a row of portraits Train guessed were past occupants of the office: Carl Sherman, Albert Ottinger, Hamilton Ward.

Bennett was a big man, taller than Hopkins or Train, broad-shouldered, with dark hair and a pointed moustache. He wore a tiny gold crucifix on the lapel of his pinstriped suit. Train felt shabby but Bennett put one arm warmly around Train's shoulder and the other around Hopkins's. 'Come on in.' He escorted Hopkins and Train into his private office. The carpeting was better. Train recognized the portraits — Al Smith, Nat Lewis, Franklin Roosevelt, Herbert Lehman. Floor-to-ceiling windows behind a massive desk let in bright spring sunlight.

Bennett consulted an ornate clock on his desk. As neat and precise as Bennett was in personal appearance, his desk was cluttered. 'You're right on time, fellas. Anybody like a cup of coffee?' Without waiting he pressed a switch on his desktop intercom and asked for a pot of coffee and three cups. 'I'm glad you're punctual, Barney.'

'News hawk's habit, John. Mr. Attorney General.'

'John is fine.'

'We've got another guest coming. I invited him for an hour after you both. Figure he'll be half an hour early, and I wanted to talk with you.' He fixed Train with a serious gaze. 'I trust you've got the documents with you.'

Train produced the notebook and worksheets.

Bennett smiled as he turned the pages. 'I've spoken with your friend Mr. Goldstein, Nicholas. May I call you Nicholas?'

Train managed to stammer, 'How did you know — '

'Of course you withheld your friend's name from Mr. Hopkins. Nothing wrong with caution. But once Barney had given me the information from the notebook and worksheets, it wasn't hard for me to find the source. Quite a chap, Jacob Goldstein. He did a remarkable job.'

The conversation paused while Bennett's secretary served coffee, then withdrew.

'You may wonder why Barney kept you under wraps since last Thursday,' Bennett resumed. 'I hope you didn't find the experience too oppressive.'

Train said, 'No, sir. In fact, I enjoyed it. I can see why tourists come to New York.'

'Had a good time, did you?' Bennett offered a broad smile. He was in his mid-forties, a few years older than Barney Hopkins, a generation separated from Train. In fact, Train was startled to realize, just a few years younger than Train's father had been at the time of his death. But strong, healthy, prosperous. No cramped apartment serviced by a creaking, unreliable elevator for the likes of the Attorney General. No smell of stale cabbage or derelict's urine in the hallway.

'Now.' Bennett paused, sipped at his coffee, and waited while Hopkins and Train followed suit. 'Now,' he repeated, 'I want you to know there was a reason for the delay. We had to verify Officer Jensen's information — his death, what a pity! — and Mr. Goldstein's good work. And your own, Officer Train. There will be a posthumous medal for Officer Jensen and suitable recognition for Mr. Goldstein and yourself.'

Bennett stood up and walked to one of the tall windows, standing with his back to the visitors, feet spread, hands clasped behind his back in the posture of a soldier — or a police officer — at parade rest. After a few seconds he whirled to face Hopkins and Train once more. 'First thing I had to do was make sure that I had reliable people checking. I was appalled, gentleman — appalled by some of the names in the Jensen notebook. We've been setting the foxes to guard the henhouse for years. Decades.'

He shook his head as if he could hardly believe his own words. 'Task forces have descended on police precincts, district attorneys' offices, congressmen, senators — yes, United States senators — this morning. We've broken up the biggest ring of racketeers since the days of Boss

Tweed! And it's your doing.'

The intercom on Bennett's desk buzzed. He pressed a toggle switch, cocked his head at his secretary's voice, and said, 'Two minutes more, then send him in.' He grinned at Train and Hopkins. 'That's Andrew James Edwards — and don't you forget to use all three names — Special Agent in Charge of the FBI office here in Albany. I'm afraid we had to let the Bureau in on this. It does involve interstate trafficking of funds and transportation of firearms across state lines.'

He heaved an exaggerated sigh, then settled into his chair as the door swung open. His secretary entered the office, followed by an immaculately groomed individual. Bennett rose from his chair and circled his desk, then crossed the office to shake the new arrival's hand. Train wasn't sure but he thought he caught a wink from Bennett as he strode past.

'Mr. Edwards, I'm so pleased to have the cooperation of the Bureau. Let me introduce Mr. Hopkins and Officer

Train.' He recited their credentials. Then he ushered Edwards to a seat. He clicked the intercom and ordered another cup for Edwards.

'The Director extends his congratulations on this successful operation, Mr. Bennett.' Edwards seemed less than wildly enthusiastic in his statement. 'It would have been wiser, though, to bring the Bureau into the case earlier. I'm sure you'll understand that. Nonetheless, we've assigned special agents to as many of the raids and arrests as our limited personnel and budget will permit. I'm sure that Congress will recognize our success and act appropriately with regard to next year's budget.'

'I'm sure they will,' Bennett agreed. This time Train was sure that he detected a twinkle in Bennett's eye, and equally sure that Edwards did not.

'Now,' Edwards said, 'If you'll just have your people turn over the necessary documents — I can accept them now, if those are the evidence on your desk, Mr. Bennett — the Bureau will take over the case.'

Bennett shook his head. 'I don't think so.' He offered Edwards a benign smile. 'I'm sure we can handle this, but please accept our thanks for the Bureau's assistance.'

'But this is an interstate matter. This is clearly a case for federal jurisdiction, for the jurisdiction of the Federal Bureau of Investigation.'

'Yes, yes. We'll send over whatever we think you folks need. I'm sure your special agents were well received this morning in the Capitol building. Those congressmen and senators must have been surprised to receive visits from the FBI.'

'I'm sure they were. Now, if you'll just turn over — I believe I see the famous Jensen notebook and telephone work-sheets.' He nodded toward Bennett's desk.

'Yes. We'll have copies made and send them right over to your office. Or would you prefer that we send them to the Director himself at the seat of government?'

Edwards seemed less than satisfied.

Instead of responding, he ignored Bennett's offer. But he soldiered on. 'I've called the local newspapers. They should have photographers here in another hour. And — and I hope you realize how privileged you are, Mr. Attorney General — the Director himself is *en route* via a commandeered army transport plane.' He checked his wristwatch and favored Bennett with a grin.

'Wonderful,' Bennett said. 'Wonderful.'

★ ★ ★

The Director arrived, preceded by an advance squad and accompanied by a pair of burly assistants. The local editors were assured that the FBI would shortly furnish them with a suitable press release detailing the Bureau's great triumph in breaking up a national and international network of illicit financial transactions. And Albany Special Agent in Charge Edwards offered the Director's personal thanks to State Attorney General Bennett for the assistance his office had rendered. Flashguns exploded, shutters clicked, and photographers knelt, ducked, and climbed on chairs to get better angles.

The Director and his entourage departed to return to Washington. Agent Edwards returned to the Albany FBI office to draft a press release for the Director's approval before releasing it to the newspapers. John Bennett burst into laughter. 'I'm sorry, boys, but if I'd had to hold that in any longer I'd have pissed my pants. And the missus would never approve of that.'

Barney Hopkins joined in Bennett's laughter. Nicholas Train wasn't sure what to make of it all.

Bennett said, 'Come on, fellas, lunch is on me.' He clicked the intercom. 'We'll be out for the next couple of hours. Oh — what's on my calendar for this afternoon?' The intercom squawked out a response. 'Okay,' Bennett said, 'nothing there that can't wait. Take care of rescheduling for me, will you? That's a good girl, thanks.' To Train and Hopkins, he said, 'How's your appetite? This kind of fun always makes me hungry.'

They wound up at a fancy joint where everybody seemed to know everybody else. The table-hopping and glad-handing never stopped. To Train the food and the surroundings were elegant, but the atmosphere was like the William Seward High School cafeteria. Once everyone had ordered, Bennett asked what Hopkins and Train planned to do.

'I've got my story half-written already,' Hopkins said. 'I can have it done and phone it in before we leave Albany. Hey, I've got the inside stuff; I've been at Nicky-here's elbow from the start of this thing. If I don't get a prize out of this I should at least get a bonus.'

Bennett said, 'You think so?'

Hopkins said, 'I also think I'll have a drink, if you don't mind.'

Bennett signaled the waiter and Hopkins was accommodated. Then Bennett turned to Train. 'What about you, Nicholas? What are your plans?'

'Sir, I'm a police officer. I have a job.'

'Not so simple, Nicholas.'

The waiter brought them soup. Bennett and Hopkins had both ordered something that Train had never heard of. He'd told the waiter he'd have the same. It was cold and white with little green flakes floating on it, and tasted of potatoes and cream and chives. It was very good.

'Not so simple,' Bennett repeated. 'To some, you're a hero now. But you're also a marked man. I don't think you can go back to your job as if nothing had happened.'

Train asked about the effect of the morning's raids on his precinct.

'Let's see.' Bennett frowned. He spooned some soup into his mouth, then wiped his moustache with his linen napkin. 'I thought you'd want to know. Precinct Captain Kober came up clean. He'll keep his job. I'm afraid Lieutenant Kessler isn't so clean.'

'I saw his name on Goldstein's worksheet,' Train said. 'That was a surprise. I'd always thought he was an honest officer.'

'I'm sorry. He'll have a chance to defend himself against both criminal charges and departmental violations. Your Sergeant Garlington turns up in the Jensen notebook and the Goldstein worksheets, but good friend On Duty McAteer cleared him.' He picked a small golden-coloured roll from a silver tray, broke it open, and spread butter on a bite-sized morsel. 'By the way, that scheme with the vitamin B12 markings was marvelous. Was that your idea, Officer Train?'

Train shook his head. 'Mr. McAteer suggested it.'

Bennett smiled approvingly. 'I knew that, Officer. Forgive me for laying a little trap. Any man who claims credit for another's work is unworthy in my book. Any man who honestly gives credit when he thinks he can get away with taking it deserves twice the points.' He turned to Barney Hopkins. 'Don't you agree?'

'It's in the story already.'

'Too bad about Inspector Clarke, though.'

Their entrees had arrived and Train cut into a small steak. He chewed and swallowed a morsel. Then he asked, 'What about Tim Charters?'

Bennett's eyebrows shot up onto his forehead. 'Didn't you know about Charters? He was working for Mr. Hoover. What the New York Police Department chooses to do with him is up to them, of course. But if I had to decide how to handle Timothy Charters, I'd tie a pretty ribbon in his hair and send him back to the Bureau.'

Bennett had been eating a piece of fish in a lemon sauce. He'd finished now. He said, 'I'm sorry, my friends, but I think I'd best get back to my office. This meal is on me, of course.' He started from his seat, then sank back into it. 'But, Nicholas, again — what do you want to do? I could use an investigator of your caliber on my staff. Or — have you ever thought about attending law school?'

'Law school? I — no, sir, I never thought about that. I've never even been to college.'

Bennett pursed his lips. 'Just a thought. It could be arranged. But the other matter — does that appeal to you?'

'Would I have to move to Albany? I mean, it's a nice town, but I don't really know how I'd feel about that. I'm just a Brooklyn boy, Mr. Bennett.'

'I understand,' Bennett said. 'Are you familiar with Park Slope? Lived there all my life. I still call it home.' He got a faraway look in his eyes. 'Sterling Place and Seventh Avenue. Home is home, eh?'

'Brownsville, sir.'

'Even so, even so.' Now he did stand up. 'Think about it, young man. Think about it. You're off to a fine start. You've got a bright future ahead of you. You think about it.'

15

They Call it Vichyssoise

Winter didn't want to give up, even though the calendar said it was spring-time and green buds had appeared on the oaks and elms of the city. A late nor' easter had borne thick clouds over the Atlantic, swept in across Long Island Sound, and was dusting the city with a final coating of snow.

Nicholas Train pulled his new Hollywood-style DeSoto to the curb in front of Keen's Steak House. The valet opened the door for Train while the restaurant's doorman opened the passenger door for Susan Chen and held an umbrella over her. Train joined Susan and they entered the restaurant. A few errant snowflakes escaped the umbrella and settled in Susan's hair, sparkling there like tiny gems.

At their table Train couldn't keep from looking around at other diners. Train and

Susan still caught the eyes of others, but not the angry glares that they received on the streets of Brownsville. Here, stylishly dressed women watched Susan, obviously studying her, seeking what they could add to their own repertoires, even as they evaluated the competition. Jealousy and admiration were mixed in equal parts. Those same women's male companions, obviously prosperous businessmen, cast surreptitious glances at Susan when they thought their wives would not notice. But notice they did. There would be sharp words tonight in uptown apartments and suburban Tudor homes.

Train had suggested Keen's for their evening out. Someplace away from Brownsville, someplace where nobody would recognize either of them. Attorney General Bennett had said that Train would be a hero, but the merchants in Brownsville seemed more nervous about not paying weekly tribute than they had been resentful in Train's days as collector. And at the precinct he was shunned by most of his colleagues. Garlington's name had gone unmentioned in the revelations of what were now known as Bennett's Raids. Lieutenant Kessler was gone. Tim Charters had discovered that family obligations required him to return to Mississippi.

'Are you dreaming, Nick?'

He blinked. Susan Chen was smiling at him.

'Sorry. No. I was just thinking about how much everything is changed.'

'Are you sorry?'

He met her eyes. They were the colour of emeralds. Her silk dress followed every curve of her slim body. Its color matched her eyes. Her hair was swept behind her head, leaving her face and her graceful neck fully visible.

'I don't know. Things were going along pretty well before this all started. I didn't want to be a big shot. I don't want to be one. I just wanted to do my job, play cards with my friends. Sometimes drink a beer, sometimes see a movie. Sometimes I think I was better off.'

'And other times?'

He picked up a silver soup spoon and gestured, dipped the spoon into the cup before him, swallowed and lowered the spoon. 'I didn't have a car. I didn't have this suit. Nobody knew who I was. Now — now, some people admire me, some people hate me. That's why I wanted to get out of Brownsville. At least here in the city nobody recognizes me.'

'You still care about the neighborhood, don't you?'

'A lot of bad things happen there.'

She looked at him, questioning. 'Poor Mr. Little. Mr. Kleinmann. You heard about him?'

'Hanged himself in the Tombs. At least he'll never have to stand trial for killing Dermott Winger. He had connections in the old country; he couldn't stand what he saw happening in Europe. He was trying to get his relatives out but he couldn't.'

'That's all, then?'

'Well, I'm an uncle now.' He grinned. 'I haven't seen Mom so happy in years, not in all the time Pop was sick, or since he died. Marie looks great. I'm still not crazy about Jocko, but even he seems a little easier to take now that he has a baby to brag about. I know he wanted a boy, but the first time I saw him holding his daughter — I've never seen anything like the look on his face. There may be hope for him yet.'

Susan sampled her soup. 'You didn't even know what this was called, did you?' she laughed.

'I do now. They call it vichyssoise.'

'Yes. You even pronounced it correctly.'

'I guess I've learned a lot.' He held a tray of rolls toward Susan, then took one for himself and broke a corner off it. 'I don't know if I'm any happier, though.'

'You're living better,' Susan countered. 'Driving that fancy DeSoto car, wearing good suits. And didn't I see some new furniture the last time your mother invited me for dinner? Even a new radio. It sounded good.'

He grunted. 'I guess so.'

'What happened? Did you fall into a pile of gold?'

Train shook his head. 'There was some reward money from the Bennett Raids. And Barney Hopkins and I are working on an article for *Collier's*. 'How I Broke the International Graft Ring,' by Nicholas Train, with Barney Hopkins. Barney thinks we might even be able to sell a book about everything that happened.'

Susan's eyes widened. 'When did you become an author?'

'I'm not. Barney's doing the writing. That's the *with* part. My dope, his words. We already got a big advance from *Collier's*. More money than I make in a year as a cop. More money than my old man ever laid eyes on.'

He paused and scanned the nearby tables. By now the diners had taken in Susan Chen's calculatedly exotic beauty. Train said, 'I'm sharing my half of the money with Benny Jensen's family and with Jackie Goldstein.' He picked up the rest of his roll, studied it, then returned it to his plate. He said, 'But what about you, Susan?'

'The restaurant is doing well.'

'I didn't mean that.'

'What did you mean, then?'

'I mean you. You and your family. Especially since your brother left.'

'He went back to China. You knew that, Nick.'

'But why? He's American. He was born here. Just as you were.'

She shook her head. The light of nearby chandeliers caught in her jet-black hair, creating a midnight-blue nimbus around her face. 'You don't understand, then. Yes, my brother is Larry Chen, an American young man who dresses just like you and speaks English without an accent. But he's also Chen Long, just as I'm just as much Chen Shu as I am Susan Chen.'

She paused while their waiter removed the cups in which their soup had been served.

'You don't have much connection to the old country, Nick. To your old country. In another generation or two you'll be so American, you won't know where you came from.' She inhaled deeply. 'Maybe that's good. Maybe someday we Chinese Americans will stop being Chinese and just be Americans. Maybe someday. But not yet. Not while Japan is doing what it is doing to China.'

Somewhere nearby silverware clattered against porcelain.

'My blood is still Chinese, Nick. I'm an

406

American girl, but my blood cries out when I see what is happening to China. That's why my brother had to go back. He's going to fight the Japanese.'

Food arrived: sole in lemon butter for Susan, broiled lamb chops with parsley and potatoes for Train. Train had ordered wine and the waiter poured a sample for his approval, then filled their glasses.

Susan asked, 'What now, Nick? What about you?'

He told her about his last conversation with James Bennett.

'Well, what about it? Are you going to work for him? Are you going back to school? Surely you don't intend to pound a beat for the next thirty years and then get a job as a bank guard.'

'No.' He cut a bit of chop, chewed and swallowed. 'Old Mike Calvert at the Citizens' and Workers' — did you ever see the picture of him holding me on his horse?'

'Your mother showed me. She loves that picture.'

'I'm starting night courses next semester. I don't know about law school, like

Mr. Bennett suggested, but at least I want to get a degree.' He paused. 'And you, Susan — '

'I'll be here for a while, but I don't know how long. I want to go out to California and see my cousin.'

'But you won't stay there?'

'I don't think so. I'll probably come back.' She smiled. 'Does it matter so much?'

'It does.'

'Oh, Nick, there are so many girls in New York. Don't be silly. Don't be so romantic.'

'I want to marry you, Susan.'

She smiled.

'That isn't so romantic, is it?' He reached for her hand, and she let him take it.

'Will you?' he asked.

She shook her head. 'No, Nick. I'll sleep with you if you want. That's the American girl in me. But I can't marry you. Not now.'

'But — '

'Can't you see what's happening? Can't you see the war coming? Nick, it's been going on in Asia for years. The Japanese have Manchuria; they're conquering China, slowly but surely. And they're committing horrible atrocities against my people.'

She stopped for breath, then went on.

'My people, don't you see? The Chinese are my people. The Americans, too. I'm two girls, one American and one Chinese. I want to go out to California and stay with my cousin Virginia and the Chinese out there. And then — but there's a war coming to America, too. Can't you see it?'

He said nothing.

'I know you, Nick. It's going to take a while but I know you'll see it too, and you'll have to go. If they don't come for you you'll go on your own. I know you will.'

He shook his head. 'No.'

'Yes, Nick. Yes. I know you. I know you better than you know yourself. After the war — I'll marry you then. I think I will. If you still want me. If you're not so changed and if I'm not so changed, if you still want to marry me when the war is over, I will say yes.'

16

Noise at the Club Lavenham, Sussex

May, 1944

The noise level dropped once the bombers returned from their day's missions over Germany and their share of the round-the-clock pounding of the Third Reich's industrial base. Schweinfurt, Cologne, Mannheim, Bremen. Wherever Hitler's minions set up their factories, the bombers would come. But now it was night. Now the RAF's Avro Lancasters and Handley Page Halifaxes would begin their work and would continue until dawn. Then the Boeing B-17s and Consolidated B-24s would take to the skies once more.

Now the sounds echoing across the 390th Bombardment Group's Lavenham base were those of roaring engines as ground crews raced to get the heavy bombers ready for the next day's missions. That was, those that returned from today's sorties against the Reich. Every day planes were lost, crews were lost. The attrition was relentless. New aircraft and new crews were pressed into service to replace those who set out each morning, never to return.

But inside the galvanized steel Quonset hut, the sounds were very different. The voices of Ginny Simms, Jo Stafford, and the Andrews Sisters poured from a jukebox. Off-duty non-coms downed beverages and sang. Some of them, lucky enough to have letters from home, crouched over wooden tables, beers or whiskeys at their elbows, reading the precious missives over and over. The wooden sign outside the iron building bore the green circular crest of the 390th. Beside it, carefully lettered, were the words *390th Non-Commissioned Officers Club, Lavenham, Sussex.*

The door swung open and for a moment the figure standing in the entrance was silhouetted against the orange dusk. Inside the club the bartender called, 'Ten-*hut!*' Silence reigned. Silence, except for the closely harmonized voices of Patty, Maxene, and LaVerne Andrews, singing 'Rum and Coca-Cola.'

'Permission to enter, Sergeant?' The man in the doorway took a step inside the building. Electric lights glinted off the polished buttons and ornaments on his tunic.

The bartender replied, 'Yes, sir.'

The officer peered around the room, barked, 'As you were,' and continued. He removed his officer's cap, revealing a black patch where one eye had been shot away. He held his cap in his right hand. The empty left sleeve of his tunic was carefully pinned up.

He circled the room, nodding and chatting briefly with air crew and ground crew corporals and sergeants. The conversation varied little. The officer acknowledged that this was the non-coms' club and he was only a visitor. The men offered him a drink, which he politely refused.

A dark-haired man sat at one table, staring into a glass of whiskey. He wore the three stripes and two rockers of a tech sergeant. The officer stopped, looking down. The enlisted man looked up. His eyes widened and he pushed himself to his feet. 'Captain Clifford!' he gasped, taking in the silver maple leaves on the older man's shoulders. 'I mean — Colonel Clifford!'

The officer laid his cap on the wooden table and offered his hand. 'Sergeant Train. Congratulations. I knew you had what it takes. OCS next for you?'

'I don't think so, sir. I wouldn't mind another rocker under my stripes, though.'

The older man smiled and nodded. 'May I join you, Nick? May I call you Nick?'

Train stammered permission.

Colonel Clifford tilted his head. 'It's been a long time since Benning's School for Boys, hasn't it, Nick?'

'Yes, sir.'

'We did some good work there, you and I. I want to thank you again for helping us put that scoundrel McWilliams away. Just between you and me, Sergeant, I never did like that fellow. Some Pointers are all right but others think they're the salt of the earth. Don't like to mix with us mustangs, that's for certain.'

He tilted his head at Train's glass. 'Come to think of it, I just might indulge. If that's all right with you.' Train signaled the bartender and in moments a bottle and another glass appeared on their table. 'I'll get this.' Colonel Clifford produced a pound note. 'I think this will be enough, will it? Can never get the hang of the funny money they use in this country.'

Train nodded approval of the note. 'My congratulations to you, too, sir. You were just a captain back at Benning.'

Colonel Clifford poured himself a hefty drink and downed half of it at a swallow. 'A long time, Nick, and a long way. Remember how eager I was to see combat?'

'I do, sir.'

'Well, I saw it all right.' He turned his face toward his empty sleeve. 'Left an eye and an arm at Anzio.' He paused. The Andrews Sisters had given way to Jo Stafford singing 'You'd Be So Nice to Come Home to.'

'Guess I shouldn't feel sorry for myself. A lot of boys lost their lives.' He paused. 'Sometimes I envy them.'

Train made a sympathetic sound. What could a sergeant say to comfort a lieutenant colonel?

Colonel Clifford shook himself. 'Never mind. I wanted to get into combat. I asked for it and I got it. That's not why I came here. Medics patched me up as best they could there in Italy, then they sent me here — God knows why — to try and get ready for . . . something, I don't know what.'

'Everybody says we're going in soon,' Train offered.

'Going in. Going in to — never mind. I'll never see combat again, Nick. We're going to win this thing, no question about it. I just wish those krauts would throw in the towel. They must know they're going to lose; they're not stupid. Why should thousands more have to die?'

'I don't know, sir.'

'Course not. Course not, Nick. Doesn't make sense.' He lifted his glass, downed some more liquor, then lifted the bottle and refilled Train's glass as well as his own. 'Look, I came here to give you something. This was mailed from China

415

to California to Brooklyn. Somebody in Brooklyn, newspaper guy named Hopkins — you remember him, Nick?'

Train smiled. 'Nice fellow. Worked with me on that shakedown case.'

'He did a feature story about you, too. I'm sure you remember that.'

'Of course. 'Brownsville Cop Trades Blues for Khaki.' Everybody likes a story with a local angle.'

'Right. And, well — ' Colonel Clifford reached inside his tunic and extracted an envelope. It was battered and covered with rubber stamp markings. 'Looks as if it's been around the world, doesn't it?' He extended the envelope and Train accepted it. 'And I guess it has.'

Train held the envelope by its ends, studying the address on it. The electric lights glinted in his eyes. Ginny Simms was singing 'It's Been a Long, Long Time.'

The sound of Colonel Clifford's chair scraping on the Quonset hut's rough floor broke Nick Train's reverie. The colonel picked up his cap and slipped it onto his iron-gray hair. Train started to rise but

Colonel Clifford laid his hand on Train's shoulder. 'Don't get up, Nick. I hope that letter is good news. Good luck to you, son. And if you change your mind about OCS just let me know. I think I can do something for you.' He left.

Train opened the letter.

Dear Nicholas,

I do not know if this will reach you. I hope it does. I tried to write to you before but I never heard back. My brother Lawrence was killed in the North African campaign. I wrote to my parents and they said that your mother had died and they did not know where you had gone. I am sorry that your mother is gone.

My Cousin Virginia in Los Angeles knew about you but she did not know where you were any longer.

I am somewhere in China now. I am not allowed to tell you where. But I am working at an American air base as an interpreter. I am billeted with a detachment of WACs.

The relationship is not entirely

417

comfortable. The American women think of me as Chinese. They try to be kind to me but I can tell that they are suspicious. I tell them that I was born in Brooklyn and raised in America but to them I am still Chinese.

Also, I am a civilian. I entered China on my own and found my way to this base and volunteered my services. The officers were happy to have someone who knows both Mandarin and English, and even a little Cantonese. They could use me, they decided, but still I am not a WAC, I am a civilian.

And the Chinese here do not like me much. They think I am an American. They make fun of my accent. They say that I sound like a foreigner trying to sound like a Chinese and not doing very well at it.

I weep for China, Nicholas. The Japanese have committed unspeakable crimes against the Chinese people, against my people. Word leaks out or is carried out by Chinese who have fled the advancing Japanese army. The Japanese bomb the cities. They murder my people. They rape Chinese women. They use old men and women and even babies for bayonet practice. They —

I cannot write any more about this. The Chinese people are themselves divided. There was a civil war in this country before the Japanese invaded. Now there is a truce, of sorts, between the warring armies of Chinese politicians and warlords. When we defeat the enemy and China is free again, I fear that the civil war will resume and more thousands of my people will suffer and die.

Nick, remember the times we had together in Brownsville. I remember our going to the movies together. I remember our one night together. It was all so long ago, as if that was some other woman who loved you. She was Susan Chen, working in her parents' restaurant. I am Chen Shu fighting in this monstrous war.

Nick, it is such a precious memory to me, our one night in that squalid old hotel in Brownsville. Please, when you read this letter, if you ever get to read *this letter, think of me. Think of me and I will think of you and maybe in some way our minds will touch or our souls will touch.*

What will I do when this war ends? Maybe I will be dead by then. Maybe not. Nick, I do not know whether I am Chinese or American. I thought I knew. I thought I was both, but now I am afraid I am neither. The American WACs do not accept me and the Chinese liaison personnel do not accept me. Each side thinks I belong with the other side.

Perhaps I will return to America. Perhaps I will stay here in China. Perhaps I will not be alive and so I will not have to decide.

Please think of me, Nicholas. Maybe — maybe we could both sleep, both dream, both dream of each other. Do you think this is possible? Do you think we could be together on some other plane of being?

Chen Shu — Susan Chen

Train folded the letter and slid the paper back into its envelope. He placed the envelope in a pocket of his service jacket. He'd reported for duty at the crack of dawn this day. The big event was coming. It was in the air. Everyone knew it. Everyone knew that the landings on the coast of France were imminent. Train wanted to be ready.

Any week now, any day now, everybody knew it. Everybody knew that Ike would say, 'Today. Today we go.' And that would be the day. And then it would happen.

THE END

Western powers plan to explode a
hydrogen bomb in a remote area of
Southern Algeria — code named Zone
Zero. The zone has to be evacuated.
Fort Ney is the smallest Foreign
Legion outpost in the zone, commanded by a young lieutenant. Here,
too, is the English legionnaire, tor-
tured by previous cowardice, as well as
a little Greek who has within him the
spark of greatness. It has always been
a peaceful place — until the twelve
travellers arrive. Now the outwitted
garrison faces the uttermost limit of
horror . . .

THE WEIRD SHADOW OVER MORECAMBE

Edmund Glasby

Professor Mandrake Smith would be unrecognisable to his former colleagues now: the shambling, drink-addled erstwhile Professor of Anthropology at Oxford is now barely surviving in Morecambe. He has many things to forget, although some don't want to forget him. Plagued by nightmares from his past, both in Oxford and Papua New Guinea, he finds himself drafted by the enigmatic Mr. Thorn, whom he grudgingly assists in trying to stop the downward spiral into darkness and insanity that awaits Morecambe — and the entire world . . .

DEATH BY GASLIGHT

Michael Kurland

London has been shocked by a series of violent murders. The victims are all aristocrats, found inside locked rooms, killed in an identical manner. Suspecting an international plot, the government calls in the services of Sherlock Holmes. Public uproar causes the police to set visible patrols on every street; fear of the murderer looks like putting the criminal class of London out of business! They in turn call in the services of Holmes's nemesis, Professor James Moriarty. What will happen when the two titans clash with the killer?

THE SECOND HOUSE

V. J. Banis

When Liza Durant is saved from drowning by Jeffrey Forrest, she little realizes how much it will change her life. Jeffrey is the heir to the old manor La Deuxieme, the 'second house'. Within days he proposes to Liza, who agrees to visit him at his country home. A series of accidents soon follows, and Liza finds herself in a web of intrigue over the inheritance of the great house. Can she escape alive? Or will the curse of the second house claim yet another victim?